Amusement Only by Richard Marsh

Richard Bernard Heldmann was born on 12th October 1857, in St Johns Wood, North London.

By his early 20's Heldmann began publishing fiction for the myriad magazine publications that had sprung up and were eager for good well-written content.

In October 1882, Heldmann was promoted to co-editor of Union Jack, a popular magazine, but his association with the publication ended suddenly in June 1883. It appears Heldman was prone to issuing forged cheques to finance his lifestyle. In April 1884 He was sentenced to 18 months hard labour.

In order to be well away from the scandal and damage this had caused to his reputation Heldmann adopted a pseudonym on his release from jail. Shortly thereafter the name 'Richard Marsh' began to appear in the literary periodicals. The use of his mother's maiden name as part of it seems both a release and a lifeline.

A stroke of very good fortune arrived with his novel The Beetle published in 1897. This would turn out to be his greatest commercial success and added some much-needed gravitas to his literary reputation.

Marsh was a prolific writer and wrote almost 80 volumes of fiction as well as many short stories, across many genres from horror and crime to romance and humour.

Index of Contents

THE LOST DUCHESS

CHAPTER I

THE DUCHESS IS LOST

"Has the Duchess returned?"

Knowles came further into the room. He had a letter on a salver. When the Duke had taken it, Knowles still lingered. The Duke glanced at him.

"Is an answer required?"

"No, your Grace." Still Knowles lingered. "Something a little singular has happened. The carriage has returned without the Duchess, and the men say that they thought her Grace was in it."

"What do you mean?"

"I hardly understand myself, your Grace. Perhaps you would like to see Barnes."

Barnes was the coachman.

"Send him up." When Knowles had gone, and he was alone, his Grace showed signs of being slightly annoyed. He looked at his watch. "I told her she'd better be in by four. She says that she's not feeling well, and yet one would think that she was not aware of the fatigue entailed in having the Prince to dinner, and a mob of people to follow. I particularly wished her to lie down for a couple of hours."

Knowles ushered in not only Barnes, the coachman, but Moysey, the footman, too. Both these persons seemed to be ill at ease. The Duke glanced at them sharply. In his voice there was a suggestion of impatience.

"What is the matter?"

Barnes explained as best he could.

"If you please, your Grace, we waited for the Duchess outside Cane and Wilson's, the drapers. The Duchess came out, got into the carriage, and Moysey shut the door, and her Grace said, 'Home!' and yet when we got home she wasn't there."

"She wasn't where?"

"Her Grace wasn't in the carriage, your Grace."

"What on earth do you mean?"

"Her Grace did get into the carriage; you shut the door, didn't you?"

Barnes turned to Moysey. Moysey brought his hand up to his brow in a sort of military salute—he had been a soldier in the regiment in which, once upon a time, the Duke had been a subaltern:

"She did. The Duchess came out of the shop. She seemed rather in a hurry, I thought. She got into the carriage, and she said, 'Home, Moysey!' I shut the door, and Barnes drove straight home. We never stopped anywhere, and we never noticed nothing happen on the way; and yet when we got home the carriage was empty."

The Duke stared.

"Do you mean to tell me that the Duchess got out of the carriage while you were driving full pelt through the streets without saying anything to you, and without you noticing it?"

"The carriage was empty when we got home, your Grace."

"Was either of the doors open?"

"No, your Grace."

"You fellows have been up to some infernal mischief. You have made a mess of it. You never picked up the Duchess, and you're trying to palm this tale off on to me to save yourselves."

Barnes was moved to adjuration:

"I'll take my Bible oath, your Grace, that the Duchess got into the carriage outside Cane and Wilson's."

Moysey seconded his colleague:

"I will swear to that, your Grace. She got into the carriage, and I shut the door, and she said, 'Home, Moysey!'"

The Duke looked as if he did not know what to make of the story and its tellers.

"What carriage did you have?"

"Her Grace's brougham, your Grace."

Knowles interposed:

"The brougham was ordered because I understood that the Duchess was not feeling very well, and there's rather a high wind, your Grace."

The Duke snapped at him:

"What has that to do with it? Are you suggesting that the Duchess was more likely to jump out of a brougham while it was dashing through the streets than out of any other kind of vehicle?"

The Duke's glance fell on the letter which Knowles had brought him when he first had entered. He had placed it on his writing-table. Now he took it up. It was addressed:

"To His Grace

"The Duke of Datchet.

"Private!

"Very Pressing!!!"

The name was written in a fine, clear, almost feminine hand. The words in the left-hand corner of the envelope were written in a different hand. They were large and bold; almost as though they had been painted with the end of the penholder instead of being written with the pen. The envelope itself was of an unusual size, and bulged out as though it contained something else besides a letter.

The Duke tore the envelope open. As he did so something fell out of it on to the writing-table. It looked as though it was a lock of a woman's hair. As he glanced at it the Duke seemed to be a trifle startled. The Duke read the letter:

"Your Grace will be so good as to bring five hundred pounds (£500) in gold to the Piccadilly end of the Burlington Arcade within an hour of the receipt of this. The Duchess of Datchet has been kidnapped. An imitation duchess got into the carriage, which was waiting outside Cane and Wilson's and she alighted on the road. Unless your Grace does as you are requested the Duchess of Datchet's left-hand little finger will be at once cut off, and sent home in time to receive the Prince to dinner. Other portions of her Grace will follow. A lock of her Grace's hair is enclosed with this as an earnest of our good intentions.

"Before 5.30 p.m. your Grace is requested to be at the Piccadilly end of the Burlington Arcade with five hundred pounds (£500) in gold. You will there be accosted by an individual in a white top-hat, and with a gardenia in his button-hole. You will be entirely at liberty to give him into custody, or to have him followed by the police. In which case the Duchess's left arm, cut off at the shoulder, will be sent home for dinner—not to mention other extremely possible contingencies. But you are advised to give the individual in question the five hundred pounds in gold, because in that case the Duchess herself will be home in time to receive the Prince to dinner, and with one of the best stories with which to entertain your distinguished guests they ever heard.

"Remember! not later than 5.30, unless you wish to receive her Grace's little finger."

The Duke stared at this amazing epistle when he had read it as though he had found it difficult to believe the evidence of his eyes. He was not a demonstrative person as a rule, but this little communication astonished even him. He read it again. Then his hands dropped to his sides and he swore.

He took up the lock of hair which had fallen out of the envelope. Was it possible that it could be his wife's, the Duchess? Was it possible that a Duchess of Datchet could be kidnapped, in broad daylight, in the heart of London, and be sent home, as it were, in pieces? Had sacrilegious hands already been playing pranks with that great lady's hair? Certainly, that hair was so like her hair that the mere resemblance made his Grace's blood run cold. He turned on Messrs. Barnes and Moysey as though he would have liked to rend them:

"You scoundrels!"

He moved forward as though the intention had entered his ducal heart to knock his servants down. But, if that were so, he did not act quite up to his intention. Instead, he stretched out his arm, pointing at them as if he were an accusing spirit:

"Will you swear that it was the Duchess who got into the carriage outside Cane and Wilson's?"

Barnes began to stammer:

"I—I'll swear, your Grace, that I—I thought—"

The Duke stormed an interruption:

"I don't ask what you thought. I ask you, will you swear it was?"

The Duke's anger was more than Barnes could face. He was silent. Moysey showed a larger courage:

"Could have sworn that it was at the time, your Grace. But now it seems to me that it's a rummy go."

"A rummy go!" The peculiarity of the phrase did not seem to strike the Duke just then—at least, he echoed it as if it didn't. "You call it a rummy go! Do you know that I am told in this letter that the woman who had entered the carriage was not the Duchess? What you were thinking about, or what case you will be able to make out for yourselves, you know better than I; but I can tell you this—that in an hour you will leave my service, and you may esteem yourselves fortunate if, to-night, you are not both of you sleeping in gaol. Knowles! take these men to a room, and lock them in it, and set some one to see that they don't get out of it, and come back at once. You understand, at once—to me!"

Knowles did not give Messrs. Barnes and Moysey a chance to offer a remonstrance, even if they had been disposed to do so. He escorted them out of the room with a dexterity and a celerity which did him credit, and in a remarkably short space of time he returned to the ducal presence. He was the Duke's own servant—his own particular man. He was a little older than the Duke, and he had been his servant almost ever since the Duke had been old enough to have a servant of his very own. Probably James Knowles knew more than any living creature of the Duke's "secret history"—as they call it in the chroniques scandaleuses—of his little peculiarities, of his strong points, and his weak ones. And, in the possession of this knowledge, he had borne himself in a manner which had caused the Duke to come to look upon him as a man in whom he might have confidence—that confidence which a penitent has in a confessor—to look upon him as a trusted and a trustworthy friend.

When Knowles reappeared the Duke handed him the curious epistle with which he had been favoured.

"Read that, and tell me what you think of it."

Knowles read it. His countenance was even more of a mask than the Duke's. He evinced no sign of astonishment.

"I am inclined, your Grace, to think that it's a hoax."

"A hoax! I don't know what you call a hoax! That is not a hoax!" The Duke held out the lock of hair which had fallen from the envelope. "I have compared it with the hair in my locket, and it is the Duchess's hair."

"May I look at it?"

The Duke handed it to Knowles. Knowles examined it closely.

"It resembles her Grace's hair."

"Resembles! It is her hair."

Knowles still continued to reflect. He offered a suggestion.

"Shall I send for the police?"

"The police! What's the good of sending for the police? If what that letter says is true, by the time I have succeeded in making a thick-skulled constable understand what has happened the Duchess will be—will be mutilated!"

The Duke turned away as if the thought were frightful—as, indeed, it was.

"Is that all you can suggest?"

"Unless your Grace proposes taking the five hundred pounds."

One might almost have suspected that the words were spoken in irony. But before he could answer another servant entered, who also brought a letter for the Duke. When his Grace's glance fell on it he uttered an exclamation. The writing on the envelope was the same writing that had been on the envelope which had contained the very singular communication—like it in all respects down to the broomstick-end thickness of the "Private!" and "Very pressing!!!" in the corner.

"Who brought this?" stormed the Duke.

The servant appeared to be a little startled by the violence of his Grace's manner.

"A lady—or, at least, your Grace, she seemed to be a lady."

"Where is she?"

"She came in a hansom, your Grace. She gave me that letter, and said, 'Give that to the Duke of Datchet at once—without a moment's delay!' Then she got into the hansom again, and drove away."

"Why didn't you stop her?"

"Your Grace!"

The man seemed surprised, as though the idea of stopping chance visitors to the ducal mansion vi et armis had not, until that moment, entered into his philosophy. The Duke continued to regard the man as if he could say a good deal, if he chose. Then he pointed to the door. His lips said nothing, but his gesture much. The servant vanished.

"Another hoax!" the Duke said, grimly, as he tore the envelope open.

This time the envelope contained a sheet of paper, and in the sheet of paper another envelope. The Duke unfolded the sheet of paper. On it some words were written. These:

"The Duchess appears so particularly anxious to drop you a line, that one really hasn't the heart to refuse her. Her Grace's communication—written amidst blinding tears!—you will find enclosed with this."

"Knowles," said the Duke, in a voice which actually trembled, "Knowles, hoax or no hoax, I will be even with the gentleman who wrote that."

Handing the sheet of paper to Mr. Knowles, his Grace turned his attention to the envelope which had been enclosed. It was a small square envelope, of the finest quality, and it reeked with perfume. The Duke's countenance assumed an added frown—he had no fondness for envelopes which were scented. In the centre of the envelope were the words "To the Duke of Datchet," written in the big, bold, sprawling hand which he knew so well.

"Mabel's writing," he said to himself, as, with shaking fingers, he tore the envelope open.

The sheet of paper which he took out was almost as stiff as cardboard. It, too, emitted what his Grace deemed the nauseous odours of the perfumer's shop.

On it was written this letter:

"My dear Hereward,—For Heaven's sake do what these people require! I don't know what has happened or where I am, but I am nearly distracted! They have already cut off some of my hair, and they tell me that, if you don't let them have five hundred pounds in gold by half-past five, they will cut off my little finger too. I would sooner die than lose my little finger—and—I don't know what else besides.

"By the token which I send you, and which has never, until now, been off my breast, I conjure you to help me.—MABEL.

"Hereward—help me!"

When he read that letter the Duke turned white—very white, as white as the paper on which it was written. He passed the epistle on to Knowles.

"I suppose that also is a hoax?"

He spoke in a tone of voice which was unpleasantly cold—a coldness which Mr. Knowles was aware, from not inconsiderable experience, betokened that the Duke was white-hot within.

Mr. Knowles's demeanour, however, betrayed no sign that he was aware of anything of the kind, he being conscious that there is a certain sort of knowledge which is apt, at times, to be dangerous to its possessor. He read the letter from beginning to end.

"This certainly does resemble her Grace's writing."

"You think it does resemble it, do you? You think that there is a certain faint and distant similarity?" The Duke asked these questions quietly—too quietly. Then, all at once, he thundered—which Mr. Knowles was quite prepared for—"Why, you idiot, don't you know it is her writing?"

Mr. Knowles gave way another point. He was, constitutionally, too much of a diplomatist to concede more than a point at a time.

"So far as appearances go, I am bound to admit that I think it possible that it is her Grace's writing."

Then the Duke let fly at him—at this perfectly innocent man. But, of course, Mr. Knowles was long since inured.

"Perhaps you would like me to send for an expert in writing? Or perhaps you would prefer that I should send for half-a-dozen? And by the time that they had sent in their reports, and you had reported on their reports, and they had reported on your report of their reports, and some one or other of you had made up his mind, the Duchess would be dead. Yes, sir, and you'd have murdered her!"

His Grace hurled this frightful accusation at Mr. Knowles, as if Mr. Knowles had been a criminal standing in the dock.

While the Duke had been collecting and discharging his nice derangement of epithets his fingers had been examining the interior of the envelope which had held the letter which purported to be written by his wife. When his fingers reappeared he was holding something between his first finger and his thumb. He glanced at this himself. Then he held it out towards Mr. Knowles.

Again his voice was trembling.

"If this letter is not from the Duchess, how came that to be in the envelope?"

Mr. Knowles endeavoured to see what the Duke was holding. It was so minute an object that it was a little difficult to make out exactly what it was, and the Duke appeared to be unwilling to let it go.

So his Grace explained:

"That is the half of a sixpence which I gave to the Duchess when I asked her to be my wife. You see it is pierced. I pierced that hole in it myself. As the Duchess says in this letter, and as I have reason to know, she has worn this broken sixpence from that hour to this. If this letter is not hers, how came this token in the envelope? How came any one to know, even, that she carried it?"

Mr. Knowles was silent. He still yielded to his constitutional disrelish to commit himself. At last he asked:

"What is it that your Grace proposes to do?"

The Duke spoke with a bitterness which almost suggested a personal animosity towards the inoffensive Mr. Knowles.

"I propose, with your permission, to release the Duchess from the custody of my estimable correspondent. I propose—always with your permission—to comply with his modest request, and to take him his five hundred pounds in gold." He paused, then continued in a tone which, coming from him, meant volumes: "Afterwards, I propose to cry quits with the concoctor of this pretty little hoax, even if it costs me every penny I possess. He shall pay more for that five hundred pounds than he supposes."

CHAPTER II

SOUGHT

The Duke of Datchet, coming out of the bank, lingered for a moment on the steps. In one hand he carried a canvas bag, which seemed well weighted. On his countenance there was an expression which to a casual observer might have suggested that his Grace was not completely at his ease. That casual observer happened to come strolling by. It took the form of Ivor Dacre.

Mr. Dacre looked the Duke of Datchet up and down in that languid way he has. He perceived the canvas bag. Then he remarked, possibly intending to be facetious:

"Been robbing the bank? Shall I call a cart?"

Nobody minds what Ivor Dacre says. Besides, he is the Duke's own cousin. Perhaps a little removed; still, there it is. So the Duke smiled a sickly smile, as if Mr. Dacre's delicate wit had given him a passing touch of indigestion.

Mr. Dacre noticed that the Duke looked sallow, so he gave his pretty sense of humour another airing:

"Kitchen boiler burst? When I saw the Duchess just now I wondered if it had."

His Grace distinctly started. He almost dropped the canvas bag.

"You saw the Duchess just now, Ivor! When?"

The Duke was evidently moved. Mr. Dacre was stirred to languid curiosity.

"I can't say I clocked it. Perhaps half an hour ago; perhaps a little more."

"Half an hour ago! Are you sure? Where did you see her?"

Mr. Dacre wondered. The Duchess of Datchet could scarcely have been eloping in broad daylight. Moreover, she had not yet been married a year. Every one knew that she and the Duke were still as fond of each other as if they were not man and wife. So, although the Duke, for some cause or other, was evidently in an odd state of agitation, Mr. Dacre saw no reason why he should not make a clean breast of all he knew.

"She was going like blazes in a hansom cab."

"In a hansom cab? Where?"

"Down Waterloo Place."

"Was she alone?"

Mr. Dacre reflected. He glanced at the Duke out of the corners of his eyes. His languid utterance became a positive drawl:

"I rather fancy she wasn't."

"Who was with her?"

"My dear fellow, if you were to offer me the bank I couldn't tell you."

"Was it a man?"

Mr. Dacre's drawl became still more pronounced:

"I rather fancy that it was."

Mr. Dacre expected something. The Duke was so excited. But he by no means expected what actually came:

"Ivor, she's been kidnapped!"

Mr. Dacre did what he had never been known to do before within the memory of man—he dropped his eye-glass.

"Datchet!"

"She has! Some scoundrel has decoyed her away, and trapped her. He's already sent me a lock of her hair, and he tells me that if I don't let him have five hundred pounds in gold by half-past five he'll let me have her little finger."

Mr. Dacre did not know what to make of his Grace at all. He was a sober man—it couldn't be that! Mr. Dacre felt really concerned.

"I'll call a cab, old man, and you'd better let me see you home."

Mr. Dacre half raised his stick to hail a passing hansom. The Duke caught him by the arm.

"You ass! What do you mean? I am telling you the simple truth. My wife's been kidnapped."

Mr. Dacre's countenance was a thing to be seen—and remembered.

"Oh! I hadn't heard that there was much of that sort of thing about just now. They talk of poodles being kidnapped, but as for duchesses— You'd really better let me call that cab."

"Ivor, do you want me to kick you? Don't you see that to me it's a question of life and death? I've been in there to get the money." His Grace motioned towards the bank. "I'm going to take it to the scoundrel who has my darling at his mercy. Let me but have her hand in mine again, and he shall continue to pay for every sovereign with tears of blood until he dies."

"Look here, Datchet, I don't know if you're having a joke with me, or if you're not well—"

The Duke stepped impatiently into the roadway.

"Ivor, you're a fool! Can't you tell jest from earnest, health from disease? I'm off! Are you coming with me? It would be as well that I should have a witness."

"Where are you off to?"

"To the other end of the Arcade."

"Who is the gentleman you expect to have the pleasure of meeting there?"

"How should I know?" The Duke took a letter from his pocket—it was the letter which had just arrived. "The fellow is to wear a white top-hat, and a gardenia in his button hole."

"What is it you have there?"

"It's the letter which brought the news—look for yourself and see; but, for God's sake make haste!" His Grace glanced at his watch. "It's already twenty after five."

"And do you mean to say that on the strength of a letter such as this you are going to hand over five hundred pounds to—"

The Duke cut Mr. Dacre short:

"What are five hundred pounds to me? Besides, you don't know all. There is another letter. And I have heard from Mabel. But I will tell you all about it later. If you are coming, come!"

Folding up the letter, Mr. Dacre returned it to the Duke.

"As you say, what are five hundred pounds to you? It's as well they are not as much to you as they are to me, or I'm afraid—"

"Hang it, Ivor, do prose afterwards!"

The Duke hurried across the road. Mr. Dacre hastened after him. As they entered the Arcade they passed a constable. Mr. Dacre touched his companion's arm.

"Don't you think we'd better ask our friend in blue to walk behind us? His neighbourhood might be handy."

"Nonsense!" The Duke stopped short. "Ivor, this is my affair, not yours. If you are not content to play the part of silent witness, be so good as to leave me."

"My dear Datchet, I'm entirely at your service. I can be every whit as insane as you, I do assure you."

Side by side they moved rapidly down the Burlington Arcade. The Duke was obviously in a state of the extremest nervous tension. Mr. Dacre was equally obviously in a state of the most supreme enjoyment. People stared as they rushed past. The Duke saw nothing. Mr. Dacre saw everything, and smiled.

When they reached the Piccadilly end of the Arcade the Duke pulled up. He looked about him. Mr. Dacre also looked about him.

"I see nothing of your white-hatted and gardenia-button-holed friend," said Ivor.

The Duke referred to his watch:

"It's not yet half-past five. I'm up to time."

Mr. Dacre held his stick in front of him and leaned on it. He indulged himself with a beatific smile:

"It strikes me, my dear Datchet, that you've been the victim of one of the finest things in hoaxes—"

"I hope I haven't kept you waiting."

The voice which interrupted Mr. Dacre came from the rear. While they were looking in front of them some one approached from behind, apparently coming out of the shop which was at their backs.

The speaker looked a gentleman. He sounded like one, too. Costume, appearance, manner were beyond reproach—even beyond the criticism of two such keen critics as were these. The glorious attire of a London dandy was surmounted with a beautiful white top-hat. In his button-hole was a magnificent gardenia.

In age the stranger was scarcely more than a boy, and a sunny-faced, handsome boy at that. His cheeks were hairless, his eyes were blue. His smile was not only innocent, it was bland. Never was there a more conspicuous illustration of that repose which stamps the caste of Vere de Vere.

The Duke looked at him, and glowered. Mr. Dacre looked at him, and smiled.

"Who are you?" asked the Duke.

"Ah—that is the question!" The newcomer's refined and musical voice breathed the very soul of affability. "I am an individual who is so unfortunate as to be in want of five hundred pounds."

"Are you the scoundrel who sent me that infamous letter?"

That charming stranger never turned a hair!

"I am the scoundrel mentioned in that infamous letter who wants to accost you at the Piccadilly end of the Burlington Arcade before half-past five—as witness my white hat and my gardenia."

"Where's my wife?"

The stranger gently swung his stick in front of him with his two hands. He regarded the Duke as a merry-hearted son might regard his father. The thing was beautiful!

"Her Grace will be home almost as soon as you are—when you have given me the money which I perceive you have all ready for me in that scarcely elegant-looking canvas bag." He shrugged his shoulders quite gracefully. "Unfortunately, in these matters one has no choice—one is forced to ask for gold."

"And suppose, instead of giving you what is in this canvas bag, I take you by the throat and choke the life right out of you?"

"Or suppose," amended Mr. Dacre, "that you do better, and commend this gentleman to the tender mercies of the first policeman we encounter."

The stranger turned to Mr. Dacre. He condescended to become conscious of his presence.

"Is this gentleman your Grace's friend? Ah—Mr. Dacre, I perceive! I have the honour of knowing Mr. Dacre, although, possibly, I am unknown to him."

"You were—until this moment."

With an airy little laugh the stranger returned to the Duke. He brushed an invisible speck of dust off the sleeve of his coat.

"As has been intimated in that infamous letter, his Grace is at perfect liberty to give me into custody— why not? Only"—he said it with his boyish smile—"if a particular communication is not received from me in certain quarters within a certain time, the Duchess of Datchet's beautiful white arm will be hacked off at the shoulder."

"You hound!"

The Duke would have taken the stranger by the throat, and have done his best to choke the life right out of him then and there, if Mr. Dacre had not intervened.

"Steady, old man!" Mr. Dacre turned to the stranger: "You appear to be a pretty sort of a scoundrel."

The stranger gave his shoulders that almost imperceptible shrug:

"Oh, my dear Dacre, I am in want of money! I believe that you sometimes are in want of money, too."

Everybody knows that nobody knows where Ivor Dacre gets his money from, so the illusion must have tickled him immensely.

"You're a cool hand," he said.

"Some men are born that way."

"So I should imagine. Men like you must be born, not made."

"Precisely—as you say!" The stranger turned, with his graceful smile, to the Duke: "But are we not wasting precious time? I can assure your Grace that, in this particular matter, moments are of value."

Mr. Dacre interposed before the Duke could answer:

"If you take my strongly urged advice, Datchet, you will summon this constable who is now coming down the Arcade, and hand over this gentleman to his keeping. I do not think that you need fear that the Duchess will lose her arm, or even her little finger. Scoundrels of this one's kidney are most amenable to reason when they have handcuffs on their wrists."

The Duke plainly hesitated. He would—and he would not. The stranger, as he eyed him, seemed much amused.

"My dear Duke, by all means act on Mr. Dacre's valuable suggestion. As I said before, why not? It would at least be interesting to see if the Duchess does or does not lose her arm—almost as interesting to you as to Mr. Dacre. Those blackmailing, kidnapping scoundrels do use such empty menaces. Besides, you would have the pleasure of seeing me locked up. My imprisonment for life would recompense you even for the loss of her Grace's arm. And five hundred pounds is such a sum to have to pay—merely for a wife! Why not, therefore, act on Mr. Dacre's suggestion? Here comes the constable." The constable referred to was advancing towards them—he was not a dozen yards away. "Let me beckon to him—I will with pleasure." He took out his watch—a gold chronograph repeater. "There are scarcely ten minutes left during which it will be possible for me to send the communication which I spoke of, so that it may arrive in time. As it will then be too late, and the instruments are already prepared for the little operation which her Grace is eagerly anticipating, it would, perhaps, be as well, after all, that you should give me into charge. You would have saved your five hundred pounds, and you would, at any rate, have something in exchange for her Grace's mutilated limb. Ah, here is the constable! Officer!"

The stranger spoke with such a pleasant little air of easy geniality that it was impossible to tell if he were in jest or earnest. This fact impressed the Duke much more than if he had gone in for a liberal indulgence of the—under the circumstances—orthodox melodramatic scowling. And, indeed, in the face of his own common sense, it impressed Mr. Ivor Dacre too.

This well-bred, well-groomed youth was just the being to realise—aux bouts des ongles—a modern type of the devil, the type which depicts him as a perfect gentleman, who keeps smiling all the time.

The constable whom this audacious rogue had signalled approached the little group. He addressed the stranger:

"Do you want me, sir?"

"No, I do not want you. I think it is the Duke of Datchet."

The constable, who knew the Duke very well by sight, saluted him as he turned to receive instructions.

The Duke looked white, even savage. There was not a pleasant look in his eyes and about his lips. He appeared to be endeavouring to put a great restraint upon himself. There was a momentary silence. Mr. Dacre made a movement as if to interpose. The Duke caught him by the arm.

He spoke: "No, constable, I do not want you. This person is mistaken."

The constable looked as if he could not quite make out how such a mistake could have arisen, hesitated, then, with another salute, he moved away.

The stranger was still holding his watch in his hand.

"Only eight minutes," he said.

The Duke seemed to experience some difficulty in giving utterance to what he had to say.

"If I give you this five hundred pounds, you—you—"

As the Duke paused, as if at a loss for language which was strong enough to convey his meaning, the stranger laughed.

"Let us take the adjectives for granted. Besides, it is only boys who call each other names—men do things. If you give me the five hundred sovereigns, which you have in that bag, at once—in five minutes it will be too late—I will promise—I will not swear; if you do not credit my simple promise, you will not believe my solemn affirmation—I will promise that, possibly within an hour, certainly within an hour and a half, the Duchess of Datchet shall return to you absolutely uninjured—except, of course, as you are already aware, with regard to a few of the hairs of her head. I will promise this on the understanding that you do not yourself attempt to see where I go, and that you will allow no one else to do so." This with a glance at Ivor Dacre. "I shall know at once if I am followed. If you entertain any such intentions, you had better, on all accounts, remain in possession of your five hundred pounds."

The Duke eyed him very grimly:

"I entertain no such intentions—until the Duchess returns."

Again the stranger indulged in that musical little laugh of his:

"Ah, until the Duchess returns! Of course, then the bargain's at an end. When you are once more in the enjoyment of her Grace's society, you will be at liberty to set all the dogs in Europe at my heels. I assure you I fully expect that you will do so—why not?" The Duke raised the canvas bag. "My dear Duke, ten thousand thanks! You shall see her Grace at Datchet House, 'pon my honour. Probably within the hour."

"Well," commented Ivor Dacre, when the stranger had vanished, with the bag, into Piccadilly, and as the Duke and himself moved towards Burlington Gardens, "if a gentleman is to be robbed, it is as well that he should have another gentleman to rob him."

CHAPTER III

AND FOUND

Mr. Dacre eyed his companion covertly as they progressed. His Grace of Datchet appeared to have some fresh cause for uneasiness. All at once he gave it utterance, in a tone of voice which was extremely sombre:

"Ivor, do you think that scoundrel will dare to play me false?"

"I think," murmured Mr. Dacre, "that he has dared to play you pretty false already."

"I don't mean that. But I mean how am I to know, now that he has his money, that he will still not keep Mabel in his clutches?"

There came an echo from Mr. Dacre:

"Just so—how are you to know?"

"I believe that something of this sort has been done in the United States."

"I thought that there they were content to kidnap them after they were dead. I was not aware that they had, as yet, got quite so far as the living."

"I believe that I have heard of something just like this."

"Possibly; they are giants over there."

"And in that case the scoundrels, when their demands were met, refused to keep to the letter of their bargain, and asked for more."

The Duke stood still. He clenched his fists, and swore:

"Ivor, if that — villain doesn't keep his word, and Mabel isn't home within the hour, by — I shall go mad!"

"My dear Datchet"—Mr. Dacre loved strong language as little as he loved a scene—"let us trust to time and, a little, to your white-hatted and gardenia-button-holed friend's word of honour. You should have thought of possible eventualities before you showed your confidence—really. Suppose, instead of going mad, we first of all go home?"

A hansom stood waiting for a fare at the end of the Arcade. Mr. Dacre had handed the Duke into it before his Grace had quite realised that the vehicle was there.

"Tell the fellow to drive faster." That was what the Duke said when the cab had started.

"My dear Datchet, the man's already driving his geegee off its legs. If a bobby catches sight of him he'll take his number."

A moment later, a murmur from the Duke:

"I don't know if you're aware that the Prince is coming to dinner?"

"I am perfectly aware of it."

"You take it uncommonly coolly. How easy it is to bear our brother's burdens! Ivor, if Mabel doesn't turn up I shall feel like murder."

"I sympathise with you, Datchet, with all my heart, though, I may observe, parenthetically, that I very far from realise the situation even yet. Take my advice. If the Duchess does not show quite so soon as we both of us desire, don't make a scene; just let me see what I can do."

Judging from the expression of his countenance, the Duke was conscious of no overwhelming desire to witness an exhibition of Mr. Dacre's prowess.

When the cab reached Datchet House his Grace dashed up the steps three at a time. The door flew open.

"Has the Duchess returned?"

"Hereward!"

A voice floated downwards from above. Some one came running down the stairs. It was her Grace of Datchet.

"Mabel!"

She actually rushed into the Duke's extended arms. And he kissed her, and she kissed him—before the servants.

"So you're not quite dead?" she cried.

"I am almost," he said.

She drew herself a little away from him.

"Hereward, were you seriously hurt?"

"Do you suppose that I could have been otherwise than seriously hurt?"

"My darling! Was it a Pickford's van?"

The Duke stared:

"A Pickford's van? I don't understand. But come in here. Come along, Ivor. Mabel, you don't see Ivor."

"How do you do, Mr. Dacre?"

Then the trio withdrew into a little ante-room; it was really time. Even then the pair conducted themselves as if Mr. Dacre had been nothing and no one. The Duke took the lady's two hands in his. He eyed her fondly.

"So you are uninjured, with the exception of that lock of hair. Where did the villain take it from?"

The lady looked a little puzzled:

"What lock of hair?"

From an envelope which he took from his pocket the Duke produced a shining tress. It was the lock of hair which had arrived in the first communication. "I will have it framed."

"You will have what framed?" The Duchess glanced at what the Duke was so tenderly caressing, almost, as it seemed, a little dubiously, "Whatever is it you have there?"

"It is the lock of hair which that scoundrel sent me." Something in the lady's face caused him to ask a question: "Didn't he tell you he had sent it me?"

"Hereward!"

"Did the brute tell you that he meant to cut off your little finger?"

A very curious look came into the lady's face. She glanced at the Duke as if she, all at once, were half afraid of him. She cast at Mr. Dacre what really seemed to be a look of enquiry. Her voice was tremulously anxious:

"Hereward, did—did the accident affect you mentally?"

"How could it not have affected me mentally? Do you think that my mental organization is of steel?"

"But you look so well?"

"Of course I look well, now that I have you back again. Tell me, darling, did that hound actually threaten you with cutting off your arm? If he did, I shall feel half inclined to kill him yet."

The Duchess seemed positively to shrink from her better-half's near neighbourhood:

"Hereward, was it a Pickford's van?"

The Duke seemed puzzled. Well he might be:

"Was what a Pickford's van?"

The lady turned to Mr. Dacre. In her voice there was a ring of anguish:

"Mr. Dacre, tell me, was it a Pickford's van?"

Ivor could only imitate his relative's repetition of her inquiry:

"I don't quite catch you—was what a Pickford's van?"

The Duchess clasped her hands in front of her: "What is it you are keeping from me? What is it you are trying to hide? I implore you to tell me the worst, whatever it may be! Do not keep me any longer in suspense; you do not know what I already have endured. Mr. Dacre, is my husband mad?"

One need scarcely observe that the lady's amazing appeal to Mr. Dacre as to her husband's sanity was received with something like surprise. As the Duke continued to stare at her, a dreadful fear began to loom upon his brain:

"My darling, your brain is unhinged!"

He advanced to take her two hands again in his; but, to his unmistakable distress, she shrank away from him:

"Hereward—don't touch me. How is it that I missed you? Why did you not wait until I came?"

"Wait until you came?"

The Duke's bewilderment increased.

"Surely, if your injuries turned out, after all, to be slight, that was all the more reason why you should have waited, after sending for me like that."

"I sent for you—I?" The Duke's tone was grave. "My darling, perhaps you had better come upstairs."

"Not until we have had an explanation. You must have known that I should come. Why did you not wait for me after you had sent me that?"

The Duchess held out something to the Duke. He took it. It was a card—his own visiting-card. Something was written on the back of it. He read aloud what was written:

"'Mabel, come to me at once with bearer. They tell me that they cannot take me home.' It looks like my own writing."

"Looks like it! It is your writing."

"It looks like it—and written with a shaky pen."

"My dear child, one's hand would shake at such a moment as that."

"Mabel, where did you get this?"

"It was brought to me in Cane and Wilson's."

"Who brought it?"

"Who brought it? Why, the man you sent."

"The man I sent?" A light burst upon the Duke's brain. He fell back a pace. "It's the decoy!"

Her Grace echoed the words:

"The decoy?"

"The scoundrel! To set a trap with such a bait! My poor, innocent darling, did you think it came from me? Tell me, Mabel, where did he cut off your hair?"

"Cut off my hair?"

Her Grace put her hand up to her head as if to make sure that her hair was there.

"Where did he take you to?"

"He took me to Draper's Buildings."

"Draper's Buildings?"

"I have never been in the City before, but he told me it was Draper's Buildings. Isn't that near the Stock Exchange?"

"Near the Stock Exchange?"

It seemed rather a curious place to which to take a kidnapped victim. The man's audacity!

"He told me that you were coming out of the Stock Exchange when a van knocked you over. He said that he thought it was a Pickford's van—was it a Pickford's van?"

"No, it was not a Pickford's van. Mabel, were you in Draper's Buildings when you wrote that letter?"

"Wrote what letter?"

"Have you forgotten it already? I do not believe that there is a word in it which will not be branded on my brain until I die."

"Hereward! What do you mean?"

"Surely you cannot have written me such a letter as that, and then have forgotten it already?"

He handed her the letter which had arrived in the second communication. She glanced at it, askance. Then she took it with a little gasp.

"Hereward, if you don't mind, I think I'll take a chair." She took a chair. "Whatever—whatever's this?" As she read the letter the varying expressions which passed across her face were, in themselves, a study in psychology. "Is it possible that you can imagine that, under any conceivable circumstances, I could have written such a letter as this?"

"Mabel!"

She rose to her feet, with emphasis:

"Hereward, don't say that you thought this came from me!"

"Not come from you?" He remembered Knowles's diplomatic reception of the epistle on its first appearance. "I suppose that you will say next that this is not a lock of your hair?"

"My dear child, what bee have you got in your bonnet? This a lock of my hair! Why, it's not in the least like my hair!"

Which was certainly inaccurate. As far as color was concerned it was an almost perfect match. The Duke turned to Mr. Dacre.

"Ivor, I've had to go through a good deal this afternoon. If I have to go through much more, something will crack!" He touched his forehead. "I think it's my turn to take a chair." He also took a chair. Not the one which the Duchess had vacated, but one which faced it. He stretched out his legs in front of him; he thrust his hands into his trousers-pockets; he said, in a tone which was not only gloomy but absolutely gruesome:

"Might I ask, Mabel, if you have been kidnapped?"

"Kidnapped?"

"The word I used was 'kidnapped.' But I will spell it if you like. Or I will get a dictionary, that you may see its meaning."

The Duchess looked as if she was beginning to be not quite sure if she was awake or sleeping. She turned to Ivor:

"Mr. Dacre, has the accident affected Hereward's brain?"

The Duke took the words out of his cousin's mouth:

"On that point, my dear, let me ease your mind. I don't know if you are under the impression that I should be the same shape after a Pickford's van had run over me as I was before; but, in any case, I have not been run over by a Pickford's van. So far as I am concerned there has been no accident. Dismiss that delusion from your mind."

"Oh!"

"You appear surprised. One might even think that you were sorry. But may I now ask what you did when you arrived at Draper's Buildings?"

"Did! I looked for you!"

"Indeed! And when you had looked in vain, what was the next item in your programme?"

The lady shrank still further from him:

"Hereward, have you been having a jest at my expense? Can you have been so cruel?" Tears stood in her eyes.

Rising, the Duke laid his hand upon her arm:

"Mabel, tell me—what did you do when you had looked for me in vain?"

"I looked for you upstairs and downstairs, and everywhere. It was quite a large place, it took me ever such a time. I thought that I should go distracted. Nobody seemed to know anything about you, or even that there had been an accident at all—it was all offices. I couldn't make it out in the least, and the people didn't seem to be able to make me out either. So when I couldn't find you anywhere I came straight home again."

The Duke was silent for a moment. Then, with funereal gravity, he turned to Mr. Dacre. He put to him this question:

"Ivor, what are you laughing at?"

Mr. Dacre drew his hand across his mouth with rather a suspicious gesture:

"My dear fellow, only a smile!"

The Duchess looked from one to the other:

"What have you two been doing? What is the joke?"

With an air of preternatural solemnity the Duke took two letters from the breast-pocket of his coat.

"Mabel, you have already seen your letter. You have already seen the lock of your hair. Just look at this—and that."

He gave her the two very singular communications which had arrived in such a mysterious manner, and so quickly one after the other. She read them with wide-open eyes.

"Hereward! Wherever did these come from?"

The Duke was standing with his legs apart, and his hands in his trousers-pockets. "I would give—I would give another five hundred pounds to know. Shall I tell you, madam, what I have been doing? I have been presenting five hundred golden sovereigns to a perfect stranger, with a top-hat, and a gardenia in his button-hole."

"Whatever for?"

"If you have perused those documents which you have in your hand, you will have some faint idea. Ivor, when its your funeral I'll smile. Mabel, Duchess of Dachet, it is beginning to dawn upon the vacuum which represents my brain that I've been the victim of one of the prettiest things in practical jokes that ever yet was planned. When that fellow brought you that card at Cane and Wilson's—which, I need scarcely tell you, never came from me—some one walked out of the front entrance who was so exactly like you that both Barnes and Moysey took her for you. Moysey showed her into the carriage, and Barnes drove her home. But when the carriage reached home it was empty. Your double had got out upon the road."

The Duchess uttered a sound which was half a gasp, half sigh:

"Hereward!"

"Barnes and Moysey, with beautiful and childlike innocence, when they found that they had brought the thing home empty, came straightway and told me that you had jumped out of the brougham while it had been driving full pelt through the streets. While I was digesting that piece of information there came the first epistle, with the lock of your hair. Before I had time to digest that there came the second epistle, with yours inside, and, as a guarantee of the authenticity of your appeal, the same envelope held this."

The Duke handed the Duchess the half of the broken sixpence. She stared at it with the most unequivocal astonishment.

"Why, it looks just like my sixpence." She put her hand to her breast, feeling something that was there. "But it isn't! What wickedness!"

"It is wickedness, isn't it? Anyhow, that seemed good enough for me; so I posted off the five hundred pounds to save your arm—not to dwell upon your little finger."

"It seems incredible!"

"Its sounds incredible; but unfathomable is the folly of man, especially of a man who loves his wife." The Duke crossed to Mr. Dacre. "I don't want, Ivor, to suggest anything in the way of bribery and corruption, but if you could keep this matter to yourself, and not mention it to your friends, our white-hatted and gardenia-button-holed acquaintance is welcome to his five hundred pounds, and—Mabel, what on earth are you laughing at?"

The Duchess appeared, all at once, to be seized with inextinguishable laughter.

"Hereward," she cried, "just think how that man must be laughing at you!"

And the Duke of Datchet thought of it.

THE STRANGE OCCURRENCES IN CANTERSTONE JAIL

CHAPTER I

MR. MANKELL DECLARES HIS INTENTION OF ACTING ON MAGISTERIAL ADVICE

Oliver Mankell was sentenced to three months' hard labour. The charge was that he had obtained money by means of false pretences. Not large sums, but shillings, half-crowns, and so on. He had given out that he was a wizard, and that he was able and willing—for a consideration—to predict the events of the future—tell fortunes, in fact. The case created a large amount of local interest, for some curious stories were told about the man in the town. Mankell was a tall, slight, wiry-looking fellow in the prime of life, with coal-black hair and olive complexion—apparently of Romany extraction. His bearing was self-possessed, courteous even, yet with something in his air which might have led one to suppose that he saw—what others did not—the humour of the thing. At one point his grave, almost saturnine visage distinctly relaxed into a smile. It was when Colonel Gregory, the chairman of the day, was passing sentence. After committing him for three months' hard labour, the Colonel added—

"During your sojourn within the walls of a prison you will have an opportunity of retrieving your reputation. You say you are a magician. During your stay in jail I would strongly advise you to prove it.

You lay claim to magic powers. Exercise them. I need scarcely point out to you how excellent a chance you will have of creating a sensation."

The people laughed. When the great Panjandrum is even dimly suspected of an intention to be funny, the people always do. But on this occasion even the prisoner smiled—rather an exceptional thing, for as a rule it is the prisoner who sees the joke the least of all.

Later in the day the prisoner was conveyed to the county jail. This necessitated a journey by rail, with a change upon the way. At the station where they changed there was a delay of twenty minutes. This the prisoner and the constable in charge of him improved by adjourning to a public house hard by. Here they had a glass—indeed they had two—and when they reached Canterstone, the town on whose outskirts stood the jail, they had one—or perhaps it was two—more. It must have been two, for when they reached the jail, instead of the constable conveying the prisoner, it was the prisoner who conveyed the constable—upon his shoulder. The warder who answered the knock seemed surprised at what he saw.

"What do you want?"

"Three months' hard labour."

The warder stared. The shades of night had fallen, and the lamp above the prison-door did not seem to cast sufficient light upon the subject to satisfy the janitor.

"Come inside," he said.

Mankell entered, the constable upon his shoulder. Having entered, he carefully placed the constable in a sitting posture on the stones, with his back against the wall. The policeman's helmet had tipped over his eyes—he scarcely presented an imposing picture of the majesty and might of the law. The warder shook him by the shoulder. "Here, come—wake up. You're a pretty sort," he said. The constable's reply, although slightly inarticulate, was yet sufficiently distinct.

"Not another drop!" he murmured.

"No, I shouldn't think so," said the warder. "You've had a pailful, it seems to me, already."

The man seemed a little puzzled. He turned and looked at Mankell.

"What do you want here?"

"Three months' hard labour."

The man looked down and saw that the new-comer had gyves upon his wrists. He went to a door at one side, and summoned another warder. The two returned together. This second official took in the situation at a glance.

"Have you come from—?" naming the town from which they in fact had come. Mankell inclined his head. This second official turned his attention to the prostrate constable. "Look in his pockets."

The janitor acted on the suggestion. The order for committal was produced.

"Are you Oliver Mankell?"

Again Mankell inclined his head. With the order in his hand, the official marched him through the side-door by which he had himself appeared. Soon Oliver Mankell was the inmate of a cell. He spent that night in the reception-cells at the gate. In the morning he had a bath, was inducted into prison clothing, and examined by the doctor. He was then taken up to the main building of the prison, and introduced to the governor. The governor was a quiet, gentlemanly man, with a straggling black beard and spectacles—the official to the tips of his fingers. As Mankell happened to be the only fresh arrival, the governor favoured him with a little speech.

"You've placed yourself in an uncomfortable position, Mankell. I hope you'll obey the rules while you're here."

"I intend to act upon the advice tendered me by the magistrate who passed sentence."

The governor looked up. Not only was the voice a musical voice, but the words were not the sort of words generally chosen by the average prisoner.

"What advice was that?"

"He said that I claimed to be a magician. He strongly advised me to prove it during my stay in jail. I intend to act upon the advice he tendered."

The governor looked Mankell steadily in the face. The speaker's bearing conveyed no suggestion of insolent intention. The governor looked down again.

"I advise you to be careful what you do. You may make your position more uncomfortable than it is already. Take the man away."

They took the man away. They introduced him to the wheel. On the treadmill he passed the remainder of the morning. At noon morning tasks were over, and the prisoners were marched into their day-cells to enjoy the meal which, in prison parlance, was called dinner. In accordance with the ordinary routine, the chaplain made his appearance in the round-house to interview those prisoners who had just come in, and those whose sentences would be completed on the morrow. When Mankell had been asked at the gate what his religion was, he had made no answer; so the warder, quite used to ignorance on the part of new arrivals as to all religions, had entered him as a member of the Church of England. As a member of the Church of England he was taken out to interview the chaplain.

The chaplain was a little fussy gentleman, considerably past middle age. Long experience of prisons and prisoners had bred in him a perhaps unconscious habit of regarding criminals as naughty boys—urchins who required a judicious combination of cakes and castigation.

"Well, my lad, I'm sorry to see a man of your appearance here." This was a remark the chaplain made to a good many of his new friends. It was intended to give them the impression that at least the chaplain perceived that they were something out of the ordinary run. Then he dropped his voice to a judicious whisper. "What's it for?"

"For telling the truth."

This reply seemed a little to surprise the chaplain. He settled his spectacles upon his nose.

"For telling the truth!" An idea seemed all at once to strike the chaplain. "Do you mean that you pleaded guilty?" The man was silent. The chaplain referred to a paper he held in his hand. "Eh, I see that here it is written 'false pretences.' Was it a stumer?"

We have seen it mentioned somewhere that "stumer" is slang for a worthless cheque. It was a way with the chaplain to let his charges see that he was at least acquainted with their phraseology. But on this occasion there was no response. The officer in charge of Mankell, who possibly wanted his dinner, put in his oar.

"Telling fortunes, sir."

"Telling fortunes! Oh! Dear me! How sad! You see what telling fortunes brings you to? There will be no difficulty in telling your fortune if you don't take care. I will see you to-morrow morning after chapel."

The chaplain turned away. But his prediction proved to be as false as Mankell's were stated to have been. He did not see him the next morning after chapel, and that for the sufficient reason that on the following morning there was no chapel. And the reasons why there was no chapel were very curious indeed—unprecedented, in fact.

Canterstone Jail was an old-fashioned prison. In it each prisoner had two cells, one for the day and one for the night. The day-cells were on the ground-floor, those for the night were overhead. At six a.m. a bell was rung, and the warders unlocked the night-cells for the occupants to go down to those beneath. That was the rule. That particular morning was an exception to the rule. The bell was rung as usual, and the warders started to unlock, but there the adherence to custom ceased, for the doors of the cells refused to be unlocked.

The night-cells were hermetically sealed by oaken doors of massive thickness, bolted and barred in accordance with the former idea that the security of prisoners should depend rather upon bolts and bars than upon the vigilance of the officers in charge. Each door was let into a twenty-four inch brick-wall, and secured by two ponderous bolts and an enormous lock of the most complicated workmanship. These locks were kept constantly oiled. When the gigantic key was inserted, it turned as easily as the key of a watch—that was the rule. When, therefore, on inserting his key into the lock of the first cell, Warder Slater found that it wouldn't turn at all, he was rather taken aback. "Who's been having a game with this lock?" he asked.

Warder Puffin, who was stationed at the head of the stairs to see that the prisoners passed down in order, at the proper distance from each other, replied to him.

"Anything the matter with the lock? Try the next."

Warder Slater did try the next, but he found that as refractory as the first had been.

"Perhaps you've got the wrong key?" suggested Warder Puffin.

"Got the wrong key!" cried Warder Slater. "Do you think I don't know my own keys when I see them?"

The oddest part of it was that all the locks were the same. Not only in Ward A, but in Wards B, C, D, E, and F—in all the wards, in fact. When this became known, a certain sensation was created, and that on both sides of the unlocked doors. The prisoners were soon conscious that their guardians were unable to release them, and they made a noise. Nothing is so precious to the average prisoner as a grievance; here was a grievance with a vengeance.

The chief warder was a man named Murray. He was short and stout, with a red face, and short, stubbly white hair—his very appearance suggested apoplexy. That suggestion was emphasised when he lost his temper—capable officer though he was, that was more than once in a while. He was in the wheel-shed, awaiting the arrival of the prisoners preparatory to being told off to their various tasks, when, instead of the prisoners, Warder Slater appeared. If Murray was stout, Slater was stouter. He was about five feet eight, and weighed at least 250 pounds. He was wont to amaze those who saw him for the first time—and wondered—by assuring them that he had a brother who was still stouter—compared to whom he was a skeleton, in fact. But he was stout enough. He and the chief warder made a striking pair.

"There's something the matter with the locks of the night-cells, sir. We can't undo the doors."

"Can't undo the doors!" Mr. Murray turned the colour of a boiled beetroot. "What do you mean?"

"It's very queer, sir, but all over the place it's the same. We can't get none of the doors unlocked."

Mr. Murray started off at a good round pace, Slater following hard at his heels. The chief warder tried his hand himself. He tried every lock in the prison; not one of them vouchsafed to budge. Not one, that is, with a single exception. The exception was in Ward B, No. 27. Mr. Murray had tried all the other doors in the ward, beginning with No. 1—tried them all in vain. But when he came to No. 27, the lock turned with the customary ease, and the door was open. Within it was Oliver Mankell, standing decorously at attention, waiting to be let out. Mr. Murray stared at him.

"Hum! there's nothing the matter with this lock, at any rate. You'd better go down."

Oliver Mankell went downstairs—he was the only man in Canterstone jail who did.

"Well, this is a pretty go!" exclaimed Mr. Murray, when he had completed his round. Two or three other warders had accompanied him. He turned on these. "Someone will smart for this—you see if they don't. Keep those men still."

The din was deafening. The prisoners, secure of a grievance, were practising step-dances in their heavy shoes on the stone floors: they made the narrow vaulted corridors ring.

"Silence those men!" shouted Mr. Jarvis, the second warder, who was tall and thin as the chief was short and stout. He might as well have shouted to the wind. Those in the cells just close at hand observed the better part of valour, but those a little distance off paid not the slightest heed. If they were locked in, the officers were locked out.

"I must go and see the governor." Mr. Murray pursed up his lips. "Keep those men still, or I'll know the reason why."

He strode off, leaving his subordinates to obey his orders—if they could, or if they couldn't.

Mr. Paley's house was in the centre of the jail. Paley, by the way, was the governor's name. The governor, when Mr. Murray arrived, was still in bed. He came down to the chief warder in rather primitive disarray.

"Anything the matter, Murray?"

"Yes, sir; there's something very much the matter, indeed."

"What is it?"

"We can't get any of the doors of the night-cells open."

"You can't get—what?"

"There seems to be something the matter with the locks."

"The locks? All of them? Absurd!"

"Well, there they are, and there's the men inside of them, and we can't get 'em out—at least I've tried my hand, and I know I can't."

"I'll come with you at once, and see what you mean."

Mr. Paley was as good as his word. He started off just as he was. As they were going, the chief warder made another remark.

"By the way, there is one cell we managed to get open—I opened it myself."

"I thought you said there was none?"

"There's that one—it's that man Mankell."

"Mankell? Who is he?"

"He came in yesterday. It's that magician."

When they reached the cells, it was easy to perceive that something was wrong. The warders hung about in twos and threes; the noise was deafening; the prisoners were keeping holiday.

"Get me the keys and let me see what I can do. It is impossible that all the locks can have been tampered with."

They presented Mr. Paley with the keys. In his turn he tried every lock in the jail This was not a work of a minute or two. The prison contained some three hundred night-cells. To visit them all necessitated not only a good deal of running up and down stairs, but a good deal of actual walking; for they were not only in different floors and in different blocks, but the prison itself was divided into two entirely separate divisions—north and south—and to pass from one division to the other entailed a walk of at least a hundred yards. By the time he had completed the round of the locks, Mr. Paley had had about enough of it. It was not surprising that he felt a little bewildered—not one of the locks had shown any more readiness to yield to him than to the others.

In passing from one ward to the other, he had passed the row of day-cells in which was situated B 27. Here they found Oliver Mankell sitting in silent state awaiting the call to work. The governor pulled up at the sight of him.

"Well, Mankell, so there was nothing the matter with the lock of your door?"

Mankell simply inclined his head.

"I suppose you know nothing about the locks of the other doors?"

Again the inclination of the head. The man seemed to be habitually chary of speech.

"What's the matter with you? Are you dumb? Can't you speak when you're spoken to?"

This time Mankell extended the palms of his hands with a gesture which might mean anything or nothing. The governor passed on. The round finished, he held a consultation with the chief warder.

"Have you any suspicions?"

"It's queer." Mr. Murray stroked his bristly chin.

"It's very queer that that man Mankell's should be the only cell in the prison left untampered with."

"Very queer, indeed."

"What are we to do? We can't leave the men locked up all day. It's breakfast-time already. I suppose the cooks haven't gone down to the cookhouse?"

"They're locked up with the rest. Barnes has been up to know what he's to do."

Barnes was the prison cook. The cooks referred to were six good-behaviour men who were told off to assist him in his duties.

"If the food were cooked, I don't see how we should give it to the men."

"That's the question." Mr. Murray pondered.

"We might pass it through the gas-holes."

"We should have to break the glass to do it. You wouldn't find it easy. It's plate-glass, an inch in thickness, and built into the solid wall."

There was a pause for consideration.

"Well, this is a pretty start. I've never come across anything like it in all my days before."

Mr. Paley passed his hand through his hair. He had never come across anything like it either.

"I shall have to telegraph to the commissioners. I can't do anything without their sanction."

The following telegram was sent:

"Cannot get prisoners out of night-cells. Something the matter with locks. Cannot give them any food. The matter is very urgent. What shall I do?"

The following answer was received:

"Inspector coming down."

The inspector came down—Major William Hardinge. A tall, portly gentleman, with a very decided manner. When he saw the governor he came to the point at once.

"What's all this stuff?"

"We can't get the prisoners out of the night-cells."

"Why?"

"There's something the matter with the locks."

"Have you given them any food?"

"We have not been able to."

"When were they locked up?"

"Yesterday evening at six o'clock."

"This is a very extraordinary state of things."

"It is, or I shouldn't have asked for instructions."

"It's now three o'clock in the afternoon. They've been without food for twenty-one hours. You've no right to keep them without food all that time."

"We are helpless. The construction of the night-cells does not permit of our introducing food into the interior when the doors are closed."

"Have they been quiet?"

"They've been as quiet as under the circumstance was to be expected."

As they were crossing towards the north division the governor spoke again:

"We've been able to get one man out."

"One!—out of the lot! How did you get him?"

"Oddly enough, the lock of his cell was the only one in the prison which had not been tampered with."

"Hum! I should like to see that man."

"His name's Mankell. He only came in yesterday. He's been pretending to magic powers—telling fortunes, and that kind of thing."

"Only came in yesterday? He's begun early. Perhaps we shall have to tell him what his fortune's likely to be."

When they reached the wards the keys were handed to the inspector, who in his turn tried his hand. A couple of locksmiths had been fetched up from the town. When the Major had tried two or three of the locks it was enough for him. He turned to the makers of locks.

"What's the matter with these locks?"

"Well, that's exactly what we can't make out. The keys go in all right, but they won't turn. Seems as though somebody had been having a lark with them."

"Can't you pick them?"

"They're not easy locks to pick, but we'll have a try!"

"Have a try!"

They had a try, but they tried in vain. As it happened, the cell on which they commenced operations was occupied by a gentleman who had had a considerable experience in picking locks—experience which had ended in placing him on the other side that door. He derided the locksmiths through the door.

"Well, you are a couple of keen ones! What, can't pick the lock! Why, there ain't a lock in England I couldn't pick with a bent 'airpin. I only wish you was this side, starving like I am, and I was where you are, it wouldn't be a lock that would keep me from giving you food."

This was not the sort of language Major Hardinge was accustomed to hear from the average prisoner, but the Major probably felt that on this occasion the candid proficient in the art of picking locks had a certain excuse. He addressed the baffled workmen.

"If you can't pick the lock, what can you do? The question is, what is the shortest way of getting inside that cell?"

"Get a watch-saw," cried the gentleman on the other side the door.

"And when you've got your watch-saw?" inquired the Major.

"Saw the whole lock right clean away. Lor' bless me! I only wish I was where you are, I'd show you a thing or two. It's as easy as winking. Here's all us chaps a-starving, all for want of a little hexperience!"

"A saw'll be no good," declared one of the locksmiths. "Neither a watch-saw nor any other kind of saw. How are you going to saw through those iron stanchions? You'll have to burst the door in, that's what it'll have to be."

"You won't find it an easy thing to do." This was from the governor.

"Why don't you take and blow the whole place up?" shouted a gentleman, also on the other side of the door, two or three cells off.

Long before this all the occupants of the corridor had been lending a very attentive ear to what was going on. The suggestion was received with roars of laughter. The Major, however, preferred to act upon the workmen's advice. A sledge hammer was sent for.

While they were awaiting its arrival something rather curious happened—curious, that is, viewed in the light of what had gone before. Warder Slater formed one of the party. More for the sake of something to do than anything else, he put his key into the lock of the cell which was just in front of him. Giving it a gentle twist, to his amazement it turned with the greatest ease, and the door was open.

"Here's a go!" he exclaimed. "Blest if this door ain't come open."

There was a yell of jubilation all along the corridor. The prisoners seemed to be amused. The official party kept silence. Possibly their feelings were too deep for words.

"Since we've got this one open," said Warder Slater, "suppose we try another?"

He tried another, the next; the same result followed—the door was opened with the greatest of ease.

"What's the meaning of this?" spluttered the Major. "Who's been playing this tomfoolery? I don't believe there's anything the matter with a lock in the place."

There did not seem to be, just then. For when the officers tried again they found no difficulty in unlocking the doors, and setting the prisoners free.

CHAPTER II

THE CHAPLAIN AS AN AUTHORITY ON WITCHCRAFT

Major Hardinge remained in the jail that night. He stayed in the governor's house as Mr. Paley's guest. He expressed himself very strongly about the events of the day.

"I'll see the thing through if it takes me a week. The whole affair is incredible to me. It strikes me, Paley, that they've been making a fool of you."

The governor combed his hair with his fingers. His official manner had temporarily gone. He seemed depressed.

"I assure you the doors were locked."

"Of course the doors were locked, and they used the wrong keys to open them! It was a got-up thing."

"Not by the officers."

"By whom then? I don't see how the prisoners could have lent a hand."

"I know the officers, and I will answer for them, every man. As for the wrong keys being used, I know the keys as well as any one. I tried them, and not a lock would yield to me."

"But they did yield. What explanation have you to give of that?"

"I wish I could explain." And again the governor combed his hair.

"I'll have an explanation to-morrow!—you see if I don't!" But the Major never did.

On the morrow, punctually at 6 a.m., an imposing procession started to unlock. There were the inspector, governor, chief warder, second warder, and the warder who carried the keys.

"I don't think we shall have much difficulty in getting the men out of their cells this time," remarked the Major. They did not. "Good—good God!" he spluttered, when they reached the corridor; "what—what on earth's the meaning of this?" He had predicted rightly. They would have no difficulty in getting the men out of their cells: they were out already—men, and bedding, and planks, and all. There was a man fast asleep in bed in front of each cell-door.

"I thought I had given instructions that a special watch was to be kept all night," the Major roared.

"So there has been," answered the chief warder, whose head and face and neck were purple. "Warder Slater here has only just gone off duty. Now then, Slater, what's the meaning of this?"

"I don't know," protested Slater, whose mountain of flesh seemed quivering like jelly. "It's not a minute ago since I went to get my keys, and they was all inside their cells when I went down."

"Who let them out, then?"

The Major glared at him, incredulity in every line of his countenance.

"I don't know. I'll swear it wasn't me!"

"I suppose they let themselves out, then. You men!"

Although this short dialogue had been conducted by no means sotto-voce, the noise did not seem to have had the slightest effect in rousing the prisoners out of slumber. Even when the Major called to them they gave no sign.

"You men!" he shouted again; "it's no good shamming Abraham with me!" He stooped to shake the man who was lying on the plank at his feet. "Good—good God! The—the—man's not dead?"

"Dead!" cried the governor, kneeling by the Major's side upon the stones.

The sleeper was very still. He was a man of some forty years of age, with nut-brown tangled hair and beard. If not a short-sentence man he was still in the early stages of his term—for he lay on the bare boards of the plank with the rug, blanket, and sheet wrapped closely round him, so that they might take, as far as possible, the place of the coir mattress, which was not there. The bed was not a bed of comfort, yet his sleep was sound—strangely sound. If he breathed at all, it was so lightly as to be inaudible. On his face was that dazed, strained expression which we sometimes see on the faces of those who, without a moment's warning, have been suddenly visited by death.

"I don't think he's dead," the governor said. "He seems to be in some sort of trance. What's the man's name?"

"'Itchcock. He's one of the 'oppickers. He's got a month."

It was Warder Slater who gave the information. The governor took the man by the shoulder, and tried to rouse him out of sleep.

"Hitchcock! Hitchcock! Come, wake up, my man! It's all right; he's coming to—he's waking up."

He did wake up, and that so suddenly as to take the party by surprise. He sprang upright on the plank, nothing on but an attenuated prison shirt, and glared at the officials with looks of unmistakable surprise.

"Holloa! What's up! What's the meaning of this?"

Major Hardinge replied, suspicion peeping from his eyes:

"That is what we want to know, and what we intend to know—what does it mean? Why aren't you in your cell?"

The man seemed for the first time to perceive where he was.

"Strike me lucky, if I ain't outside! Somebody must have took me out when I was asleep." Then, realising in whose presence he was—"I beg your pardon, sir, but someone's took me out."

"The one who took you out took all the others too."

The Major gave a side glance at Warder Slater. That intelligent officer seemed to be suffering agonies. The prisoner glanced along the corridor. "If all the blessed lot of 'em ain't out too!"

They were not only all out, but they were all in the same curiously trance-like sleep. Each man had to be separately roused, and each woke with the same startling, sudden bound. No one seemed more surprised to find themselves where they were than the men themselves. And this was not the case in one ward only but in all the wards in the prison. No wonder the officials felt bewildered by the time they had gone the round.

"There's one thing certain," remarked Warder Slater to Warder Puffin, wiping the perspiration from his—Warder Slater's—brow, "if I let them out in one ward, I couldn't 'ardly let them out in all. Not to mention that I don't see how a man of my build's going to carry eight-and-forty men, bed, bedding, and all, out bodily, and that without disturbing one of them from sleep."

As the official party was returning through B ward, inspecting the men, who were standing at attention in their day-cells, the officer in charge advanced to the governor.

"One man missing, sir! No. 27, sir! Mankell, sir!"

The chief warder started. If possible, he turned a shade more purple even than before.

"Fetch me the key of the night-cells," he said.

It was brought. They went upstairs—the Major, the governor, the chief and second warders. Sure enough they found the missing man, standing at attention in his night-cell, waiting to be let out—the only man in the prison whom they had found in his place. The chief warder unlocked him. In silence they followed him as he went downstairs.

When the Major and Mr. Paley found themselves alone, both of them seemed a little bewildered.

"Well, Major, what do you think of it now?"

"It's a got-up thing! I'll stake my life, it's a got-up thing!"

"What do you mean—a got-up thing?"

"Some of the officers know more about it than they have chosen to say—that man Slater, for instance. But I'll have the thing sifted to the bottom before I go. I never heard of anything more audacious in the whole of my career."

The governor smiled, but he made no comment on the Major's observation. It was arranged that an inquiry should be held after chapel. During chapel a fresh subject was added to the list of those which already called for prompt inquiry.

Probably there is no more delicate and difficult position than that of a prison chaplain. If any man doubt this, let him step into a prison chaplain's shoes and see. He must have two faces, and each face must look in an exactly opposite way. The one towards authority—he is an official, an upholder of the law; the other towards the defiers of authority—he is the criminal's best friend. It requires the wisest of men to do his duty, so as to please both sides; and he must please both sides—or fail. As has already been hinted, Mr. Hewett, the Chaplain of Canterstone Jail, was not the wisest of men. He was in the uncomfortable—but not uncommon—position of being disliked by both the rival houses. He meant well, but he was not an apt interpreter of his own meaning. He blundered, sometimes on the prisoners' toes, and sometimes on the toes of the officials. Before the service began, the governor thought of giving him a hint, not—in the course of it—to touch on the events of the last two days. But previous hints of the same kind had not by any means been well received, and he refrained. Exactly what he feared would happen, happened. Both the inspector and the governor were present at the service. Possibly the chaplain supposed this to be an excellent opportunity of showing the sort of man he was—one full of zeal. At any rate, before the service was over, before pronouncing the benediction, he came down to the altar-rail, in the way they knew so well. The governor, outwardly unruffled, inwardly groaned.

"I have something to say to you."

When he said this, those who knew him knew exactly what was coming; or they thought they did, for, for once in a way, they were grievously wrong. When the chaplain had got so far he paused. It was his habit to indulge in these eloquent pauses, but it was not his habit to behave as he immediately did. While they were waiting for him to go on, almost forecasting the words he would use, a spasm seemed to go all over him, and he clutched the rail and spoke. And what he said was this—

"Bust the screws and blast 'em!"

The words were shouted rather than spoken. In the very act of utterance he clung on to the rail as though he needed its support to enable him to stand. The chapel was intensely still. The men stared at him as though unable to believe their eyes and ears. The chaplain was noted for his little eccentricities, but it was the first time they had taken such a shape as this.

"That's not what I meant to say." The words came out with a gasp. Mr. Hewett put his hand up to his brow. "That's not what I meant to say."

He gave a frightened glance around. Suddenly his gaze became fixed, and he looked intently at some object right in front of him. His eyes assumed a dull and fish-like stare. He hung on to the rail, his surpliced figure trembling as with palsy. Words fell from his lips with feverish volubility.

"What's the good of a screw, I'd like to know? Did you ever know one what was worth his salt? I never did. Look at that beast, Slater, great fat brute, what'd get a man three days' bread-and-water as soon as look at him. A little bread and water'd do him good. Look at old Murray—call a man like that chief warder. I wonder what a chief fat-head's like? As for the governor—as for the governor—as—for—the—governor—"

The chapel was in confusion. The officers rose in their seats. Mr. Paley stood up in his pew, looking whiter than he was wont to do. It seemed as though the chaplain was struggling with an unseen antagonist. He writhed and twisted, contending, as it were, with something—or some one—which appeared to be in front of him. His sentence remained unfinished. All at once he collapsed, and, sinking into a heap, lay upon the steps of the altar—still.

"Take the men out," said the governor's quiet voice.

The men were taken out. The schoolmaster was already at the chaplain's side. With him were two or three of the prisoners who sang in the choir. The governor and the inspector came and looked down at the senseless man.

"Seems to be in a sort of fit," the schoolmaster said.

"Let some one go and see if the doctor has arrived. Ask him to come up here at once." With that the governor left the chapel, the inspector going with him. "It's no good our staying. He'll be all right. I—I don't feel quite well."

Major Hardinge looked at him shrewdly out of the corner of his eyes. "Does he drink?"

"Not that I am aware of. I have never heard of it before. I should say certainly not."

"Is he mad?"

"No-o—he has his peculiarities—but he certainly is not mad."

"Is he subject to fits?"

"I have not known of his having one before."

When they reached the office the Major began to pace about.

"That chaplain of yours must be stark mad."

"If so, it is a very sudden attack."

"Did you hear what he said?"

"Very well indeed."

"Never heard such a thing in my life! Is he in the habit of using such language?"

"Hardly. Perhaps we had better leave it till we hear what the doctor says. Possibly there is some simple explanation. I am afraid the chaplain is unwell."

"If he isn't unwell, I don't know what he is. Upon my word, Paley, I can't congratulate you upon the figure Canterstone Jail has cut during the last few days. I don't know what sort of report I shall have to make."

The governor winced. When, a few minutes afterwards, the doctor entered, he began upon the subject at once.

"How is the chaplain, doctor?"

Dr. Livermore gave a curious glance about him. Then he shook hands with the inspector. Then he sat down. Taking off his hat, he wiped his brow.

"Well? Anything wrong?"

"The chaplain says he is bewitched."

The governor looked at the inspector, and the inspector looked at him.

"Bewitched?" said Mr. Paley.

"I told you the man was mad," the inspector muttered.

"Hush!" the doctor whispered. "Here he comes."

Even as he spoke the chaplain entered, leaning on the chief warder's arm. He advanced to the table at which the governor sat, looking Mr. Paley steadily in the face.

"Mr. Paley, I have to report to you that I have been bewitched."

"I am sorry to hear that, Mr. Hewett." He could not resist a smile. "Though I am afraid I do not understand exactly what you mean."

"It is no laughing matter." The chaplain's tone was cool and collected—more impressive than it was used to be. "The man whose name I believe is Oliver Mankell has bewitched me. He was the second man in the third row on my right-hand side in chapel. I could make out that his number was B 27. He cast on me a spell."

There was silence. Even the inspector felt that it was a delicate matter to accuse the chaplain outright of lunacy. An interruption came from an unexpected quarter—from the chief warder.

"It's my belief that man Mankell's been up to his games about those cells."

The interruption was the more remarkable, because there was generally war—not always passive—between the chief warder and the chaplain. Every one looked at Mr. Murray.

"What is this I hear about the cells?" asked Dr. Livermore.

The governor answered:

"Yesterday the men were all locked in their night-cells. This morning they were all locked out—that is, we found them all seemingly fast asleep, each man in front of his cell-door."

"They were all locked in except one man, and that man was Mankell—and he was the only man who was not locked out." Thus the chief warder.

"And do you suggest," said the doctor, "that he had a finger in the pie?"

"It's my belief he did it all. Directly I set eyes upon the man I knew there was something about him I couldn't quite make out. He did it all! Have you heard, sir, how he came to the gate?"

Mr. Murray was, in general, a reticent man. It was not his way to express decided opinions in the presence of authorities, or indeed of any one else. Mr. Paley, who knew his man, eyed him with curiosity.

"What was there odd about that?"

"Why, instead of the constable bringing him, it was him who brought the constable. When they opened the gate there was him with the policeman over his shoulder."

In spite of Mr. Murray's evident earnestness, there were some of his hearers who were unable to repress a smile.

"Do you mean that the constable was drunk?"

"That's the queer part of it. It was John Mitchell. I've known him for two-and-twenty years. I never knew him have a glass too much before. I saw him soon afterwards—he was all right then. He said he had only had three half-pints. He was quite himself till he got near the gate, when all of a sudden he went queer all over."

"Possibly the ale was drugged," suggested the doctor.

"I don't know nothing about that, but I do know that the same hand that played that trick was the same hand that played the tricks with the cells."

"Consider a moment what you are saying, Murray. How are three hundred locks to be tampered with in the middle of the night by a man who is himself a prisoner? One moment—But even that is nothing compared to the feat of carrying three hundred men fast asleep in bed—bed and all—through three hundred closed doors, under the very noses of the officers on guard—think of doing all that singlehanded!"

"It was witchcraft."

When the chief warder said this, Major Hardinge exploded.

"Witchcraft! The idea of the chief warder of an English prison talking about witchcraft at this time of day! It's quite time you were superannuated, sir."

"The man, Mankell, certainly bewitched me."

"Bewitched you!" As the Major faced the chaplain he seemed to find it difficult to restrain his feelings. "May I ask what sort of idea you mean to convey by saying he bewitched you?"

"I will explain so far as I am able." The chaplain paused to collect his thoughts. All eyes were fixed upon him. "I intended to say something to the men touching the events of yesterday and this morning. As I came down to the altar-rail I was conscious of a curious sensation—as though I was being fascinated by a terrible gaze which was burning into my brain. I managed to pronounce the first few words. Involuntarily looking round, I met the eyes of the man Mankell. The instant I did so I was conscious that something had passed from him to me, something that made my tongue utter the words you heard. Struggling with all my might, I momentarily regained the exercise of my own will. It was only for a moment, for in an instant he had mastered me again. Although I continued to struggle, my tongue uttered the words he bade it utter, until I suppose my efforts to repel his dominion brought on a kind of fit. That he laid on me a spell I am assured."

There was a pause when the chaplain ceased. That he had made what he supposed to be a plain and simple statement of facts was evident. But then the facts were remarkable ones. It was the doctor who broke the silence.

"Suppose we have the man in here, so that we can put him through his facings?"

The governor stroked his beard

"What are you going to say to him? You can hardly charge him with witchcraft. He is here because he has been pretending to magic powers."

The doctor started.

"No! Is that so? Then I fancy we have the case in a nutshell. The man is what old-fashioned people used to call a mesmerist—hypnotism they call it nowadays, and all sorts of things."

"But mesmerism won't explain the cells!"

"I'm not so sure of that—at any rate, it would explain the policeman who was suddenly taken queer. Let's have the man in here."

"The whole thing is balderdash," said the Major with solemnity. "I am surprised, as a man of sane and healthy mind, to hear such stuff talked in an English prison of to-day."

"At least there will be no harm in our interviewing Mr. Mankell. Murray, see that they send him here." The chief warder departed to do the governor's bidding. Mr. Paley turned to the chaplain. "According to you, Mr. Hewett, we are subjecting ourselves to some personal risk by bringing him here. Is that so?"

"You may smile, Mr. Paley, but you may find it no laughing matter after all. There are more things in heaven and earth than are dreamt of in man's philosophy."

"You don't mean to say," burst out the Major, "that you, a man of education, a clergyman, chaplain of an English prison, believe in witchcraft?"

"It is not a question of belief—it is a question of fact. That the man cast on me a spell, I am well assured. Take care that he does not do the same to you."

The governor smiled. The doctor laughed. The enormity of the suggestion kept the Major tongue-tied till Mankell appeared.

CHAPTER III

THE SINGULAR BEHAVIOUR OF THE PRISON OFFICIALS

Although Mankell was ushered in by the chief warder, he was in actual charge of Warder Slater. The apartment into which he was shown was not that in which prisoners ordinarily interviewed the governor. There a cord, stretched from wall to wall, divided the room nearly in half. On one side stood the prisoner, with the officer in charge of him; on the other sat the governor. Here there was no cord. The room—which was a small one—contained a single table. At one end sat Mr. Paley, on his right sat Major Hardinge, the chaplain stood at his left, and just behind the Major sat Dr. Livermore. Mankell was told to stand at the end which faced the governor. A momentary pause followed his entrance—all four pairs of eyes were examining his countenance. He for his part bore himself quite easily, his eyes being fixed upon the governor, and about the corners of his lips hovered what was certainly more than the suspicion of a smile.

"I have sent for you," Mr. Paley began, "because I wish to ask you a question. You understand that I make no charge against you, but—do you know who has been tampering with the locks of the cells?"

The smile was unmistakable now. It lighted up his saturnine visage, suggesting that here was a man who had an eye—possibly almost too keen an eye—for the ridiculous. But he gave no answer.

"Do you hear my question, Mankell? Do you know who has been tampering with the locks of the cells?"

Mankell extended his hands with a little graceful gesture which smacked of more southern climes.

"How shall I tell you?"

"Tell the truth, sir, and don't treat us to any of your high faluting."

This remark came from the Major—not in too amiable a tone of voice.

"But in this land it would seem that truth is a thing that wise men shun. It is for telling the truth that I am here."

"We don't want any of your insolence, my man! Answer the governor's question if you don't want to be severely punished. Do you know who has been playing hanky-panky with the cells?"

"Spirits of the air."

As he said this Mankell inclined his head and looked at the Major with laughter in his eyes.

"Spirits of the air! What the devil do you mean by spirits of the air?"

"Ah! what do I mean? To tell you that," laying a stress upon the pronoun, "would take a year."

"The fellow's an insolent scoundrel," spluttered the Major.

"Come, Mankell, that won't do," struck in Mr. Paley. "Do I understand you to say that you do know something about the matter?"

"Know!" The man drew himself up, laying the index finger of his right hand upon the table with a curiously impressive air. "What is there that I do not know?"

"I see. You still pretend, then, to the possession of magic powers?"

"Pretend!" Mankell laughed. He stretched out his hands in front of him with what seemed to be his favourite gesture, and laughed—in the face of the authorities.

"Suppose you give us an example of your powers?"

The suggestion came from the doctor. The Major exploded.

"Don't talk stuff and nonsense! Give the man three days' bread and water. That is what he wants."

"You do not believe in magic, then?" Mankell turned to the Major with his laughing eyes.

"What's it matter to you what I believe? You may take my word for it that I don't believe in impudent mountebanks like you."

The only reply Mankell gave was to raise his hand—if that might be called a reply—in the way we sometimes do when we call for silence, and there was silence in the room. All eyes were fixed upon the prisoner. He looked each in turn steadily in the face. Then, still serenely smiling, he gently murmured, "If you please."

There still was silence, but only for a moment. It was broken by Warder Slater. That usually decorous officer tilted his cap to the back of his head, and thrust his hands into his breeches pockets—hardly the regulation attitude in the presence of superiors.

"I should blooming well like to know what this means! 'Ere have I been in this 'ere jail eleven years, and I've never been accused before of letting men out of their night-cells, let alone their beds and bedding, and I don't like it, so I tell you straight."

The chief warder turned with automatic suddenness towards the unexpectedly and unusually plain-spoken officer.

"Slater, you're a fool!"

"I'm not the only one in the place! There's more fools here besides me, and some of them bigger ones as well!"

While these compliments were being exchanged, the higher officials sat mutely looking on. When the chief warder seemed at a loss for an answer, the chaplain volunteered a remark. He addressed himself to Warder Slater.

"It's my opinion that the governor's a bigger fool than you are, and that the inspector's a still bigger fool than he is."

"And it's my belief, Mr. Hewett," observed the doctor, "that you're the biggest fool of all."

"It would serve him right," remarked the governor, quietly, "if somebody were to knock him down."

"Knock him down! I should think it would—and kick him too!"

As he said this the Major glared at the chaplain with threatening eyes.

There was silence again, broken by Warder Slater taking off his cap and then his tunic, which he folded up carefully and placed upon the floor, and turning his shirt-sleeves up above his elbows, revealing as he did so a pair of really gigantic arms.

"If any man says I let them men out of the cells, I'm ready to fight that man, either for a gallon of beer or nothing. I don't care if it's the inspector, or who it is."

"I suspect," declared the chaplain, "that the inspector's too great a coward to take you on, but if he does I'm willing to back Slater for half-a-crown. I am even prepared to second him."

Putting his hands under his coat-tails, the chaplain looked up at the ceiling with a resolute air.

"If you do fight Slater, Hardinge, I should certainly commence by giving the chaplain a punch in the eye."

So saying, the governor leaned back in his chair, and began drumming on the table with the tips of his fingers. The doctor rose from his seat. He gave the inspector a hearty slap on the back.

"Give him beans!" he cried. "You ought to be able to knock an over-fed animal like Slater into the middle of next week before he's counted five."

"I've no quarrel with Slater," the inspector growled, "and I've no intention of fighting him; but as the chaplain seems to be so anxious for a row, I'll fight him with the greatest pleasure."

"If there's goin' to be any fighting," interposed the chief warder, "don't you think I'd better get a couple of sponges and a pail of water?"

"I don't know about the sponges," said the governor; "I don't fancy you will find any just at hand. But you might get a pail of water, I think."

The chief warder left the room.

"I'm not a fighting man," the chaplain announced; "and in any case, I should decline to soil my hands by touching such an ill-mannered ruffian as Major Hardinge."

"I say," exclaimed the doctor, "Hardinge, you're not going to stand that?"

The Major sprang from his seat, tore off his coat, and flung it on to the ground with considerably less care than Warder Slater had done. He strode up to the chaplain.

"Beg my pardon, or take a licking!"

The Major clenched his fists. He assumed an attitude which, if not exactly reminiscent of the pets of the fancy, was at least intended to be pugilistic. The chaplain did not flinch.

"You dare to lay a finger on me, you bullying blackguard."

The Major did dare. He struck out, if not with considerable science, at any rate with considerable execution. The chaplain went down like a log. At that moment the chief warder entered the room. He had a pail of water in his hand. For some reason, which was not altogether plain, he threw its contents upon the chaplain as he lay upon the floor.

While these—considering the persons engaged—somewhat irregular proceedings had been taking place, Mankell remained motionless, his hand upraised—still with that smile upon his face. Now he lowered his hand.

"Thank you very much," he said.

There was silence again—a tolerably prolonged silence. While it lasted, a change seemed to be passing over the chief actors in the scene. They seemed to be awaking, with more or less rapidity, to the fact that a certain incongruity characterised their actions and their language. There stood Warder Slater, apparently surprised and overwhelmed at the discovery that his hat and coat were off, and his shirtsleeves tucked up above his elbows. The chief warder, with the empty pail in his hand, presented a really ludicrous picture of amazement. He seemed quite unable to realise the fact that he had thrown the contents over the chaplain. The inspector's surprise appeared to be no less on finding that, in his pugilistic ardour, he had torn off his coat and knocked the chaplain down. The doctor, supporting him in the rear, seemed to be taken a little aback. The governor, smoothing his hair with his hand, seemed to be in a hopeless mist. It was the chaplain, who rose from the floor with his handkerchief to his nose, who brought it home to them that the scene which had just transpired had not been the grotesque imaginings of some waking dream.

"I call you to witness that Major Hardinge has struck me to the ground, and the chief warder has thrown on me a pail of water. What conduct may be expected from ignorant criminals when such is the behaviour of those who are in charge of them, must be left for others to judge."

They looked at one another. Their feelings were momentarily too deep for words.

"I think," suggested the governor, with quavering intonation, "I think—that this man—had better—be taken away."

Warder Slater picked up his hat and coat, and left the room, Mankell walking quietly beside him. Mr. Murray followed after, seeming particularly anxious to conceal the presence of the pail. Mr. Hewett, still stanching the blood which flowed from his nose, fixed his eyes on the inspector.

"Major Hardinge, if, twenty-four hours after this, you are still an Inspector of Prisons, all England shall ring with your shame. Behind bureaucracy—above it—is the English press." The chaplain moved towards the door. On the threshold he paused. "As for the chief warder, I shall commence by indicting him for assault." He took another step, and paused again. "Nor shall I forget that the governor aided and abetted the inspector, and that the doctor egged him on."

Then the chaplain disappeared. His disappearance was followed by what might be described as an abject silence. The governor eyed his colleagues furtively. At last he stammered out a question.

"Well, Major, what do you think of this?"

The Major sank into a chair, expressing his thoughts by a gasp. Mr. Paley turned his attention to the doctor.

"What do you say, doctor?"

"I say?—I say nothing."

"I suppose," murmured the Major, in what seemed to be the ghost of his natural voice, "that I did knock him down?"

The doctor seemed to have something to say on that point, at any rate.

"Knock him down!—I should think you did! Like a log of wood!"

The Major glanced at the governor. Mr. Paley shook his head. The Major groaned. The governor began to be a little agitated.

"Something must be done. It is out of the question that such a scandal should be allowed to go out into the world. I do not hesitate to say that if the chaplain sends in to the commissioners the report which he threatens to send, the situation will be to the last degree unpleasant for all of us."

"The point is," observed the doctor—"are we, collectively and individually, subject to periodical attacks of temporary insanity?"

"Speaking for myself, I should say certainly not."

Dr. Livermore turned on the governor.

"Then perhaps you will suggest a hypothesis which will reasonably account for what has just occurred." The governor was silent. "Unless you are prepared to seek for a cause in the regions of phenomena."

"Supposing," murmured the Major, "there is such a thing as witchcraft after all?"

"We should have the Psychical Research Society down on us, if we had nobody else, if we appended our names to a confession of faith." The doctor thrust his thumbs into his waistcoat arm-holes. "And I should lose every patient I have."

There was a tapping at the door. In response to the governor's invitation, the chief warder entered. In general there was in Mr. Murray's bearing a not distant suggestion of an inflated bantam-cock or pouter-pigeon. It was curious to observe how anything in the shape of inflation was absent now. He touched his hat to the governor—his honest, rubicund, somewhat pugnacious face, eloquent of the weight that was on his mind.

"Excuse me, sir. I said he was a witch."

"Your saying that he was a witch—or wizard," remarked the governor, dryly, "will not, I fear, be sufficient excuse, in the eyes of the commissioners, for your throwing a pail of water over the chaplain."

"But a man's not answerable for what he does when he's bewitched," persisted the chief warder, with characteristic sturdiness.

"It is exactly that reflection which has constrained me to return."

They looked up. There was the chaplain standing in the doorway—still with his handkerchief to his nose.

"Mr. Murray, you threw a pail of water over me. If you assert that you did it under the influence of witchcraft, I, who have myself been under a spell, am willing to excuse you."

"Mr. Hewett, sir, you yourself know I was bewitched."

"I do; as I believe it of myself. Murray, give me your hand." The chaplain and the chief warder solemnly shook hands. "There is an end of the matter as it concerns us two. Major Hardinge, do I understand you to assert that you too were under the influence of witchcraft?"

This was rather a delicate inquiry to address to the Major. Apparently the Major seemed to find it so.

"I don't know about witchcraft," he growled; "but I am prepared to take my oath in any court in England that I had no more intention of striking you than I had of striking the moon."

"That is sufficient, Major Hardinge. I forgive you from my heart. Perhaps you too will take my hand."

The Major took it—rather awkwardly—much more awkwardly than the chief warder had done. When the chaplain relinquished it, he turned aside, and picking up his coat, began to put it on—scarcely with that air of dignity which is proper to a prison inspector.

"I presume," continued Mr. Hewett, "that we all allow that what has occurred has been owing to the malign influence of the man Oliver Mankell?"

There was silence. Apparently they did not all allow it even yet: it was a pill to swallow.

"Hypnotism," muttered the doctor, half aside.

"Hypnotism! I believe that the word simply expresses some sort of mesmeric power—hardly a sufficient explanation in the present case."

"I would suggest, Major Hardinge," interposed the governor, "all theorising aside, that the man be transferred to another prison at the earliest possible moment."

"He shall be transferred to-morrow," affirmed the Major. "If there is anything in Mr. Hewett's suggestion, the fellow shall have a chance to prove it—in some other jail. Oh, good Lord! Don't! He's killing me! Help—p!"

"Hardinge!" exclaimed the doctor; "what's the matter now?"

There seemed to be something the matter. The Major had been delivering himself in his most pompously official manner. Suddenly he put his hands to the pit of his stomach, and began to cry out as if in an ecstacy of pain, his official manner altogether gone.

"He'll murder me! I know he will!"

"Murder you? Who?"

"Mankell."

"Oddly enough, I too was conscious of a very curious sensation."

As he said this, the governor wiped the cold dew of perspiration from his brow. He seemed unnaturally white. As he adjusted his spectacles, there was an odd, tremulous appearance about his eyes.

"It was because you spoke of transferring him to some other jail." The chaplain's tone was solemn. "He dislikes the idea of being trifled with."

The Major resented the suggestion.

"Trifled with? He seems uncommonly fond of trifling with other people. Confound the man! Oh—h!"

The Major sprang from the floor with an exclamation which amounted to a positive yell. They looked each other in the face. Each man seemed a little paler than his wont.

"Something must be done," the governor gasped.

The chaplain made a proposition.

"I propose that we summon him into our presence, and inquire of him what he wishes us to do."

The proposition was not received with acclamation. They probably felt that a certain amount of complication might be expected to ensue if such inquiries began to be addressed to prisoners.

"I think I'll go my rounds," observed the doctor. "This matter scarcely concerns me. I wish you gentlemen well out of it."

He reached out his hand to take his hat, which he had placed upon a chair. As he did so, the hat disappeared, and a small brown terrier dog appeared in its place. The dog barked viciously at the outstretched hand. The doctor started back just in time to escape its teeth. The dog disappeared—there was the hat again. The appearance was but momentary, but it was none the less suggestive on that account. The doctor seemed particularly affected.

"We must have all been drinking, if we are taking to seeing things," he cried.

"I think," suggested the chaplain, almost in a whisper, "that we had better inquire what it is he wishes us to do." There was silence. "We—we have all clear consciences. There—there is no reason why we should be afraid."

"We're—we're not afraid," gasped the governor. "I—I don't think you are entitled to infer such a thing."

The Major stammeringly supported him.

"Of—of course we—we're not afraid. The—the idea is preposterously absurd."

"Still," said the doctor, "a man doesn't care to have hanky-panky tricks played with his top hat."

There was a pause—of considerable duration. It was again broken by the chaplain.

"Don't you think, Mr. Paley, that we had better send for this man?" Apparently Mr. Paley did.

"Murray," he said, "go and see that he is sent here."

Mr. Murray went, not too willingly—still he went.

CHAPTER IV

THE CIRCUMSTANCES UNDER WHICH THE OFFICIALS OF CANTERSTONE JAIL PRESENTED MR. MANKELL WITH A TESTIMONIAL

Oliver Mankell was again in the charge of Warder Slater. Warder Slater looked very queer indeed—he actually seemed to have lost in bulk. The same phenomenon was observable in the chief warder, who followed close upon the prisoner's heels. Mankell seemed, as ever, completely at his ease. There was again a suspicion of a smile in his eyes and about the corners of his lips. His bearing was in striking contrast to that of the officials. His self-possession in the presence of their evident uneasiness gave him the appearance, in a sense, of being a giant among pigmies; yet the Major, at least, was in every way a bigger man than he was. There was silence as he entered, a continuation of that silence which had prevailed until he came. The governor fumbled with a paper-knife which was in front of him. The inspector, leaning forward in his chair, seemed engrossed by his boots. The doctor kept glancing, perhaps unconsciously, at his hat. The chaplain, though conspicuously uneasy, seemed to have his wits about him most. It was he who, temporarily usurping the governor's functions, addressed the prisoner.

"Your name is Oliver Mankell?" The prisoner merely smiled. "You are sentenced to three months' hard labour?" The prisoner smiled again. "For—for pretending to tell fortunes?" The smile became more pronounced. The chaplain cleared his throat. "Oliver Mankell, I am a clergyman. I know that there are such things as good and evil. I know that, for causes which are hidden from me, the Almighty may permit evil to take visible shape and walk abroad upon the earth; but I also know that, though evil may destroy my body, it cannot destroy my soul."

The chaplain pulled up. His words and manner, though evidently sincere, were not particularly impressive. While they evidently had the effect of increasing his colleagues' uneasiness, they only had the effect of enlarging the prisoner's smile. When he was about to continue, the governor interposed.

"I think, Mr. Hewett, if you will permit me. Mankell, I am not a clergyman." The prisoner's smile almost degenerated into a grin. "I have sent for you, for the second time this morning, to ask you frankly if you have any reason to complain of your treatment here?" The prisoner stretched out his hands with his familiar gesture. "Have you any complaint to make? Is there anything, within the range of the prison rules, you would wish me to do for you?" Again the hands went out. "Then tell me, quite candidly, what is the cause of your behaviour?"

When the governor ceased, the prisoner seemed to be considering what answer he should make. Then, inclining his head with that almost saturnine grace, if one may coin a phrase, which seemed to accompany every movement he made:

"Sir, what have I done?" he asked.

"Eh—eh—we—we won't dwell upon that. The question is, What did you do it for?"

"It is perhaps within your recollection, sir, that I have my reputation to redeem, my character to reinstate."

"Your character? What do you mean?"

"In the first interview with which you favoured me, I ventured to observe that it would be my endeavour, during my sojourn within these walls, to act upon the advice the magistrate tendered me."

"What"—the governor rather faltered—"what advice was that?"

"He said I claimed to be a magician. He advised me, for my character's sake, to prove it during my sojourn here."

"I see. And—and you're trying to prove it—for your character's sake?"

"For my character's sake! I am but beginning, you perceive."

"Oh, you're but beginning! You call this but beginning, do you? May I ask if you have any intention of going on?"

"Oh, sir, I have still nearly the whole three months in front of me! Until my term expires I shall go on, with gathering strength, unto the end."

As he said this Mankell drew himself up in such a way that it almost seemed as though some inches were added to his stature.

"You will, will you? Well, you seem to be a pleasant kind of man!" The criticism seemed to have been extracted from the governor almost against his will. He looked round upon his colleagues with what could only be described as a ghastly grin. "Have you any objection, Mankell, to being transferred to another prison?"

"Sir!" the prisoner's voice rang out, and his hearers started—perceptibly. Perhaps that was because their nerves were already so disorganised. "It is here I was sent, it is here I must remain—until the end."

The governor took out his handkerchief and wiped his brow.

"I am bound to tell you, Mankell, judging from the experiences of the last two days, if this sort of thing is to continue—with gathering strength!—the end will not be long."

The prisoner seemed lost in reflection. The officials seemed lost in reflection too; but their reflections were probably of a different kind.

"There is one suggestion I might offer."

"Let's have it by all means. We have reached a point at which we shall be glad to receive any suggestion—from you."

"You might give me a testimonial."

"Give you what?"

"You might give me a testimonial."

The governor looked at the prisoner, then at his friends.

"A testimonial! Might we indeed! What sort of testimonial do you allude to?"

"You might testify that I had regained my reputation, redeemed my character—that I had proved to your entire satisfaction that I was the magician I claimed to be."

The governor leaned back in his seat.

"Your suggestion has at least the force of novelty. I should like to search the registers of remarkable cases, to know if such an application has ever been made to the governor of an English jail before. What do you say, Hardinge?"

The Major shuffled in his chair.

"I—I think I must return to town."

The prisoner smiled. The Major winced.

"That—that fellow's pinned me to my chair," he gasped. He appeared to be making futile efforts to rise from his seat.

"You cannot return to town. Dismiss the idea from your mind."

The Major only groaned. He took out his handkerchief and wiped his brow. The governor looked up from the paper-knife with which he was again trifling.

"Am I to understand that the testimonial is to take the shape of a voluntary offering?"

"Oh, sir! Of what value is a testimonial which is not voluntary?"

"Quite so. How do you suggest it should be worded?"

"May I ask you for paper, pens, and ink?"

The prisoner bent over the table and wrote on the paper which was handed him. What he had written he passed to the governor. Mr. Paley found inscribed, in a beautifully fair round hand, as clear as copperplate, the following "testimonial":—

"The undersigned persons present their compliments to Colonel Gregory. Oliver Mankell, sentenced by Colonel Gregory to three months' hard labour, has been in Canterstone Jail two days. That short space of time has, however, convinced them that Colonel Gregory acted wrongly in distrusting his magic powers, and so casting a stain upon his character. This is to testify that he has proved, to the entire satisfaction of the undersigned inspector of prisons and officials of Canterstone Jail, that he is a magician of quite the highest class."

"The signatures of all those present should be placed at the bottom," observed the prisoner, as the governor was reading the "testimonial."

Apparently at a loss for words with which to comment upon the paper he had read, the governor handed it to the inspector. The Major shrank from taking it.

"I—I'd rather not," he mumbled.

"I think you had better read it," said the governor. Thus urged, the Major did read it.

"Good Lord!" he gasped, and passed it to the doctor.

The doctor silently, having read it, passed it to the chaplain.

"I will read it aloud," said Mr. Hewett. He did so—for the benefit, probably, of Slater and Mr. Murray.

"Supposing we were to sign that document, what would you propose to do with it?" inquired the governor.

"I should convey it to Colonel Gregory."

"Indeed! In that case he would have as high an opinion of our characters as of yours. And yourself—what sort of action might we expect from you?"

"I should go."

The governor's jaw dropped.

"Go? Oh, would you!"

"My character regained, for what have I to stop?"

"Exactly. What have you? There's that point of view, no doubt. Well, Mankell, we will think the matter over."

The prisoner dropped his hands to his sides, looking the governor steadily in the face.

"Sir, I conceive that answer to convey a negative. The proposition thus refused will not be made again. It only remains for me to continue earnestly my endeavours to retrieve my character—until the three months are at an end."

The chaplain was holding the testimonial loosely between his finger and thumb. Stretching out his arm, Mankell pointed at it with his hand. It was immediately in flames. The chaplain releasing it, it was consumed to ashes before it reached the floor. Returning to face the governor gain, the prisoner laid his right hand, palm downwards, on the table: "Spirits of the air, in whose presence I now stand, I ask you if I am not justified in whatever I may do?"

His voice was very musical. His upturned eyes seemed to pierce through the ceiling to what there was beyond. The room grew darker. There was a rumbling in the air. The ground began to shake. The chaplain, who was caressing the hand which had been scorched by the flames, burst out with what was for him a passionate appeal:

"Mr. Mankell, you are over hasty. I was about to explain that I should esteem it quite an honour to sign your testimonial."

"So should I—upon my soul, I should!" declared the Major.

"There's nothing I wouldn't do to oblige you, Mr. Mankell," stammered the chief warder.

"Same 'ere!" cried Warder Slater.

"You really are too rapid in arriving at conclusions, Mr. Mankell," remarked the governor. "I do beg you will not suppose there was any negative intention."

The darkness, the rumbling, and the shaking ceased as suddenly as they began. The prisoner smiled.

"Perhaps I was too hasty," he confessed. "It is an error which can easily be rectified."

He raised his hand. A piece of paper fluttered from the ceiling. It fell upon the table. It was the testimonial.

"Your signature, Major Hardinge, should head the list."

"I—I—I'd rather somebody else signed first."

"That would never do: it is for you to lead the van. You are free to leave your seat."

The Major left his seat, apparently not rejoicing in his freedom. He wrote "William Hardinge" in great sprawling characters.

"Add 'Inspector of Prisons.'"

The Major added "Inspector of Prisons," with a very rueful countenance.

"Mr. Paley, it is your turn."

Mr. Paley took his turn, with a really tolerable imitation of being both ready and willing. Acting on the hint which had been given the Major, he added "Governor" of his own accord.

"Now, doctor, it is you."

The doctor thrust his hands into his trousers' pockets. "I'll sign, if you'll tell me how it is done."

"Tell you how it is done? How what is done?"

"How you do that hanky-panky, of course."

"Hanky-panky!" The prisoner drew himself straight up. "Is it possible that you suspect me of hanky-panky? Yes, sir, I will show you how it's done. If you wish it, you shall be torn asunder where you stand."

"Thank you,—you needn't trouble. I'll sign."

He signed. The chaplain shook his head and sighed.

"I always placed a literal interpretation on the twenty-eighth chapter of the first book of Samuel. It is singular how my faith is justified!"

The chief warder placed his spectacles upon his nose, where they seemed uneasy, and made quite a business of signing. And such was Warder Slater's agitation, that he could scarcely sign at all. But at last the "testimonial" was complete. The prisoner smiled as he carefully folded it in two.

"I will convey it to Colonel Gregory," he said. "It is a gratification to me to have been able to retrieve my character in so short a space of time."

They watched him—a little spellbound, perhaps; and as they watched him, even before their eyes—behold, he was gone!

CHAPTER I

THE FIRST LADY

"Mrs. And Miss Danvers."

Mr. Herbert Buxton, standing at the office window of the hotel, glancing at the visitors' book on the desk at his right, saw the names among the latest arrivals. They caught his eye. "Pontresina" was stated to be the place from which they had lately come.

"It is the Danvers, for a fiver—Cecil's Danvers."

Strolling from the office window, he took a letter—a frayed letter—from his pocket-book. It was post-marked "Pontresina." The signature was "Cecil Buxton"—it was from his brother.

"Dear Hubert," it ran, "you really must get something to do! Your request for what you call an advance is absurd. So far from advancing you anything I shall have to cut short the allowance I have been making you. I have met here a Mrs. and Miss Danvers. I have asked Miss Danvers to do me the honour to marry me. She has consented. When that event comes to pass—which will be very shortly—your allowance will recede to a vanishing point. That you will get something to do is, therefore, the advice of your affectionate brother, Cecil Buxton."

"It would be an odd coincidence," reflected Hubert, "if that Miss Danvers is this Miss Danvers."

An idea occurred to his fertile—too fertile—brain. As the first glimmerings of the idea burst on him, Hubert smiled.

In giving birth to Cecil and Hubert Buxton, Nature had been indulging in one of her freaks. They were twins—born within a few seconds of each other. Cecil came first. Hubert came, with all possible expedition, immediately after. Babies are proverbially alike. These babies were so much alike that, when they were undressed, no one ever pretended to be able to tell one from the other. The resemblance outlived babyhood. As the years went on, Cecil was always being taken for Hubert, Hubert for Cecil. The unfortunate part of the business was that the resemblance was merely superficial. Inside, they were altogether different. Cecil was solid and steady, while Hubert—well, at that particular moment he was quartered at that fashionable Bournemouth hotel, without money in his pocket with which to pay his hotel bill, and with nobody within reach from whom he could borrow a five-pound note.

"If," he told himself, "this Danvers is that Danvers, I might make something out of that fatal likeness after all."

It would not be, by any means, the first time he had made something out of the "fatal likeness," but on that, in this place, we need not dwell. He strolled along the corridor, the open letter in his hand, biting his nails and thinking over things as he went. As he approached the glass door which led into the grounds, it opened to admit a lady. At sight of him she stopped.

"Cecil!" she exclaimed.

Hubert looked at her. She was a magnificent woman, planned altogether on a magnificent scale, with a profusion of red-gold hair, and a pair of the biggest and brightest eyes Hubert, with all his wide experience, ever remembered to have seen.

"It is the Danvers!" he inwardly decided. "What a 'oner'!"

But he was equal to the occasion. He generally was—more than equal. He held out his hand to her with a little sudden burst.

"You!" he cried.

The lady, however, did not immediately respond to his advances. On the contrary, she put her hands behind her back.

"This is an unexpected pleasure. I didn't expect to see you here. I thought you were in Paris."

As a matter of fact according to the most recent advices, Cecil was in Paris. But, of course, Hubert had nothing to do with that.

"I only arrived last night. You—you don't seem glad to see me?"

"It is rather I who should ask the question. Are you glad to see me?"

There was a dryness in her tone which grated on Hubert's ears.

"This is a case in which diplomacy is required. I wonder what there's been between them." Aloud he remarked, "Can you not forget and forgive?"

"Cecil, do you mean it?" She glanced behind her as if in sudden agitation. "I cannot stop now. Meet me in the garden after dinner."

She was gone before he even had a ghost of a chance of feeling his way.

CHAPTER II

THE SECOND LADY

"Cecil! Where are you? Here?"

Hubert, who had been leaning against the wall, came out into the moonlight. The lady stood on the top of the steps. The moon shone full upon her. It lit up the glory of her red-gold hair. She was clad in full evening dress. Her little opera cloak, which had slipped off her shoulders, revealed, rather than concealed, her magnificent proportions. Hubert, eying her critically from below, told himself that she was certainly a "oner!"

"I am afraid I am late. I hope you haven't been waiting long."

"Nothing to speak of. Just time enough to enjoy a cigar—and to dream of you."

"Cecil! For shame! Is it damp? I have only my thin shoes on."

She held one out in evidence. Hubert liked the look of it.

"It is as dry as tinder; just the night for lovers."

"I really think it is." She came down the steps. "How glorious!" Laying her hand upon his arm, she looked into his eyes with her big ones. "As you say, it is just the night for lovers."

They began to stroll. She spoke—

"It seems strange, after all that has passed between us, that you and I should be walking here together."

"It does seem strange." It certainly did.

"After all the hard things you have thought and said of me." There was a pause. She looked down, speaking softly. "Call me by my pet name."

He slightly started. But he was not the sort of man to remain long at a loss. As he turned to her and answered, in his voice there was a ring of passionate intensity.

"Tell me by what name to call you!"

"Call me Angel."

"Angel! My angel of love! My angel of all good things!"

"Cecil!"

Their lips met in a kiss. As they did so, he told himself that if she was Cecil's idea of an angel, she wasn't his. But she was certainly a "oner." He wondered if she had been christened "Angel" Danvers. What a weapon with which to chastise a wife!

"Cecil, let us understand each other. You are not trifling with me again?"

"Need you ask?" This time he was fairly startled. "I am afraid that after all which has passed between us, I need—"

"You do mean to make me your wife?"

"Make you my wife? Good heavens! What do you suppose I mean?"

"Then you do not believe I cheated?"

"Cheated!"

"Then you do not believe that man? You don't believe the lies they said of me?"

"Never for one single instant."

His outspoken denial seemed to take her aback.

"Then, if you didn't believe it, why—but never mind! Cecil, it would be useless to pretend to you that I have been the best of women, but I swear that I will be a good wife to you until I die."

"My own," he murmured. To himself he said, "There seems to have been a good deal more romance about this little affair of Cecil's than I supposed."

Her manner changed.

"Let us talk of something else! Let us talk of you. Tell me of yourself, my love!"

"Well," said Hubert, the ever-ready, "for the moment I am in rather an awkward predicament."

"What is it?"

"The fact is"—he looked her straight in the face, and never turned a hair—"my remittances seem to have all gone wrong. I am landed here with empty pockets."

She laughed. "Let me be your banker, will you?"

"With pleasure."

"I'm quite rich, for me. I've got a heap of money in my purse, if I can only find it." She found it, after long seeking. "How much would you like—twenty pounds?"

"Thank you."

"Should I make it thirty?"

"If you could make it thirty."

Some bank-notes changed hands. He thrust them into his waistcoat-pocket, telling himself that that was something on account at any rate.

"Now, your remittances must make haste and come. Thirty pounds is nothing to you; it is a deal to me. Now I am destitute."

She held out her purse for him to see. It still contained a couple of bank-notes and some gold.

"I suppose you couldn't manage to spare the rest?" he said.

"You greedy thing! I can scarcely believe you are the Cecil Buxton I used to know—he would never have condescended to borrow thirty pounds from me. Do you know, it isn't only that you are nicer, but, somehow, even your manner and your voice seem different."

"Do you think so?" They were standing under the shadow of a tree. He leaned back against the tree. "By the way, I have been remiss. I ought to have inquired after your mother."

"My mother?" She started.

"I see your names are bracketed in the visitors' book together."

"Our names bracketed in the visitors book together! You are dreaming!"

"I saw them there—Mrs. and Miss Danvers."

"Mrs. and Miss Danvers! Cecil! what do you mean?"

It was his turn to stare. Her manner had all at once become quite singular.

"What do you mean? Isn't your mother with you?"

"Cecil, are you making fun of me?"

Hubert felt that, in some way, he was putting his foot in it—though he did not quite see how.

"Nothing is further from my thoughts than to make fun of you. But when I saw Mrs. Danvers' name in the visitors' book—"

"Whose name?"

"When I saw Mrs. and Miss Danvers there as large as life—"

The lady moved a step away from him. All at once she became, as it were, a different woman entirely.

"I see that you are the same man after all. The same Mr. Cecil Buxton. The same cold, calculating, sneering cynic. Only you happen to have broken out in another place. I presume you have been having a little amusement at my expense on a novel plan of your own. But this time, my friend, you have gone too far. You have asked me, in so many words, to be your wife—I dare you to deny it! You have borrowed money—I dare you to deny that too! I am not so unprotected as you may possibly imagine. I took the precaution to wire this morning for a friend. You will marry me, or we shall see!"

The lady swept him a splendid curtsey, and—walked off. He was so taken aback by the sudden change in her deportment that he made not the slightest attempt to arrest her progress. He stared after her, in the moonlight, open-eyed and open-mouthed.

"Well—! I've done something, though I don't know what. And I've done it somehow, though I don't know how. Cecil ought to be grateful to me for ridding him of her. They'd never have been happy together, I'll stake my life on it. Hallo! Who's this? More adventures!"

There was a rustling behind him. He turned. Someone came out of the shadow of the tree. It was a young girl. She was clad in a plain black silk dinner dress. A shawl was thrown over her shoulders. He could see that she had brown hair and pleasant features. She addressed to him a question which surprised him.

"Who is that woman?" she asked.

She pointed after the rapidly retreating "Angel" with a gesture which was almost tragic. He raised his hat.

"I beg your pardon? I don't think I have the pleasure—"

She paid no attention to his words.

"Who is that woman?" she repeated.

"Which woman?"

"That woman?"

"Really I—I think there's some mistake—"

To his amazement she burst into a passion of tears. "Cecil, don't speak to me like that—don't! don't! don't!"

Hubert stared. The young lady dropped her hands from before her face. She looked at him with streaming eyes.

"Who is that woman? Tell me! I've been longing for your coming, thinking of all that I should say to you, wishing that the minutes were but seconds—and you've been here all the time! You must have come hours before you told me that your train was due. What is the meaning of it all?"

"That is precisely what I should like to know."

"I came out here that I might be alone before our meeting. I heard the sound of voices, and I thought that one of them was yours—I could not believe it. I listened. I heard you talking to that woman. I saw her kiss you. Oh, Cecil! Cecil! my heart is broken!"

She tottered forward, all but falling into Hubert's arms. He tried to soothe her. Sotto voce he told himself that Cecil had more romance in his nature than he had given him credit for. His complications in the feminine line appeared to be worthy of the farces at the Palais Royal. In the midst of her emotion, the young lady in his arms continued to address him.

"Why—did you—tell me—you were coming—by one train—when—all the time—you must have meant—to come by another. I—have your letter here—"

From the bosom of her dress she drew an envelope. Hubert made a dash at it.

"My letter? Permit me for an instant!"

With scant ceremony he took it from her hand. He glanced at the address—recognising Cecil's well-known writing.

"Miss—Miss Danvers! Are you—are you—Miss Danvers?"

The girl shrank from him. Her tears were dried. Her face grew white. "Cecil!" she exclaimed.

"Forgive me if my question seems a curious one, but—are you Miss Danvers?"

The girl shrank away still more. Her face grew whiter. She spoke so faintly her words were scarcely audible.

"Cecil! Give me back my letter, if you please!"

He handed her back her envelope. "Miss Danvers, I entreat you—"

But the look of scorn which was on her face brought even Hubert to a standstill. As he hesitated, she "fixed him with her eyes." He had seldom felt so uncomfortable as he did just then. He seemed to feel himself growing smaller simply because of the scorn which was in her glance.

"Good evening, Mister Buxton."

She slightly inclined her head—and was gone. Hubert stared after her dumfounded. When he did recover the faculty of speech he hardly knew what use to make of it.

"Well—I've done it! If she's Miss Danvers—who is 'Angel?' Cecil will thank me for the treat which I'm preparing for him. I knew this fatal likeness would dog me to the grave. Why was I born a twin?"

He strolled slowly toward the building. As he entered the hall a lady was coming along the corridor. At sight of him she quickened her pace. She advanced to him with outstretched hands. She was a lady of perhaps forty years of age.

"Cecil!" she cried.

But Hubert was not to be caught with salt. He had had enough, for the present, of Cecil and—of Cecil's feminine friends. Ignoring her outstretched hands, he slightly raised his hat.

"Pardon me, you have the advantage of me, Madame."

The lady seemed bewildered. She stared at him as if she could not believe her eyes and ears. The door through which Hubert had just entered from the grounds was re-opened at his back. A figure glided past him. It was the young girl from whom he had just parted—in not too cordial a manner. She went straight to the lady, slipping her arm through hers.

"Mamma, Mr. Buxton has declined to acknowledge my acquaintance as he declined to acknowledge yours. I think I can give you a sufficient reason for his doing so, if you will come with me, dear mother."

"Hetty!" murmured the elder woman, still plainly at a loss.

"Come!" said the girl. They went, leaving Hubert to stare.

"Well—I've gone one better! That's Mrs. Danvers, I presume. So I've contrived to insult the mother and the daughter too. Cecil will shower blessings on my head. Who can that Angel be?"

As he was about to follow the ladies along the corridor, someone touched him on the arm. Turning, he saw that a stranger in a black frock coat stood at his side.

"What were you saying to those ladies?" this person asked.

"What the deuce is that to do with you? And who the devil are you?"

"It has this to do with me, that I am the manager of this hotel, and that it is sufficiently obvious that your presence is objectionable to those ladies. Moreover, under existing circumstances, it is objectionable to me. It is a rule of this hotel that accounts are paid weekly. You have been here more than three weeks, and your first week's bill is yet unpaid. You have made sundry promises, but you have not kept them. I don't wish to have any unpleasantness with you, sir, but I regret that I am unable to accommodate you with a bed, in this hotel, to-night."

Hubert felt a trifle wild. He was capable of that feeling now and then. As they were advancing in one direction, two gentlemen, a tall and a short one, were advancing towards them in the other. They were coming to close quarters. Hubert was conscious that the manager's outspoken observations could not be altogether inaudible to the approaching strangers. So he rode as high a horse as he conveniently could.

"As for your bill, I will see it hanged first. As for your insolence, I will report it to your employers. As for myself, I shall only be too glad to go at once."

One of the approaching strangers—the tall one—suddenly standing still, placed himself in front of Hubert in such a way as to bar his progress. With the finger tips of his right hand he tapped him lightly on the chest.

"Not just at once, dear Buxton, not just at once. Not before you have said a few words to me."

"And to me," said the short man, who stood beside his taller companion. Hubert looked from one to the other.

"And pray who may you be?" he inquired.

"You do not know me?" asked the big stranger.

"Nor me?" echoed the little one.

"But it does not matter. Perhaps you have a bad memory, my dear Buxton."

The big man's manner was affable. He turned to the manager. "You must excuse us for one moment, we have just a word to say to our friend Buxton. Here is our little private sitting-room most convenient—just a word."

Before Hubert had altogether realised the situation, the big man had thrust his arm through his, and drawn him into a sitting-room which opened off the corridor from the left. When they were in, the big man locked the door—he not only locked the door, but in an ostentatious manner he pocketed the key.

CHAPTER III

THE UNFORTUNATE RESULT OF BEING A TWIN

"So, Mr. Buxton, you don't know me?"

"Nor me?"

The larger stranger stood against the door. The lesser one, who appeared to be acting as echo, leaned against a table. He began, with a slightly overacted air of carelessness, to roll a cigarette. There was something about this little man which Hubert did not like at all. He was a short, wiry individual, with long, straight black hair, hollow, sallow, shaven cheeks, high projecting cheek-bones, and a pair of small black eyes, which he had a trick of screwing up until only the pupils could be seen. His personal attractions were not enhanced by a huge mole which occupied a conspicuous place in the middle of his left cheek. But if he liked the appearance of the small man little, it was not because he liked the appearance of the tall man more. This was a great hulking fellow, with sandy whiskers and moustache, and a manner which, in spite of its greasy insinuation, Hubert felt was distinctly threatening.

"Is it really possible, Mr. Buxton, that I have had the misfortune to escape your memory?"

"And me?"

Hubert glanced from one to the other. That the little man was a foreigner, probably an Italian, he made up his mind at once. As to the nationality of the big man he was not so sure. He had had dealings with some strange people in his time, both at home and abroad. But he could not recollect encountering either of these gentlemen before.

"I do not remember having ever seen either of you."

"Oh, you do not remember?" The big man came a step nearer. "You do not remember that pleasant evening in that little room at Nice?"

"You do not remember slapping my face?" quickly exclaimed the little man, suddenly slapping his own right cheek with startling vigour.

"You do not remember accusing me of cheating you at cards?"

"You do not remember placing an insult on me! on me! on me?"

All at once, abandoning the process of manufacturing his cigarette, the little man came and placed himself in even uncomfortable proximity to Hubert's person. "My friend, my cheek is burning to this very hour."

Hubert did not like the look of things at all. He was sure he had never seen these men before.

"I understand the position exactly. You are doing what people constantly are doing—you are mistaking me for my brother."

"Mistaking you for your brother? I am mistaking you for your brother?"

"And me!" cried the little man, again saluting his own cheek smartly. "You liar!"

The big man's manner was insulting. Hubert felt he must resent it.

"How dare you—"

But the sentiment died down into his boots as the big man came at him with a sudden ferocity which seemed to cause the beating of his heart to cease.

"How dare I! You dare to speak a word to me. Liar! I will kill you where you stand."

"As for me," remarked the short man, affably, "I have this, and this." From one recess in his clothing he took a revolver. From another, a long, glittering, and business-like, if elegant, knife.

"All these years I have not been able to make up my mind if I will shoot you like a dog, or stick you like a pig—which you are."

"Gentlemen," explained Hubert, with surprising mildness, "I assure you you are under a misapprehension. The likeness between my brother and myself is so striking that our most intimate friends mistake one for the other."

"For whom, then, did my sister mistake you this morning and to-night?"

A light flashed upon Hubert's brain. "You mean Angel?"

"You call her Angel! He calls her Angel!"

"I hear," observed the little man.

"If you will allow me to explain!"

The big man made a gesture of refusal. But the little man caught him by the arm. "Let the liar speak," he said.

The big man, acting on his friend's advice, let the—that is, he let Hubert speak. Availing himself of the courteously offered permission, Hubert did his best to make things clear.

"I am not—as I would have told you before if you would have let me—I am not Cecil, but Hubert Buxton." The big man made another gesture. Again the little man restrained him. "We are twins. All our lives it has been difficult to tell one from the other. Of recent years, I understand, the resemblance between us has grown even greater. But the likeness is only skin deep. Cecil is the elder by, I believe, about thirty seconds. He is a rich man, and I am a poor man—bitterly poor."

The big man spoke. "And you dare to tell me that you have been making love to my sister under a false name? Very good, I have killed a man for less. But I will not kill you—not yet—Is your handwriting as much like your brother's as you are?"

"My fist is like Cecil's."

"So! Sit down." Hubert sat down. "Take that pen." He took the pen. He dipped it in the ink. "Write, 'I promise to marry—'"

"What's the good of my promising to marry anyone? Don't I tell you that I'm without a sou with which to bless myself?"

"Write, my friend, what I dictate. 'I promise to marry—'" Hubert wrote it—"'Marian Philipson Peters—'"

"And who the—something is Marian Philipson Peters?"

"Marian Philipson Peters—Mrs. Philipson Peters, is my sister."

It seemed to be a tolerably prosaic paraphrase of "Angel." Hubert, if the expression of his features could be trusted, appeared to think so.

"And what possible advantage does your sister propose to derive from my promising, either in black and white or in any other way, to marry her? Does the lady propose to pay my debts, or to provide me with an income?"

"Attend to me, my friend—write what I dictate." The big man laid his hand on Hubert's shoulder with an amount of pressure which might mean much—or more! Hubert looked up. The pressure increased. "Write it."

The little man was standing on the other side of the unwilling scribe. He had his revolver in one hand, his knife in the other. "Write it!" he said.

Up went Hubert's shoulders—he wrote it. The big man continued his dictation.

"'Within three months after date.'"

"What on earth—"

"Write—'Within three months after date.'"

"Oh, I'll write anything. I'll promise to marry her within three minutes—to oblige you."

The big man examined what Hubert had written.

"Very like!—very like indeed. So like Cecil Buxton's handwriting that I plainly perceive, my friend, that you are the prince of all the liars. Now sign it." He arrested Hubert's hand. "Sign it—'Cecil Buxton.'"

Hubert glanced up. He dropped his pen. "Now I see!"

"Pick up that pen."

"With pleasure." He picked it up.

"Sign it—'Cecil Buxton.'"

The big man spoke in a tone of voice which could not, truthfully, be described as friendly.

"In other words—commit forgery."

The tall man turned to the short one.

"Eugene, who is to use your revolver? Is it you or I? I swear to you that if this scoundrel, this contemptible villain, does not make all the reparation to my sister that is in his miserable power, I will blow his brains out as he is sitting here."

The short man smiled—not pleasantly.

"Leave to me, my friend, that sacred duty—the sacred duty of being executioner. I have long had a little grudge of my own against Mr. Cecil Buxton. I have one of those little insults to wipe out which can only be wiped out by—blood. I have not doubted all the time that this is Mr. Cecil Buxton. I doubt it still less now that I have seen him write."

"I swear to you—"

The big man cut Hubert uncivilly short. He repeated his command. "Sign it—'Cecil Buxton.'"

Hubert looked from one face to the other. He was conscious—painfully conscious!—that his was not a pleasant situation. He saw murder on the short man's face. He did not like the look of his revolver. He held it far too carelessly. That he was the sort of man who would entertain no kind of conscientious scruple against shooting him, to use his own words, like a dog, he felt quite certain.

"Let me say one word?" he pleaded.

The big man refused him even that grace. "Not one!"

While Hubert hesitated, the pen between his fingers, there came a rapping at the door.

The cause of that rapping at the door was this.

Cecil Buxton arrived by the train by which he had informed Miss Danvers, by letter, that he would arrive. Hastily seeing his luggage on to a cab, he drove off to the hotel. In the hall he encountered a porter.

The porter greeted him in rather a singular manner, scarcely as hotel porters are wont to greet arriving guests.

"What! Back again!" Cecil stared, as, under the circumstances, any man would stare. "This won't do, you know. I know all about it—you've been chucked. My orders is, not let you into the place again."

"My good man," said Cecil, fully believing that what he said was true, "you're drunk."

Just then a lady came down the staircase. He recognised her—recognised her well. He rushed towards her.

"Hetty!" he cried.

The lady gave a start, but not the sort of start he had reason, and good reason, to expect. She turned, she looked at him—with scornful eyes. She drew back, seeming to remove her very gown from any risk of personal contact.

"I half expected to see you at the station. Hetty, what—what's the matter?"

The lady said nothing, but she looked at him—and she walked away, her head held very high in the air.

"Now you've got to come out of this!" The porter who had followed him across the hall laid his hand upon his shoulder. Cecil swung round. And he not only swung round, but he swung the porter off, and that with a degree of vigour which possibly took that official by surprise.

"Remove your hand!" he cried.

There was a moment's pause, and during that moment's pause another lady came down the stairs. The bewildered Cecil rushed to her.

"Mrs. Danvers, has everybody gone mad? What is the matter with Hetty?" There was no mistake about it this time. The lady was so desirous that none of her garments should come into contact with Cecil that, the better to draw them away from him, she clutched her skirts with both her hands. She spoke—

"How dare you, sir, address yourself to me?" She turned to the porter with an air of command. "Desire this person to stand out of my way."

And she swept off, Cecil staring at her like a man in a dream.

"Well, sir?" Cecil turned. A decently-attired, and even gentlemanly, individual was standing at his side. "Have you returned to pay your bill?"

Cecil looked him up and down. In his appearance he noted no signs of insanity, nor of intoxication either.

"Are you the manager of this establishment?"

"You know very well that I am. Pray don't let's have any nonsense."

"Allow me to give you my card." Cecil handed him his "pasteboard." "I left Paris last night. I have been travelling all day. I arrived five minutes ago in your hotel. What is the meaning of the treatment which has been accorded me?"

The manager regarded him with a smile which scarcely came within the definition of a "courteous smile."

"You are certainly a character."

"Explain yourself."

"Surely not much explanation is required. It is only a few minutes ago since I informed you that your presence in this establishment could no longer be permitted, and now you favour me with this amazing story."

Cecil started forward. A new light came into his eyes.

"Has anyone been staying here resembling me?"

"So much resembling you that we shall be obliged if you will pay his bill, which lies, unpaid, on the cashier's desk."

Cecil gave an exclamation—not of pleasure.

"By Jove! It's Hubert! I see it all! He has been up to some of his infernal tricks with Hetty and her mother! If he has!" He turned upon the manager, "Where is he?"

The manager hesitated.

"Where is who? You are standing here. When I last saw you, you were entering a private sitting-room with two gentlemen who happened to have a particular desire for your society."

"Where is this sitting-room?"

"I will show you if you really don't know." The manager led the way—still smiling. Cecil went after him. As they moved along a corridor, into which the manager turned, they came upon a lady who was standing outside one of the sitting-rooms, and who, not to put too fine a point on it, seemed listening at the door. Her back was turned towards them as they advanced. It was only when they were quite close to her that she seemed to become conscious of their approach. When she arrived at such a state of consciousness she sprang up—she had been stooping a good deal forward before—and sprang round. She was in evening dress. A fine, tall, generously proportioned woman, with big bright eyes, and red-gold hair, she was Hubert's "oner"—"Angel." As her glance fell upon Cecil she gave a start—a most melodramatic start—so melodramatic a start that she bumped herself, quite unintentionally, but with considerable force, against the wall.

"You!" she exclaimed.

Cecil, on his part, appeared to recognise the lady.

"You!" he said—without any appearance of undue deference in his manner.

His arrival on the scene seemed to have thrown the lady into a state of really curious agitation. She stood with her back against the wall, staring at him as if he were a ghost. She positively trembled.

"How—how did you get out?" she asked—speaking in a sort of gasp.

"I was never in." Cecil turned to the manager. "It's a little complicated, but I think that I begin to understand the situation." He turned to the lady. He pointed to the sitting-room, outside which she was standing. "Who is in there?"

Angel did not answer. Leaning forward, she rapped with her knuckles against the panel of the door.

CHAPTER V

THE TWINS CONFRONT EACH OTHER

When there came that rapping at the door, Hubert started back.

"Who's that?" he cried.

The big man still retained his grasp on Hubert's shoulder. He tightened it.

"Never mind who it is. Sign that paper."

There was a voice without. "Open the door!"

Hubert slipped from the man's grasp. He sprang to his feet. He threw the pen from him on to the floor. "It's Cecil!"

The two men looked at him. He looked at them. Again there was the voice without. "Open the door!"

"It's Cecil! It's my brother! Now you will see if I lied."

In Hubert's manner there was positively something approaching an air of triumph. The associates exchanged glances. The big man addressed himself again to Hubert.

"Look here, my friend, you will sign that paper."

He moved a step forward. Hubert grasped the back of a chair.

"You touch me! By George! I'll smash you!"

The big man hesitated. Hubert seemed to have gained a sudden access of energy. He continued to address his companions in a strain which was distinctly not pacific. "You couple of cowardly curs! You get me into a room, you lock the door, you come at me, the pair of you, with a revolver and a knife, when you know that I haven't got so much as a toothpick in my pocket! Why, you miserable brutes, I'll smash you both!"

Hubert brandished the chair about his head. The big man still hesitated. The shorter gentleman addressed this inquiry to his friend, "Shall I shoot him? Shall I put six shots into his carcass—shall I?"

Hubert did not wait to hear the other's answer. He turned to the door. "Cecil! Cecil! break down the door. The brutes will murder me! Break down the door!"

These words, uttered with the full force of Hubert's lungs, seemed to create, as was not unnatural, some sensation without. Several voices were heard speaking together. There was a loud knocking at the door. Someone said, evidently not Cecil, "Open the door immediately! I am the manager of the hotel! Open at once!"

The associates looked at each other. The clamour without seemed to mean business. Hubert had slipped from their control. If they were not careful their friendly little interview might be disagreeably interrupted. The shorter man shrugged his shoulders right up to his ears.

"What is the use? You had better open the door. What is the use of playing a losing game too far?" Then, to Hubert, "With you, my friend, I will settle some other time."

"And I," chimed in the big man, playing the part of echo for once.

"I don't care that," Hubert snapped his fingers in the air, "for either, or both of you, you curs!"

The comrades still hesitated—they probably resented the alteration in the young gentleman's demeanour. But the clamour at the door continued. The big man, doubtless perceiving that the position was becoming desperate, took the key out of his pocket. He unlocked the door. As he did so, his companion's weapons disappeared into the hidden recess of his apparel. The moment the door was opened Hubert advanced.

"Cecil! so it is you. Now, gentlemen, you will be able to see if I lied. These gentlemen, Cecil, are friends of yours, not of mine. I have never seen them before to-night. You appear to have offended them. They have been endeavouring to visit your offence on me. I cannot congratulate you on your acquaintance. That little scoundrel there, who appears to be an Italian bravo, has a knife in one pocket, and a revolver in the other. He would have murdered me if you had delayed your appearance on the scene."

"Bah!" Again the little man's shoulders went up to his ears. "It was but a little game."

"And was this a little game?"

Hubert snatched up the paper, the unsigned promise of marriage, from the table on which it was lying; he held it out in front of him. The big man, in his turn, snatched it from his grasp. He tore it into minute shreds. While Hubert still was staring, a lady advanced. It was Angel.

"So, all the time you were amusing yourself at my expense. You are a charming person. Where are my thirty pounds?"

Hubert was not at all embarrassed. He twirled his moustache.

"Cecil, this lady appears to be a friend of yours. Where are her thirty pounds?"

Cecil stepped up to him. "What confounded tricks have you been up to?"

Hubert's air of injured innocence was, in its way, superb.

"Cecil, this is too much; too much! In mistake for you I have been insulted, all but murdered, and all"—he turned to the assembled company—"and all, upon my word of honour, because I was so unfortunate as to have been born a twin."

A VISION OF THE NIGHT

CHAPTER I

ASLEEP

"Charlie, do you believe in dreams?"

It was in the great hall of the Pouhon spring at Spa. The band was playing. The motley crowd which gathers in the season at Spa to drink, or not to drink, the waters, were talking, smoking, drinking coffee, something stronger, looking at the papers, or listening to the music. Among the crowd were Gerald Lovell and his friend Charles Warren. At the particular moment in which Mr. Lovell put his question, Mr. Warren was puffing rings of cigarette smoke into the air.

"Ask me," he said, with distinct irreverence, "another."

"A queer thing happened to me last night."

"If you have any malicious intention of inflicting on me a dream, young man, there'll be a row. I have an aunt who dreams. She's a dreaming sort. She's always dreaming. And she tells her dreams—such dreams! Ye Goths! At the mere mention of the word 'dreams' the nightmare figure of my aunt rises to my mind's eye. So beware."

"But I'm not sure that this was a dream. Anyhow, just listen."

"If I must!" said Mr. Warren. And he sighed.

"I dreamt that a woman kissed me!"

"If I could only dream such a thing. Some men have all the luck."

"The queer thing was, that it was so real. I dreamt that a woman came into my room. She came to my bedside. She stood looking down upon me as I slept. Suddenly she stooped and kissed me. That same instant I awoke. I felt her kiss still tingling on my lips. I could have sworn that someone had just kissed me. I sat up in bed and called out to know if anyone was there. I got up and lit the gas and searched the room. There was nothing and no one."

"It was a dream!"

"If it was, it was the most vivid dream I remember to have heard of; certainly the most vivid dream I ever dreamt. I saw the woman so distinctly, and her face, as she stooped over me, with laughter in her eyes. To begin with, it was the most beautiful face I ever saw, and hers were the most beautiful eyes. The whole thing had impressed me so intensely that I took my sketch-book and made a drawing of her then and there. I have my sketch-book in my pocket—here is the drawing."

Mr. Lovell handed his open sketch-book to his friend. It was open at a page on which was a drawing of a woman's face. When Mr. Warren's eyes fell on this drawing, he sat up in his chair with a show of sudden interest.

"Gerald! I say! You'll excuse my saying so, but I didn't think you were capable of anything so good as this. Do you know that this is the best drawing of yours I have ever seen, young man?"

"I believe it is."

"It looks to me—I don't want to flatter you; goodness knows you've conceit enough already!—but it looks to me as though it were a genuine bit of inspiration."

"Joking apart, it seems to me almost as if it were an inspiration."

"I wish an inspiration of the same kind would come to me. I'd be considerably grateful—even for a nightmare. Do you know what I should do with this? I should use it for a picture."

"I thought of doing something of the kind myself."

"Just a study of a woman's face. And you might call it—the title would be apposite—'A Vision of the Night!'"

"A good idea. I will."

And Mr. Lovell did. When he returned to his Chelsea studio, he chose a moderate-sized canvas, and he began to paint on it a woman's face—just a woman's face, and nothing more. She was looking a little downwards, as a woman might look who was about to stoop to kiss someone lying asleep in bed—say a sleeping child—and she glanced from the canvas with laughing eyes. Mr. Warren came in to look at it several times while it was progressing. When it was finished, he regarded it for some moments in silent contemplation.

"I call that," he declared, sententiously, with what he supposed, perhaps erroneously, to be a Yankee twang, "a gen-u-ine work of art. I do. The thing. Young man, if you forward that, with your compliments, or without 'em, to the President, Fellows, and Associates of the Royal Academy, I'll bet you five to one it's hung!"

His prediction was verified—it was hung. It was the first of Mr. Lovell's pictures which ever had been hung—which made the fact none the less gratifying to Mr. Lovell. It was hung very well, too, considering. And it attracted quite a considerable amount of attention in its way. It was sold on the opening day. That fact was not displeasing to Mr. Lovell.

One morning, about the middle of June, a card was brought in to Mr. Lovell, while he was working in his studio. On it was inscribed a name—Vicomte d'Humières. The card was immediately followed by its owner, a tall, slightly built gentleman; unmistakably a foreigner. He saluted Mr. Lovell with a bow which was undoubtedly Parisian.

"Mr. Gerald Lovell?"

The accent was French, but, for a Frenchman, the English was fair.

"I am Gerald Lovell."

"Ah! That is good! You are a gentleman, Mr. Lovell, whom I particularly wish to see." The stranger had been carrying his stick in one hand and his hat in the other. These he now deposited upon one chair; himself he placed upon a second—uninvited. He crossed his legs. He folded his black gloved hands in front of him. "I believe, Mr. Lovell, that we are not strangers—you and I."

Mr. Lovell glanced at the card which he still was holding.

"You are the Vicomte d'Humières?"

"I am."

"I am afraid—it is unpardonable remissness on my part; but I am afraid that, if I have ever had the pleasure of meeting you before, it is a pleasure which has escaped my memory."

"It is not that we have ever met before—no, it is not that. It is my name to which you are not a stranger."

Mr. Lovell glanced again at the card. "Your name? I am afraid, Vicomte, that I do not remember having ever heard your name before."

"Ah! Is that so?" The stranger regarded his polished boots. He spoke as if he were addressing himself to them. "Is it possible that she can have given another name? No, it is not possible. She is capable of many things. I do not believe she is capable of that." He looked up again at Mr. Lovell. "My business with you, Mr. Lovell, is of rather a peculiar kind. You will think, perhaps, that mine is rather a singular errand. I have come to ask you to acquaint me with the residence of my wife."

"With the—did you say, with the—residence of your wife?"

"That is what I said. I have come to ask you to acquaint me with the residence of my wife." The artist stared.

"But, so far as I am aware, I do not know your wife."

"That is absurd. I do not say, Mr. Lovell, that you are conscious of the absurdity. But still—it is absurd—I was not aware that you were acquainted with my wife until I learned the fact, this morning, at your Academy."

"At our Academy?"

"Precisely. Upon the walls of your Academy of Painting, Mr. Lovell."

Mr. Lovell began to wonder if his visitor was not an amiable French lunatic.

"Is that not rather a singular place in which to learn such a fact?"

"It is a singular place. It is a very singular place, indeed. But that has nothing to do with the matter. It is as I say. You have a picture, Mr. Lovell, at the Academy?"

"I have."

"It is a portrait."

"Pardon me, it is not a portrait."

"Pardon me, Mr. Lovell, in my turn; it is a portrait. As a portrait, it is a perfect portrait. It is a portrait of my wife."

"Of your wife! You are dreaming!"

"You flatter me, Mr. Lovell. Is it that you suppose I am an imbecile? Are not the features of a wife familiar to a husband? Very good. I am the husband of my wife. Your picture, Mr. Lovell, is a portrait of my wife."

"I cannot but think you have mistaken some other picture for mine. Mine is a simple study of a woman's face. It is called 'A Vision of the Night.'"

"Precisely. And 'A Vision of the Night'—is my wife."

"It is impossible!"

"Do I understand you to say, Mr. Lovell, of a thing which I say is so—that it is impossible?"

The Vicomte rose. His voice had a very significant intonation. Mr. Lovell resented it.

"I do not know, Vicomte, that I am called upon to explain to you. But, in face of your remarkable statement, I will volunteer an explanation. I saw the face, which I have painted, in a dream."

"Indeed; is that so? What sort of dream was it in which you saw my wife's face, Mr. Lovell?"

The young man flushed. The stranger's tone was distinctly offensive.

"It was in a dream which I dreamt last August, at Spa."

"Ah! This is curious. At what hotel were you stopping last August at Spa?"

"At the Hôtel de Flandre—though I don't know why you ask."

"So! We approach a point at last. Last August, my wife and I, we were at Spa. We stayed, my wife and I, at the Hôtel de Flandre. It was at the Hôtel de Flandre my wife left me. I have never seen her since. Perhaps, Mr. Gerald Lovell, you will be so good as to inform me what sort of dream it was in which you saw my wife's face, at the Hôtel de Flandre, last August, at Spa?"

Mr. Lovell hesitated. He perceived that caution was advisable. He felt that if he entered into minute particulars of his dream, there might be a misunderstanding with the Vicomte. So he temporized—or he endeavoured to.

"I have already told you that I saw the face in my picture in a dream. It is the simple fact—that I have no other explanation to offer."

"Is that so?"

"That is so."

"Very good, so far, Mr. Gerald Lovell. I thought it possible that you might have some explanation of this kind to offer. I was at the Academy with a friend. When I perceived my wife's portrait on the walls, and that it was painted by a Mr. Gerald Lovell, I said to my friend: 'I will go to this Mr. Lovell, and I will ask him, among other things, who authorized him to exhibit my wife's portrait in the absence of her husband, in a place of public resort, as if it were an advertisement.' My friend proposed to accompany me. But I said: 'No. I will go, first of all, alone. I will see what sort of explanation Mr. Gerald Lovell has to offer. If it is not a satisfactory explanation, then we will go together, you and I.' I go to seek my friend,

Mr. Lovell. He is not very far away. Shortly we will return. Then I will request, of your courtesy, an explanation of that very curious dream in which you saw my wife's face at the Hôtel de Flandre. Mr. Lovell, I wish you, until then, good day."

The Vicomte withdrew, with the same extremely courteous salutation with which he had entered. The artist, left alone, looked at his visitor's card, which he still retained in his hand, with a very puzzled expression of countenance.

"If the Vicomte d'Humières returns, it strikes me there'll be a little interesting conversation."

He laid down the card. He resumed the work which had been interrupted. But the work hung fire. A painter paints, not only with his hand, but with his brain. Mr. Lovell's brain was, just then, preoccupied.

"It was a dream. And yet, as I told Warren at the time, it certainly was the most vivid dream I ever dreamt." Deserting his canvas he began to move about the room. "Supposing it wasn't a dream, and the woman was a creature of flesh and blood! Then she must have come into my room, and kissed me while I slept. I'll swear that someone kissed me. By Jove! the Vicomte won't like to be told a tale like that! As he says, a man ought to know his own wife's face when he sees it, even in a portrait. And if the picture is a portrait of his wife, then it was his wife who came into my room—and kissed me. But whatever made her do a thing like that? There's no knowing what things some women will do. I rather fancy that I ought to have made a few inquiries before I took it for granted that it was nothing but a dream. They would have been able to tell me at the hotel if the original of my dream had been staying there. As it is, unless I mind my P's and Q's, I rather fancy there'll be a row."

"Pardon!—may I enter?"

Mr. Lovell was standing with his back to the door. The inquiry, therefore, was addressed to him from behind. The voice in which it was uttered was feminine, and the accent foreign. The artist turned—and stared. For there, peeping through the partly open door, was the woman of his dream! There could not be the slightest doubt about it. Although the head was covered with the latest thing in Parisian hats, there was no mistaking, when one once had seen it—as he had seen it—that lovely face, those laughing eyes. He stared—and gaped. The lady seemed to take his silence to imply consent. She advanced into the room.

"You are Mr. Gerald Lovell?"

As she came into the room, he perceived that she was not only most divinely fair, but most divinely tall. Her figure, clad in the most recent coquetries of Paris, was the most exquisite thing in figures he had lately seen. So completely had she taken his faculties of astonishment by storm, that he could only stammer a response.

"You are the painter of my portrait?" For the life of him, he knew not what to say. "But, if you are Mr. Gerald Lovell, it is certain that you are. Besides, I see it in your face. There is genius in your eyes. Mr. Lovell, how am I to thank you for the honour you have done me?" Moving to him, she held out to him her hand. He gave her his. She retained it—or, rather, part of it—in her small palm. "If I am ever destined to attain to immortality, it is to your brush it will be owing. Monsieur, permit me to salute the master!"

Before he had an inkling of her intention, she raised his hand and touched it with her lips. He withdrew it quickly.

"Madame!"

She exhibited no signs of discomposure.

"I was at your Academy, with a friend—not half an hour ago. I beheld miles of mediocrity. Suddenly I saw—my face! my own face! glancing at me from the walls! Ah, quel plaisir! But my face—how many times more lovely! How many times more beautiful! My face—depicted by the hand of a great artist! by the brush of a poet, and a genius!—Monsieur, you have placed on me ten thousand obligations."

She gave him the most sweeping curtsey with which he ever had been favoured—and in her eyes was laughter all the time. He was recovering his presence of mind. He felt that it was time to put a stop to the lady's flow of flowery language. He was about to do so—when a question she put to him again sent half his senses flying.

"There is one thing which I wished to ask you, Monsieur. When and where did I sit to you for my portrait? I do not remember to have had the pleasure and the honour of meeting you before." The lady's laughing eyes were fixed intently on his face. "And yet, as I look at you, a sort of shadowy recollection comes to me of a previous encounter; it is very strange! Monsieur, where was it we encountered—you and I?"

"Madame!"

Seeing how evidently he was at a loss for words, she put out her hand to him as if to give him courage.

"Do not be afraid. Tell me—where was it that you saw me?"

"I saw you in a dream."

"A dream? Monsieur! To hear you speak—it is like a poem. Monsieur, where did you dream this dream in which you dreamt of me?"

"It was last year, at Spa."

"At Spa—that horrible place?"

"I did not find it a horrible place."

"No? Was it that dream which you dreamt of me which robbed it of its horror?" He did not speak. He allowed her to infer a compliment, but he did not proffer one. "But Monsieur, I was only at Spa one afternoon and a single night."

"It was that night I dreamed of you."

"You dreamed? How? Tell me about this dream."

"I dreamed that you came into my room while I was asleep in bed, and kissed me!"

She continued to look at him intently a moment longer, as if she did not realize the full meaning of his words. Then—let us do her justice!—the blood rushed to her face, her cheeks flamed fiery red. With her hands she veiled her eyes. She gave a little cry.

"Ah, mon Dieu! It was you—I remember. Quelle horreur!"

There was silence. Before she removed her hands from her eyes she turned away. She stood with her back towards him, trifling with a brush which he had placed upon the table. She spoke scarcely above a whisper.

"Monsieur, I thought you were asleep."

"I was asleep. I saw you in a dream."

"Then did—did I wake you?"

"You must have done. I woke—you must forgive my saying so—with a kiss tingling on my lips." The lady put her hands up to her eyes again. "The dream had been so vivid I could not understand it. I got up to see if anyone was in the room."

"If you had caught me!"

"There was no one. But so acutely had your face impressed itself on my imagination that I took my sketch-book, and made a drawing of it then and there. In the morning I showed this drawing to a friend. He advised me to use it for a picture I did. That picture is 'A Vision of the Night'!"

"It is the most extraordinary thing, Monsieur; you will suppose I am a very peculiar person. It is but a lame explanation I have to offer. Of that I am but too conscious. But such as it is, I entreat that you will suffer me to give it you. Monsieur, I am married"—Mr. Lovell bowed. He did not mention that he was aware of that already—"to the most capricious husband in the world—to a husband whom I love, but whom I cannot respect." Mr. Lovell thought that that was good—from her. "He is a man who is extremely difficile, Monsieur. I do not think you have a word which expresses what I would say in English. He is extremely jealous; he is enraged that his wife should use the eyes which are in her head! The very day on which we arrived at Spa we had a dreadful quarrel. I will not speak of the treatment to which I was subjected; it is enough to say that he locked the door so that I should not leave the room—he wished to make of me a prisoner. Monsieur, directly he was gone, I perceived that there were two doors to the room—the one which he had locked, and another, which I tried I found that it was open. Monsieur, when a prisoner desires to escape, he escapes by any road which offers. I was a prisoner; I desired to escape; I made use of the only road which I could find. I entered the door; I found myself in a room in which there was—how shall I say it?—in which there was a man asleep. Monsieur, it was you!"

It must be owned that at this point the lady certainly did look down.

"I was, that night, in a wicked mood. I glanced at you; I perceived that you were but a boy"—Mr. Lovell flushed: he did not consider himself a boy—"but a handsome boy." She peeped at him with malicious laughter in her eyes. "I regarded myself as your mother, or your sister, or your guardian angel. Monsieur will perceive how much I am the elder." Again, a glance of laughing malice from those bewitching eyes. "I am afraid it is too true that I approached the sleeping lips." There was silence. Then, so softly that her listener was only able to catch the words: "I pray that Monsieur will forgive me."

"There is nothing for which Madame needs forgiveness."

"Monsieur but says so to give me pleasure. But one thing Monsieur must permit me to observe: If every woman were to be rewarded, as I have been, for what I did, half the women in France would commit—a similar little indiscretion." Mr. Lovell was silent; he did not know exactly what to say. "Monsieur will permit me to regard him, from this day forward, as my friend? Mr. Gerald Lovell, permit me to introduce to you—the Vicomtesse d'Humières!"

The lady favoured him with another sweeping curtsey.

"I have already the pleasure of being acquainted with Madame's name."

"From whom did you learn it? From the people at the hotel?"

"I but learned it a few minutes before Madame herself came here."

"So! From whom?"

"I learnt it from the Vicomte d'Humières."

"The Vicomte d'Humières! My husband! Are you acquainted with him, then?"

"I can scarcely claim to be acquainted with the Vicomte. It seems, Madame, that this has been a morning of coincidences. It would appear that just before Madame perceived my little picture at the Academy, the Vicomte d'Humières perceived it too."

"Truly! But how magnificent!"

The lady clasped her hands in a little ecstacy.

"The Vicomte d'Humières did not seem to consider it magnificent. He took a distinctly contrary view."

"But that is certain!"

"He requested me to furnish him with your address. When I informed him that I was not acquainted with Madame, he desired to know who had authorized me to send your portrait to a public exhibition. I observed that I was not aware that it was the portrait of Madame, since the face in the picture was but the study of a face which I had seen in a dream."

"In a dream! You did not tell him—the little history?"

"I entered into no particulars."

"I entreat you, Monsieur, not to tell him the little history. There will be a scandal; he is so quick to misconceive."

"I will endeavour to observe Madame's wishes."

"It is like a little romance, is it not, Monsieur? Perhaps I should explain myself a little further. That night"—she emphasized the that—"I left my husband. In effect, he had become unbearable. I have seen and heard nothing of him since. But I am beginning to become conscious of a desire to meet with him again. I know not why! I suppose, when one loves one's husband truly, one wishes to meet him—once a year. I do not wish our reconciliation to be inaugurated by a quarrel—no, I entreat you, Monsieur, not recount to him that little history."

"I should inform Madame that I expect the Vicomte d'Humières to return."

"Return? Where? Here? When?"

"Very shortly—with a friend. In fact, unless I am mistaken, he comes already."

The lady listened.

"It is Philippe's voice! Mon Dieu! He must not find me here."

"But, Madame—"

"Ah, the screen! It is like a farce at the Palais Royal—is it not a fact? I will be your model, Monsieur, behind the screen!"

"Madame!"

Before he could interpose to prevent her, the lady vanished behind the screen. The door of the studio opened, and the Vicomte d'Humières entered, accompanied by his friend.

CHAPTER II

AND AWAKE

The Vicomte's friend was a gentleman of a figure which is not uncommon in France, even to-day. His attitude suggested a ramrod, he breathed powder and shot; and he bristled—what shall we say?—with bayonets. The last person in the world with whom a modern Briton should have a serious difference of opinion. The ideas of that sort of person upon matters which involve a difference of opinion are in such contrast to ours. The Vicomte performed the ceremony of introduction.

"Mr. Gerald Lovell, permit me to introduce to your courteous consideration my friend, M. Victor Berigny!"

M. Berigny bowed, ceremoniously. Mr. Lovell only nodded—his thoughts were behind the screen. The Vicomte turned to his friend.

"Victor, I have explained to you that I have already had the pleasure of an interview with Mr. Gerald Lovell." M. Berigny bowed. "I have also explained to you that I have desired him to inform me by whose authority he exhibits a portrait of my wife in a public exhibition. To that he has replied that his picture, 'A Vision of the Night,' is not a portrait of my wife. I request you, Victor, to state, in Mr. Gerald Lovell's presence, whether that picture, in your opinion, is or is not a portrait of my wife."

"Certainly, it is a portrait."

M. Berigny's accent was more marked than the Vicomte's, but still he did speak English.

"I thank you, Victor. It remains for me to once more request, in your presence, Mr. Gerald Lovell to explain how it was that he happened to dream of the face of my wife last August, in the Hôtel de Flandre, at Spa. Mr. Gerald Lovell, I have the honour to await your explanation."

The Vicomte, his arms crossed upon his chest, his left foot a little protruding, his head thrown back, awaited the explanation.

Mr. Lovell's thoughts ran screenwards.

"What the deuce shall I do if he discovers her behind the screen?"

"Monsieur, I am waiting."

"If he does discover her—there'll be a row."

"I still am waiting, Mr. Gerald Lovell."

With each repetition of the statement the Vicomte's tone became more acidulated. The artist arrived at a sudden resolution.

"Then I am afraid, Vicomte, that you will have to wait."

The Vicomte looked at the artist with an evident inclination to add a cubit to his own stature.

"Is it possible that I understand your meaning, Mr. Gerald Lovell?"

"My language is sufficiently simple."

"In France, Mr. Gerald Lovell, an artist is supposed to be a gentleman."

"And so in England, Vicomte. And therefore, when an artist is interrupted at his work by another gentleman, he feels himself at liberty to beg that other gentleman—to excuse him."

Mr. Lovell waved his hand, affably, in the direction of the door. The Vicomte's countenance assumed a peculiar pallor.

"You are a curious person, Mr. Gerald Lovell."

His friend interposed.

"Philippe, you had better leave the matter to me."

M. Berigny approached the painter—with a ramrod down his back.

"I have the honour, Monsieur, to request from you the name of a friend."

"Of a friend? What for?"

"Ah, Monsieur—to arrange the preliminaries!"

"What preliminaries?"

"Is it that Monsieur amuses himself?"

"Is it possible that you suppose that I am going to fight a duel?"

"Monsieur intends, then, to offer an explanation to my friend?"

"M. Berigny, I do not wish to say to you anything uncourteous, or anything unworthy an English gentleman; but I do beg you to believe that, because you choose to be an idiot, and your friend chooses to be an idiot, it does not follow that I choose to be an idiot, too."

"Monsieur!"

"One other observation. I have not seen much of you, M. Beringy, but that little has not disposed me to see more. May I therefore ask you—to leave my studio?"

"Monsieur!"

"Or—must I turn you out?"

"Turn me out!"

The Vicomte had been listening to this little dialogue. He now turned towards his friend.

"Ah, my friend, it is as he says! He will turn you out, neck and crop, as the English say. He will throw you down the stairs, he will heave half a brick at your head, to help you on your way. Then, when you require satisfaction, he will refer you to a magistrate. You will summon him—it will be in the papers—he will be fined half-a-crown! That is how they manage these affairs in England. It is true!"

"But—among gentlemen!"

"Ah, mon ami, voila! In England, nowadays, there are no gentlemen!"

Mr. Lovell moved a step towards M. Berigny.

"I have asked you, as a gentleman, to leave my studio."

"Monsieur, you are a coward!"

The painter's eyes gleamed. But he kept his temper pretty well, considering.

"You appear to have been taught singularly ill manners in your native country, sir. I will endeavour to teach you better manners here. Are you going? Or must I eject you?"

"Polison!"

That was M. Berigny's answer. There was just a momentary hesitation. Then, grasping M. Berigny firmly by the shoulders, Mr. Lovell began to move him, more rapidly than gently, in the direction of the door. The Vicomte came forward, with the evident intention of interposing. There would probably have been a slightly undignified scramble had not a diversion been created by the opening of the door, and the entrance of Mr. Warren. That gentleman glanced from one person to another.

"I beg your pardon," he observed. "I hope I don't intrude!"

Mr. Lovell laughed, a little forcedly. His complexion was distinctly ruddy.

"Not at all! I wish you had come in sooner. The most ridiculous thing has happened."

"Indeed! I have an eye for the ridiculous."

"You know that picture of mine, 'A Vision of the Night'?"

"I've heard of it."

"This gentleman says that it's a portrait of his wife."

Mr. Lovell pointed to the Vicomte d'Humières.

"No? Then, in that case, this gentleman's wife came into your bedroom in the middle of the night, and—kissed you, wasn't it?"

Mr. Warren spoke in the innocence of his heart, but, at that moment, Mr. Lovell could have struck his boyhood's friend. There was a listener behind the screen. The young gentleman's cheeks grew crimson, as the lady's had done a few minutes before. He was conscious, too, that the Vicomte's unfriendly eyes were fixed upon his face.

"So! That is it! You—you—" The Vicomte moved a step forward, then checked himself. "Tell me, where is my wife at this instant?"

Mr. Lovell could have told him, but he refrained.

"I decline to give you any information of any kind whatever."

"You decline?" The Vicomte raised his hand. He would have struck the artist. Mr. Warren interposed to avert the blow.

"He declines for the very simple reason that he has never seen your wife; isn't that so, Gerald?"

Mr. Lovell hesitated. He scarcely saw his way to a denial while the lady was behind the screen.

"You see! He does not even dare to lie!"

"Don't talk nonsense, sir! Gerald, why don't you tell the man that you have never seen the woman in your life?"

"I repeat that I decline to give this person any information of any kind whatever."

"You decline?"

The Vicomte uttered the words in a kind of strangled screech. His patience was exhausted. He seemed to think that he was being subjected to treatment which was more than flesh and blood could bear. He rushed at Mr. Lovell. Mr. Lovell, probably forgetting himself on the impulse of the moment—or he would have been more careful—swung the Vicomte round against the screen. It tottered, reeled, and, raising a cloud of dust, it fell with a bang to the floor!

It was a leaf out of Sheridan.

For an instant the several members of that little party did not distinctly realize what it was that had happened. Then they saw. There was a pause—a curious pause. Their attitudes betrayed a charming diversity of emotions. The Vicomte, his coat a little disarranged, owing to the somewhat rough handling which he had just received, stood and glared. M. Berigny, more ramroddy than ever, stared. Mr. Warren gasped. Mr. Lovell's quickened breathing, crimsoned cheeks, and flashing eyes seemed to suggest that his breast was a tumult of conflicting feelings. The lady, whose presence had been so unexpectedly revealed, stood behind the fallen screen, with the most charming air of innocence in the world, and she smiled.

It was she who broke the silence. She held out her hand to the Vicomte.

"Bon jour, Philippe!"

"Ah-h-h!" The Vicomte drew himself away with a sort of shuddering exclamation. "Antoinette! It is you! It cannot be!"

"My dear Philippe—why not?"

"Why not?"

"Why not? She asks why not!" The Vicomte held out his hands, as though he appealed to the eternal verities. "Traîtresse! Once more is woman false and man betrayed!"

The Vicomte's gesture was worthy of the tragic stage—in France. The lady still held out her hand, and still she smiled.

"My dear Philippe—try comedy!"

"Comedy? Ah, yes, I will try comedy—the comedy of r-r-revenge!" The Vicomte distinctly rolled his r's. He turned to Mr. Lovell. "I will kill you, even though for killing you, by the law of England, I am hanged. Victor, where is my hat?"

The Vicomte put this question to his friend with a peculiar coldness. M. Berigny shrugged his shoulders.

"How should I know? It is not a question of a hat."

"As you say, it is not a question of a hat. It is a question"—the Vicomte moved towards Mr. Lovell—"of that!"

He raised his hand with the intention of striking the artist on the cheek. Mr. Lovell never flinched; but the lady, rushing forward, caught her husband by the wrist. She looked at him, still with laughter in her eyes.

"Try not to be insane."

The Vicomte glared at her with a glare which, at least, was characteristic.

"Why do I not kill her—why?"

The lady only smiled.

"They say that a woman is devoid of humour. How is it then sometimes with a man? You, Philippe, are always thinking of the Porte St. Martin—I, of the Bouffes Parisiens."

The Vicomte turned to his friend.

"Victor, why do I not kill this woman?"

M. Berigny only shrugged his shoulders. Possibly because he was not ready with a more adequate reply. The lady turned to the artist.

"Monsieur, I offer you ten thousand apologies, which my husband will one day offer you himself, as becomes a gentleman of France."

The Vicomte repeated his inquiry:

"Victor, why do I not kill this woman?"

Only a shrug in reply. The lady went on:

"You have immortalized my poor face, Monsieur; my husband insults you in return."

The Vicomte folded his arms across his chest.

"It is certain, Victor, that she still lives!"

"One night, Monsieur, my husband locked me in my room. He designed to make of me a prisoner. Why? Ah, do not ask me why? When he had left me, I escaped, not by the door which he had locked, but by a door he had not noticed. This door led into an apartment in which there was a stranger sleeping. I was but an instant in that apartment—but the instant in which it was necessary to pass through. The sleeper never spoke to me; he never saw me with his waking eyes. But, even in his sleep, my poor, frightened face so flashed upon his brain that, even in his waking hours, it haunted him so that he made of it a picture—a picture of that Vision of the Night!"

The Vicomte approached closer to his friend. He addressed him in a sort of confidential, but still distinctly audible, aside:

"Victor, is it possible that this is true?"

"I beg, my friend, that of me you will ask nothing."

"Monsieur, this morning I was at your Academy. I saw my own countenance looking at me from the walls. For the first time I learned that my poor, frightened woman's face had appeared to a sleeping stranger in a Vision of the Night. Oh, Monsieur, Monsieur!"

The lady covered her face with her hands. It would, perhaps, be rash to say that she cried; but, at least, she seemed to cry, and if it was only seeming, she did it very well.

"Victor," again inquired the Vicomte of his friend, "is it possible that this is true?"

M. Berigny wagged his finger in the Vicomte's face.

"D'Humières, it now becomes a question of hats." The Vicomte laid his hand on his companion's arm.

"One instant, Victor—still one instant more."

The lady, uncovering her eyes—which actually were sparkling with tears—continued to address the artist.

"Monsieur, I will not speak to you of my love for my husband—my Philippe! I will not speak to you of how we have been parted for a year—a whole, long year—mon Dieu, Monsieur, mon Dieu! I will not speak to you of how, every instant of that long, long year I have thought of him, of how I have yearned for him, of how I have longed for one touch of his hand, one word from his lips, one glance from his eyes. No, Monsieur, I will not speak to you of all these things. And for this reason: That, with me all things are finished. I go, never to return again. My face—you have made immortal; the rest of me—will perish. For the woman whose heart is broken there remains but one place—the grave. It is to that place I go!"

The lady had become as tragic as her husband—even more so, in her way. She moved across the room with the air of a tragedy queen—Parisian. The Vicomte was visibly affected. He fastened a convulsive clutch upon M. Berigny's arm.

"Victor, tell me, what shall I do? Advise me, oh, my friend! This is a critical moment in my life! It is impossible that I should let her go. Antoinette!"

The Vicomte advanced, just in time, between the lady and the door.

"Monsieur, I entreat of you this last boon, to let me go. You have insulted me in the presence of a stranger; for me, therefore, nothing else remains. You have inquired if you should kill me. No, Philippe, you need not kill me; it is myself I will kill!"

"Antoinette!"

"I am no longer Antoinette; I am the woman whose happiness you have destroyed. It is only when I am dead that you will learn what is written on my heart for you."

"Antoinette," the strong man's voice faltered, "Antoinette, am I never, then, to be forgiven?"

There was a momentary pause. Then the lady held out both her hands. "Philippe!"

"My heart! my soul! thou treasure of my life! thou star of my existence! Is it possible that a cloud should have interposed itself between thy path and mine?"

He took her in his arms. He pressed her to his breast. M. Berigny turned away. From his attitude it almost seemed as if the soldier—the man of ramrods and of bayonets!—wiped away a tear.

"Philippe! Take care, or you will derange my hat!"

"Antoinette! My beautiful, my own!"

"Philippe, do you not think you should apologize—take care, my friend, or you certainly will derange my hat!—to the stranger who has made immortal the face of the woman who loved you better than her life—my friend, take care!—who has made her appear on canvas so much more beautiful than she is in life?"

"No, Antoinette, that I will not have. It is impossible. Beauty such as yours in not to be rendered by a painter's brush!"

"If that be so, all the more reason why we should be grateful to Mr. Lovell for endeavouring the impossible."

The lady peeped at Mr. Lovell with the quaintest malice in her eyes.

"Certainly, Antoinette, there is something in what you say. And, after all, it is a charming painting. I said, Victor, when I saw it, there can be no doubt, as a painting, it is charming—did I not say so?" M. Berigny inclined his head. With his handkerchief the Vicomte smoothed his moustache. He advanced towards Mr. Lovell: "Monsieur, a Frenchman—a true Frenchman—seldom errs. On those rare occasions on which he errs he is always willing, under proper conditions, to confess his error. Monsieur, I perceive that I have done you an injustice. For the injustice which I have done you—I desire to apologize."

Mr. Lovell smiled. He held out his hand.

"My dear fellow! There's nothing for which you need apologize."

The Vicomte grasped the artist's hand in both of his.

"My dear friend!" he cried.

"Philippe," whispered the lady into her husband's ear, "do you not think that you would like Mr. Lovell and his friend to favour us with their company at luncheon?"

The Vicomte seemed to think he would. They lunched together—all the five! Why not?

THE WAY OF A MAID WITH A   MAN.

(Miss Whitby writes to her Mother.)

MY DEAREST MAMMA,—You will be surprised, and I hope you will be pleased to hear that I am engaged to be married! You are not to smile—it would be cruel—this, really, is serious. Charlie is all that a husband should be—you are not to laugh at that—you know exactly what I mean. I am nearly twenty, and, this time, I feel that my happiness really is at stake. I may not be able to keep my looks for long—some girls lose them when they are quite young—and something seems to tell me that I ought to begin to look life seriously in the face, and become responsible. I almost wish that I had taken to district visiting, like Emma Mortimer—it might have balanced me. Poor Emma! what a pity she is so plain.

Will you mind hinting to Tom Wilson that I think he might be happy with Nora Cathcart? It is true that I made him promise that he would never speak to her again, but all that is over. I hope you will not think me fickle, dear mamma. I enclose the ring Tom gave me. Will you please give it to him? And point out to him that I am now persuaded that boy and girl attachments never come to anything serious.

By the way, do not forget to tell them to send two pairs of evening shoes. Those which I have are quite worn out. Let both pairs be perfectly plain bronze. Charlie thinks that they make my feet look almost ethereal. Is he not absurd? But I hope that you will not think so, when you come to know him, for he loves your child. You might also ask them to send me a dozen pairs of stockings—nice ones. All mine seem to be in holes. You know I like them as long as you can get them.

I have been here nearly a month, and I have been almost engaged to three different men. How time does seem to fly! Lily says I am a heartless little flirt. I think that perhaps I was, until he came. He has been here just a week, and I seem to have known him years.

Lily seems to be under the impression that I was engaged to Captain Pentland. She is wrong. Captain Pentland has some very noble qualities. He is destined to make some true woman profoundly happy. Of that I have no doubt whatever. But I am not that woman. No, dear mamma, I feel that now. Besides, he wears an eyeglass. As you are aware, I have always had an insuperable objection to an eyeglass. It seems to savour of affectation. And affectation I cannot stand. And then he lisps. As I told you, when I wrote you last, when I sprained my ankle on Highdown Hill, he carried me in his arms for over a mile. Of course, I was grateful. And, between you and me, dear mamma, he held me so very closely to him, that, afterwards I felt as if I ought to marry him. I have explained everything to Charlie. He quite agrees with me that it is absurd for Captain Pentland to think himself ill-used.

While I think of it, when you are in town will you tell them to send me a box of assorted chocolates? You know the kind I like. There is nothing of that sort to be had here, and I do so long for some.

Charlie is Lily's cousin. Do you think that cousins ought to kiss each other? I wish I could get the opinion of someone on whose judgment I could implicitly rely. At any rate, even supposing that they ought I am quite sure that there should be limits. Before long I am afraid that I shall have to give Charlie a hint that I do not think, under the circumstances, that he ought to kiss Lily quite as much as he does me. She may be his cousin, but she is young, and she is pretty. And cousins are not sisters. It is nonsense for people to pretend they are.

The odd part of it is that if Charlie had not been so fond of kissing Lily I might not be going to marry him now. I knew that he was coming. And I was sitting alone in the drawing-room, in a half-light, with my back to the door, when suddenly someone, putting his arm round my waist, lifting me off my feet, twisted me right round, and began kissing me on my eyes and lips and everywhere.

I thought it was Captain Pentland. Though I was astonished at such behaviour even from him—because it was only that morning we quarrelled. You may judge of my astonishment when I was again able to look out of my own eyes, to find myself being held, as if I were a baby, or a doll, in the arms of a perfect giant of a man, whom I had never seen before. You may imagine how shocked I felt, because, as you know well, my views on such subjects—which I owe to your dear teaching—are, if anything, too severe. I will do him the justice to admit that he seemed to be almost as much shocked as I was.

"I beg your pardon," he said, "ten thousand times. I thought that you were Lily."

He put me down very much as you handle your Chelsea cups, mamma—softly and delicately, as if he had been afraid of chipping pieces off me.

"I suppose you're Charlie?"

I spoke more lightly and more cheerfully than I felt. He seemed so ashamed of himself, and so confused, that I pitied him. You know, dear mamma, that when people know, and feel, that they have done wrong, I always pity them. I cannot help it. It is my nature. All flesh is weak. I myself am prone to err. When Lily did appear, we were talking quite as if we knew each other. And that is how it began. It is odd how these sort of things sometimes do begin. As you are aware, I speak as one who has had experience. I shall always believe that it was only the breaking of a shoelace which first brought Norman Eliot and me together.

But those chapters in my life are closed. In the days which are past I may have seemed to hesitate, to occasionally have changed my mind. But now my life is linked to Charlie's by bonds which never shall be broken. I feel as if I were already married. The gravity of existence is commencing to weigh upon my mind. A woman when she is nearly twenty is no longer young.

While I remember it, when you send the chocolates don't send any walnuts. I am sick of them. Variously flavoured creams are what I really like. And let two pairs of the stockings be light blue, with bronze stripes high up the leg.

I cannot truly say that Lily is behaving to me quite nicely in my relations with Charlie. I do not wish to wrong her, even in my thoughts—she is the very dearest friend I have!—but, sometimes, I cannot help thinking that she had an eye on Charlie for herself. Because when the other morning I was telling her how strongly I disapproved of cousins marrying, if she had not been Lily—whose single-hearted affection I have every faith in—I should have said that she was positively rude. Charlie only proposed to me last night, yet, although she must have seen what was coming, in the afternoon she was actually talking to me of Norman Eliot—as if I had been to blame! Mr. Eliot and I never really were engaged—some people jump to conclusions without proper justification. And am I compelled to answer a person's letters if, for reasons of my own—quite private reasons—I do not choose to?

She came to my bedroom last night, just as I was going to bed. I told her what Charlie had said, and what I had said. Of course I expected her to congratulate me—as, in circumstances such as mine, a girl's best friend ought to do. She heard me to an end, and she looked at me, and said:

"So you've done it again."

"I don't know about again, dear Lily," I replied. "But it would seem as if I had done it at last. I am feeling so happy that it almost makes me afraid."

"Some girls would feel afraid if they had reason to be conscious of the fact that they had engaged themselves to marry three men at once."

I could not help but notice that a jarring something was in her tone. But I paid no heed to it.

My thoughts were elsewhere.

"How wrong it is," I murmured, "for people to scoff at love. They cannot know what love is—as I do."

"Perhaps not. I should think that what you don't know about love, May, isn't worth knowing." I sighed.

"I fancy, Lily dear, that I have heard stories about you."

"I daresay; but I never snapped up your favourite cousin from under your nose. Possibly you will not mind telling me if you do mean to marry one of them, and, if so, which."

"Lily! How can you ask me such a question? Have I not just been telling you that there is only one man in the world for me, henceforth and for ever, and that his name is Charlie?"

"Exactly. Only last week you told me precisely the same story, and his name was Jim, while about a fortnight ago, it was Norman."

My dearest mamma, you see I am making a clean breast of everything to you. I own, quite candidly, that since I have been here I have not behaved precisely as I might have done, and, indeed, ought to have done. I do not know how it is, I meant to be good; I am sure that nothing could have been better than my resolutions. I had no idea that they could have been so easily broken. It only shows, after all, how fragile we are. I felt that, strange and sad though it seems, Lily was not wholly unjust. I got up from my chair, and I knelt at her feet, and I pillowed my head in her lap and I cried:

"Oh, Lily, I've been so wicked! You can't think how sorry I am, now that it's too late. I wish you'd help me, and tell me what I ought to do."

"I'm a bit of a dab at a cry myself," she said. "So, if you take my advice, to begin with, you'll literally dry up."

Was it not unkind? And was it not vulgar? But I sometimes think that Lily's heart is like the nether millstone—so hard, you know. She went on:

"If you do mean business with Charlie, and you do want my advice, you'll just tell him everything you have been doing, and leave the solution of the situation to him."

I made up my mind there and then that that was exactly what I would do. I resolved that I would have no secrets from my husband—particularly as he would be sure to be told them by unfriendly lips if he did not learn them from mine. Besides, in such matters, a man is so much more generous, and so much more sympathetic than a woman—especially the man. Nor does he value you any the less because he finds that someone else happens to value you a little too.

So, directly Lily had gone I let my hair down, and I put on my light blue dressing-jacket and a touch of powder, and I waited. Presently I heard steps coming along the passage. I opened the door. Sure enough it was Charlie, just going to bed. At sight of me he started. I was conscious that I was, perhaps, acting with some imprudence. But I could not help it. My entire happiness was at stake. You know, dear mamma, that I do look nice in that pretty dressing-jacket, with my hair, not at all untidy, but simply let down. You yourself have told me that, in every sense of the word, I look so young. He held out his hands to me—under a misapprehension. I shrank back.

"Mr. Mason," I began very softly, with, in my voice, a sort of sob, "I could not rest until I had told you all that has passed between us to-night must be considered as unsaid."

He started as if I had struck him. I could see that his face went white.

"Miss Whitby! May! What do you mean?" He seemed to gasp for breath. "After all, it is only natural that you should not love a great hulking idiot such as I am."

"You are mistaken. You are not a great hulking idiot. And I do love you. I shall never love anyone but you. It is you who will not love me when you have heard all I have to say."

"What nonsense are you talking?"

Again he held out his arms to me. And again I shrank away.

"It is not nonsense. I wish it were. So far is it from being nonsense that I felt that I could not be at peace until my conscience was unburdened." I paused. I felt the crucial moment was arriving. My voice sank lower. "Someone else was staying here before you came."

"Yes, I know; Lily told me—a man named Pentland."

"Oh, Lily told you so much, did she? Did Lily also tell you that the man named Pentland had bad taste enough to fancy that he had fallen in love with me?"

"Bad taste, you call it. I know nothing about the man, but there, evidently, can be no sort of doubt about his perfect taste."

"But, Charlie—I mean, Mr. Mason."

"You don't—you mean Charlie."

Dear mamma, once more I sighed. I perceived that it would have to be. Some men are so dictatorial.

"The worst of it is that he worried and worried me so—I was staying in the same house, and couldn't get away from him, you see—that he made me almost think I cared for him. But now you have come, and made me see what a mistake it was."

"My little love."

For the third time he held out his arms to me. And, this time, he took me in them. I could not find it in my heart to resist him any longer; it might be the last time he would ever hold me there. I continued my remarks with my head not very far away from his waistcoat. He smoothed my hair, very softly, with his great right hand.

"Unfortunately, I am not at all sure that Captain Pentland does not think that, in a sort of way, I am engaged to him. Oh, Charlie, whatever shall I do?"

"Tell him the truth. Say that you're sorry for him, poor chap, but even the best regulated girls will make mistakes. I'm the mistake you've made."

I was silent. Then I whispered:

"Will you forgive me?"

"It strikes me that it is I who ought to ask you to forgive me—for not having been the first to come upon the scene."

This was throwing a new light upon the subject. It had not occurred to me to look at it from that point of view before. But I had not come to the end of my confessions. Dear mamma, how careful we women ought to be! It is these crises in our lives which make us feel what short-sighted mortals we actually are.

"Before Captain Pentland came"—I was pulling at one of the buttons on his waistcoat as I spoke, and I realised what a big heart Charlie's must be, if it was at all in proportion to his chest—"another friend of Lily's was stopping in the house."

"Ye-es."

I could not help but be conscious of a certain hesitation in his pronunciation of the word.

"His name was Eliot."

"Well?"

There had been a moment's silence before he spoke. And, when he had spoken, there ensued a portentous pause. I hid my face still more from his examining gaze. My voice seemed almost to die away.

"He, also, professed to bestow on me the gift of his affection."

"The devil he did!"

Yes, mamma, that was precisely what he said. It made me shiver. But he was sorry as soon as the words had passed his lips.

"Forgive me! I didn't mean it! After all, it is only to be expected that every man who sees you will fall in love with you at sight."

I wondered if he would talk to me like that in years to come. Do husbands of ten years' standing say such things unto their wives? Oh, how ashamed of myself I felt as I thought of what I still had to admit! Dear mamma, I will try hard never again to do what my conscience tells me is not right. If only we would always listen to the still small voice which seeks to guide us!

"Charlie, you have no notion how foolish I have been! Until you came I had no proper conception of the actualities of existence. Mr. Eliot caused me to confuse the issues just as Captain Pentland did."

He held me out a little way in front of him, trying to look into my face. I was careful not to let him see too much of it. I hung down my head with what, I do hope, mamma, was proper penitence.

"Let me know, clearly, where we are, little girl. Am I to understand you to say that both these men asked you to marry them?"

"I am afraid, Charlie, that you are to understand something of the kind."

"And that you gave both of them encouragement?"

I looked up at him—such a look, mamma! My eyes were swimming in tears. I knew he would not tell me to "dry up." My heart seemed to be rising to my lips.

"Not real encouragement. I never gave anyone real encouragement, Charlie, till I knew you. Even in your case I fear I ought to have been more reticent. But you cannot have the least idea of what a wide world of love you seem to have opened out to me. Won't you forgive me for encouraging you?"

Dear mamma, he collapsed. Of what took place during the moments which immediately followed. I can give you no definite description. I know I began to think that the end of the world had come. When he had quite finished, he said:

"Look here, young lady, what is past is past. We will make no further allusions to what took place before the war. But, in the future, perhaps you will kindly manage not, as you put it, to confuse the issues, but will continue to confine yourself to encouraging me."

Was it not noble of him? And so sweet! I am persuaded that his character is one of singular beauty.

Dear mamma, the passages which ensued were too sacred even for your dear eyes. When he left me I felt certain it was to dream of him. I know that, all night long, I dreamt of him. And, on my knees, beside my bed, I registered a vow that, in the time to come, I will be as good as I possibly can.

Do not forget the shoes, and the stockings, and the chocolates! And do give Tom his ring! I am registering this letter, so you are sure to get it safe.

I will bring, or send, Charlie to you, on approval, whenever you please.

I am, my dearest mamma,

Your ever loving daughter,

MAY.

AUNT JANE'S JALAP

CHAPTER I

BEFORE TAKING

"There's a fortune in it!"

"For the bottlemakers."

"If for them, then what for us? We shan't want more bottles than we can sell. Besides, we can make our own bottles if it comes to that. Cost of bottle, contents, cork, label, and all, one penny. Selling price, eightpence. Sale, at a moderate estimate, one million bottles a year. How does that figure for a profit?"

"It figures nicely. But give me facts. How long do you suppose it will take us to reach that sale?"

"No time. The name will sell it! 'Aunt Jane's Jalap!' There isn't an old woman in England who, seeing those words staring her in the face, won't press a longing hand to her inside."

"Outside, I presume, you mean. But no matter."

Hughes placed the bottle on the table. He looked at it with loving eyes. Then he shook his head.

"There's only one thing we want."

"Customers?"

"Testimonials! There's something in it. I know there is."

"Not much, perhaps, but still something."

"That bottle, sir, contains a remedy for all known diseases, and all unknown ones, for all that I can tell. In fact, I have a suspicion that it is to the unknown diseases that it will come as the greatest blessing. Patent medicines generally do. Those mysterious maladies which, up to the advent of 'Aunt Jane's Jalap,' have baffled all the resources of medical science. Give me a day or two and I will prove it. I will bring you testimonials which will make your hair stand up on end, and—" He paused, looking me fixedly in the face—"all genuine."

That evening I had a small dinner-party. It was rather an occasion. The suggestion, I am bound to admit, had come from Margaret.

"My dear George, it's the easiest thing in the world, and you could do it nicely! Why don't you ask us to dinner? Aunt and I, and old Pybus to round it off." Square it off, I suspect she meant, because, of course, that would make four with me. But I didn't correct her. "And then you and I could look over the house together—after dinner."

So I asked them. And they came. Old Pybus said he would be delighted. I don't care for Pybus myself, but Mrs. Chalmers does, and this was an occasion on which her taste had to be consulted rather than mine. And during dinner I began on "Aunt Jane's Jalap."

"Well, it's all settled with Hughes."

I addressed myself to Margaret.

"What about?"

"'Aunt Jane's Jalap.'"

Mrs. Chalmers put down her spoon. This was while the soup was on.

"'Aunt Jane's Jalap!' Whatever's that?"

"The new patent medicine—the coming boom. You must know that my friend Francis Hughes has a wonderful old nurse, and this wonderful old nurse has the most wonderful medicine, which she used to administer to all her charges. Hughes has obtained the receipt from her."

"How much did he give her for it? Half-a-crown?"

I crushed Pybus.

"That is a private matter, but rather more than half-a-crown."

As a plain statement of fact he hadn't given her anything as yet. But, of course, we should both of us see that she made a good thing of it when the sale got up.

"I need scarcely observe what fortunes have been made in patent medicines."

"And lost in them, my boy."

This was just like Pybus—but I let it pass.

"Millions, literally millions, have been made, and, I may safely say, that none of them can compare with 'Aunt Jane's Jalap.'"

"Have you tried the stuff upon yourself?"

"No, Pybus, I have not. I am ready at any time to try it upon you. Well, Hughes has supplied the medicine, and I am going to supply part of the capital."

"What part?"

"That is another private matter, Pybus. Sufficient, I trust, to bring the matter before the public eye."

"Don't you think the name is rather a funny one?—'Aunt Jane's Jalap!'"

This was hard, coming from Margaret.

"My dear Margaret, the name is half the battle. Hughes thinks it's a splendid one."

"But don't you think it makes one think of indigestion?"

"That's exactly what it's meant to do."

"Before, or afterwards?"

This, of course, was Pybus.

"Let those laugh who win. Wait till you see the name blazoned on every dead wall. Then you'll welcome 'Aunt Jane's Jalap' as a friend."

That dinner, I confess, was a little patent mediciney. More than once I rather wished that I had kept the subject out of it. Pybus told some pleasant and characteristic anecdotes about injurious effects of patent medicines. How he had known whole families killed by taking them. How more than half the infant mortality of Great Britain was owing to their unrestricted sale. How the habit of taking patent medicines was worse than the habit of dram drinking, and the why, and the wherefore, and so on. I could not, at my own table, take the man by the scruff of the neck and drop him from the first floor window. But I know that Margaret didn't like it—and I didn't either. Mrs. Chalmers seemed undecided. She herself swears by some noxious compound, which is absurdly named "Daddy's Delight," and which I know, by the mere smell of it, is nothing else but poison.

"Have you any of the stuff in the house?" she asked.

"I have a bottle of 'Aunt Jane's Jalap,' which is not stuff, my dear Mrs. Chalmers, but a most invaluable medicine. Hughes brought it this afternoon as a sample."

"Trot it out," said Pybus.

Pybus is fifty-five, if he is a day, but he uses the slang of a schoolboy. I was not going to act on such a hint as that, but when Mrs. Chalmers expressed a wish to look at it I fetched the bottle. It was a small black bottle, such as is used for "samples" of wines, about quarter-bottle size. I held it in my hand.

"This, ladies and gentlemen, is 'Aunt Jane's Jalap.' It is a name which I trust will soon be familiar in your mouths as household words. This, however, is its first appearance on the scene, and I propose, to mark the importance of the occasion, that we drink to its success. I propose, ladies and gentlemen, that we drink to 'Aunt Jane's Jalap' in 'Aunt Jane's Jalap.' Brooks, bring four claret glasses."

I drew the cork.

"George, you don't mean that we're to drink the stuff?"

"I do, my dear Margaret, why not? The dose is a wine-glassful, to be taken immediately after meals. Mrs. Chalmers, allow me to offer you a glass of 'Aunt Jane's Jalap.'"

She sniffed at it.

"It has a very disagreeable smell."

That was good. I protest that I have smelt "Daddy's Delight" when I was passing the house, and took it—till I knew better—for drains.

"Margaret, a glass of 'Aunt Jane's Jalap.'"

"But, George, I assure you that I never do take medicine."

"Some people's wine is no better than medicine. We drink that, and pretend we like it. Why not jalap?"

This was Pybus! As he had just before been making insinuations about my wine, the allusion was pointed. But the man's proverbial.

"No heeltraps—'Aunt Jane's Jalap'—with the honours!"

We all stood up. I drained my glass. I immediately wished I hadn't. The others drained their glasses. I saw they wished they hadn't too. I do not think I ever tasted anything quite so nasty. I wished I had sampled it before. As it was, it took me by surprise, so much by surprise that my first impulse was to fly for shelter. It was like—well, the taste was really so exceedingly disagreeable that comparison fails me.

"It is a case of kill or cure," observed Pybus, with the most extraordinary expression of countenance I ever saw. "The man who takes much of that stuff will be killed if he isn't cured. Death for me, rather than 'Aunt Jane's Jalap'—if it is jalap."

"It is rather pungent," I owned.

"I don't know about pungent," continued Pybus, who certainly seemed to be suffering; "but with ice pudding it's a failure."

"Never," declared Mrs. Chalmers, who was leaning back in her chair, and had her handkerchief in her hand, "never did I taste anything like it! Never! and after dinner, too!"

Margaret's feelings seemed for the moment to be too strong for speech. I perceived the thing had been a failure. Still, I endeavoured to pass it off, which was difficult, for I myself felt really ill.

"Ah! it is to the after effects we must look forward."

"It is the after effects I'm thinking of," said Pybus.

That was almost more than I could bear; it was the after effects I was thinking of as well.

"Come, let's adjourn and have a little music."

"Have we finished the bottle of jalap?" inquired Pybus.

"I really must apologise; I confess I had no idea what a peculiar taste it had; it certainly is peculiar." Mrs. Chalmers put her handkerchief up to her eyes.

"And after dinner, too!"

We accompanied the ladies to the drawing-room, as well as we could. Pybus went with Mrs. Chalmers, I took Margaret. As we went I whispered in her ear:

"Now, you and I can look over the house together."

"I am afraid, George, you must excuse me. I—I couldn't walk about just yet. Do take me to a chair!"

We had planned that we would examine the house together from attic to basement; indeed, the whole affair had been got up for that express purpose. Everything was in apple-pie order and ready for inspection. The servants were on the tiptoe of expectation. As we went, Margaret was to make suggestions for alterations which would fit the house for its mistress. And opportunities might arise for a little confidential intercourse. But, of course, I could not drag the girl about the place against her will. Love works wonders. But there are circumstances which prove too strong.

The atmosphere of the drawing-room was depressing. It was no use my talking to Margaret, because she wouldn't talk to me. And general conversation seemed out of the question. So I tried another line.

"Pybus, give us a song." (Pybus thinks he can sing. He may have been able to—once.) "Here's 'Drink to me only.' That's a favourite of yours." (You should hear him sing it.) "Margaret will play the accompaniment."

"Lucas," he said, "Do you think, by any chance, that dose of jalap was too strong? I ask the question because I remember, when I was a boy, hearing of a family being poisoned by an overdose of jalap. In their case they took it by mistake. Though, judging from the taste of your jalap, I can't see how that could be. Still, if there is likely to be any danger it is as well that we should be prepared for it."

"Margaret," murmured Mrs. Chalmers, "let's go home."

"Why, aunt? It will pass off in time."

In time! At that moment I heartily wished that Hughes had been at Jericho before he induced me to dabble in his patent medicines. I always did hate them, even as a child.

"It is quite impossible," continued Pybus, "that the sensations which I am now experiencing are the ordinary and natural outcome of a dose of jalap."

"Margaret," groaned Mrs. Chalmers, "I insist upon your coming home."

"Aunt, what is the use of going home?"

"You haven't got a book in the house, Lucas, treating of poisons?"

"I wish you wouldn't talk like that, Pybus. It really is unfair. I quite perceive that I made a mistake in administering the dose after dinner; in fact, I am myself inclined to believe that I misunderstood Hughes, and that the dose ought to be administered before a meal."

"Good God!"

"Pybus!"

"I can't help it. I really cannot help it, sir. The idea of a reasonable person voluntarily swallowing such a concoction as that before his dinner is enough to make any man profane!"

"I don't think, Mr. Lucas," murmured Mrs. Chalmers, "that you have the least idea how ill I feel."

"My dear Mrs. Chalmers, if—if there is anything I can do for you." "Yes," said Pybus, "another bottle."

Just then Brooks came in.

"Mr. Hughes, sir, wishes to speak to you."

"Excuse me one moment—I'll be back directly."

I found Hughes waiting for me in my snuggery.

"Sorry to interrupt you, old man, but I just called in to prevent accidents."

"What do you mean?"

"You know that bottle I brought you this afternoon. I thought it was 'Aunt Jane's Jalap,' but it isn't. I found it out directly I got home. You see, I keep all sorts of bottles in my cupboard—regular chemist's shop!—and I caught hold of the wrong one by mistake."

"Not 'Aunt Jane's Jalap!'"

"No, it's laudanum."

"Laudanum? Hughes!"

"The fact is—Lucas!—What's the matter?—You don't mean to say you have been drinking some?"

"Is—is it poison?"

"Poison!—Why, it's pure laudanum!"

"Would—would a wineglassful do any harm?"

"A wineglassful! Lucas, old man, don't say you've drank a wineglassful!"

"We all have."

"All have!"

"Margaret, and Mrs. Chalmers, and Pybus.

"Great powers!"

"We—we thought it was 'Aunt Jane's Jalap,' and we drank to its success."

"Are they dead?"

"Dead! Hughes!"

"How long ago is it since they took it?"

"Not long. After dinner."

"But—a wineglassful! Are they conscious?"

"They were when I just now left them. But they weren't feeling well. I—I'm not either. We couldn't understand it. This—this explains it. Hughes, you—you've murdered us!"

"Never mind, old man. Keep your head; I'll pull you through. Trust all to me. The great thing in a case like this is to keep your head. Don't sit down; keep yourself in constant circulation! Just one second! Brooks! Brooks! Run, Brooks, to the nearest doctor, and then to half-a-dozen others, and tell them there's a case of laudanum poisoning, and they're to come at once."

"Laudanum poisoning, sir! What, in the house?"

"Yes, in the house. Don't stand there like a pig in a fit. It's a question of life or death!"

"One moment, sir, while I get my hat."

"Go without your hat. Here; take mine. Now, run for your life. Remember, if anything happens through you, you will be held responsible in the eyes of the law. Come along, Lucas, let's go in to them. Keep yourself awake, old man; jump about. Don't say a word to them about what has happened. Don't let them even suspect from your manner that anything is wrong. The great thing is to keep them in entire ignorance. And keep cool—keep cool."

He gave a jerk at my arm which almost pulled me forward on my face.

"I say, Hughes, don't!"

"But I must, old man, I must. I must keep you alive, at any cost. Oh, Lucas, old man, if anything should happen— But I won't talk like that, or I shall make a fool of myself. Come along, old man, and mind what I say. Keep cool."

We went along—that is to say, he took me by the arm and dragged me towards the drawing-room. My emotions I am unable to describe. I always think that when a man is able to describe his emotions he hasn't had any worth describing. But through it all I had a dim perception that, in spite of his repeated adjurations, Hughes himself kept anything but cool. Outside the drawing-room door I brought the procession to a standstill. I gripped his arm.

"Hughes, do you think that she will die?"

"Who?"

"Margaret."

"Nonsense! Don't I tell you no one's going to die? For goodness' sake don't talk like that. Don't I keep telling you to keep cool?"

He did. But it was scarcely with an air of coolness that he threw the door wide open, and with so much force that it seemed as if he were trying to wrench it from its hinges. I fancy our entry made a slight sensation. It was strange if it didn't. They were certainly not unconscious—yet! Even amidst my own agitation it was with quite a sensation of relief that I perceived so much. Mrs. Chalmers was reclining on the couch, with her head thrown back, and a look about her which I did not like. Margaret was on a settee, seeming as though the proceedings had lost all interest for her. Pybus sat in an arm chair, his hands crossed upon his stomach.

"Good evening," said Hughes. I could see he did not like the look of things. "I—I've just dropped in."

Pybus rose.

"I'm just dropping out. Good evening, Lucas. I have to thank you for a very pleasant evening. I'll send you the doctor's bill when I get it."

Hughes looked at me, then at Pybus.

"You're not going, Mr. Pybus?"

"Do you wish me to be ill here?"

"But I was looking forward to a song, or a dance, or something."

"Dance! I feel like dancing; and singing, too. I've been the victim of an outrage, Mr. Hughes. I've been introduced to 'Aunt Jane's Jalap.'"

"I've heard of it. Lucas ought not to have given it you."

"And after dinner!"

This was a murmur from the couch.

"That was wrong—quite wrong. The dose should have been administered before the meal."

"In that case," I observed, a little nettled, "we should all of us been dead by now."

Pybus glanced at me sharply.

"Dead! What do you mean?"

Hughes turned on me in a rage.

"Yes. What do you mean?"

I felt I had made a mistake.

"I—I mean nothing. Only—only I think Hughes was as much to blame as I was."

Hughes took Pybus away. They went to Mrs. Chalmers. So far as I could judge, the lady was rapidly sinking into a lethargic condition. I remained standing where I was. I began gradually to realise my situation—the approaching tragedy in which, by fate or circumstance, I was cast as an actor. A strange leaden feeling seemed to be stealing over me, but, in spite of it, I began to understand that at any moment the drawing-room, this drawing-room, my drawing-room, might be strewed with corpses. I knew nothing of the effects of laudanum poisoning, but Hughes seemed to be surprised that we were not all of us dead already. Here was Margaret, the woman I loved best in all the world, upon my right. There was her aunt, for whom, I own, my love was less, upon the couch. There was old Pybus. That old man's blood was also on my hands.

What would they call me? A suicide? The irony! In the full flush of health and strength, with fortune, all the world before me, and a wife. A wife whom I loved with a great fulness of love which was quite old-fashioned. I had wrought this hecatomb. I felt impelled to scream aloud. To warn my victims of the frightful fate which was stealing fast upon them, and of which they were still unconscious.

Someone touched me on the arm. I turned. It was Margaret!

"George, what is the matter?"

"Margaret!"

My voice trembled. There was a choking in my throat. I wished to take her in my arms before them all. It might be a last embrace.

"George, tell me, what is wrong?"

I made an effort to pull myself together.

"Oh! there's nothing wrong. I—I'm only a bit upset."

She put her arm through mine. She led me across the room. I required leading. She drew me into an alcove, which was formed by a window bay.

"Now, George, tell me what is wrong. I know there is something wrong. Tell me what it is."

I was at a loss for words. I trifled with her.

"Margaret! What do you mean?"

"George, was"—her voice sank to a whisper—"was there anything wrong about that stuff you gave us?"

What could I say to her?

"It—it was a mistake drinking it after dinner."

"Is that all? Was it the right stuff, George?"

"It—it was the stuff Hughes gave me."

"You are trifling with me? I know that there is something wrong. I can see it in your manner and in Mr. Hughes's. See how strangely Mr. Hughes is behaving now."

I peeped round the corner. Hughes was behaving strangely. He was frantically urging Mrs. Chalmers to stand up and dance, though anyone looking less like dancing than she did I never saw. He was evidently forgetting his own axiom—keep cool. A curious qualm came over me. Almost without knowing it I leaned for support against the wall.

"George! What is the matter? You are ill."

Margaret's eager face looked into mine.

"It will be all right in a minute."

"It won't! I know it won't! Tell me what it is. There was something the matter with that stuff you gave us. I knew it directly I had swallowed it. Do you think I am a coward? Do you think I am afraid? But it is only fair that you should tell me. If you won't tell me, George, I will go to Mr. Hughes and insist upon his telling me."

"Don't, Margaret. The doctor will be here directly."

"The doctor?" She drew herself straight up. A strange look came into her eyes.

She spoke almost in a whisper. "What is the doctor coming for?"

"Hughes thought that he had better come."

"Is it so bad as that? George, what was that stuff you gave us?"

"I have not said that it was anything. The—the dose was too strong."

"Was it poison?"

"Margaret!"

I took her two hands in mine. She came into my arms. I held her to my breast.

"Was it poison? If you love me half as much as I love you you will tell me, George."

"Margaret!"

"What poison was it?"

"Laudanum!"

She drew herself away from me. She looked at me with her great wide open eyes. Then her eyes were closed. Before I had the least suspicion of what was going to happen she had fallen to the ground. I knelt beside her.

"Margaret!" I cried. I cried to her in vain. I was seized with a great horror. "She is dead!" I exclaimed.

Hughes came running forward. I almost sprang at him.

"You have killed her!"

"Don't be an idiot, Lucas! She can't be dead!"

"She is dead. And it is your work. For the matter of that, all our blood is upon your head. But we shall not die alone. You shall come, too, my friend."

"If you don't take your hands away, Lucas, I shall have to do you a mischief."

"Mr. Lucas! Mr. Hughes! Have you both of you gone mad? Are you aware that there are ladies present?"

The interference came from Pybus. He dragged us asunder. He showed more presence of mind, and more coolness, too, than I had credited him with. He was a great deal calmer than either Lucas or I.

"What is the meaning of this extraordinary behaviour? And what is the matter with Miss Hammond?"

"He has killed her."

"Who has killed her?"

"That scamp; with his infernal negligence."

"I don't in the least understand you. And I think that instead of wrangling here your attentions were better bestowed upon Miss Hammond."

I threw myself at her side. I was like a man distraught in the whirlwind of conflicting emotions which came sweeping over me.

"My darling! Oh, my darling! I shall soon be with you. Already the poison is stealing through my veins. May my end be as rapid as was yours. Why doesn't the doctor come? I don't believe that you have sent for him. Go and fetch him."

Again I sprang at Hughes. And again Pybus interposed.

"Mr. Lucas, may I ask for an explanation of your singular conduct? Has Miss Hammond fainted?"

"Fainted! He has poisoned her!"

"Poisoned her!"

"Yes, and you and me and all of us! We all, like her, are doomed to die."

"Mr. Lucas!"

"Lucas, you're—you're mad, you know."

This was Hughes. But a piercing scream came from the couch.

"I knew that I was poisoned!"

Mrs. Chalmers might know that she was poisoned, but that was no reason why, on the strength of her knowledge, she should develope violent hysterics, which she immediately did. I had never seen so much of the man in Pybus as he showed just then. He gave one look at Mrs. Chalmers, and then he turned to Hughes.

"Mr. Hughes, will you be so good as to tell me if there is any meaning in Mr. Lucas's words?"

Hughes was ghastly white.

"The great point is to bring Miss Hammond back to life again. While we are talking here she may be dying at our feet. I appeal to your manhood, Mr. Pybus, to help me bring her back to consciousness."

Hughes knelt down by Margaret. Pybus turned to me.

"What does he mean?" he said.

I did not answer. I knelt down by Hughes. He had my darling's hand in his. I saw that he was putting great restraint upon himself. Beads of perspiration were on his brow.

"She is not dead," he stammered. "She is in a faint or something. At any cost we must bring her back to consciousness. Be a man, Lucas, and help me. Her life should be even more precious to you than to me."

"Don't talk like that, Hughes. Don't you see that I am nearly mad already? What can I do?"

"Help me to raise her."

Between us we raised her to a perpendicular position.

"Mr. Pybus, can I trouble you to order some brandy? Stay, she is coming back to life again!"

She was. She sighed. She opened her eyes, as if she were waking out of sleep. She turned to me.

"George!"

"My darling!"

I caught her in my arms. I held her to my breast. What mattered it if there were others there? We were standing by an open grave!

"I do so love you, George!"

She was dreaming. She thought we were alone.

"Margaret!"

I kissed her. Something caused her to look round. There was old Pybus standing at her side. She drew herself away from me. She blushed a rosy red; then her glance travelled round the room. She pressed her hands against her bosom. A startled look came into her eyes.

"Then—it wasn't all a dream."

Hughes slipped his arm through hers.

"Miss Hammond, I must insist upon your taking exercise. Take a sharp turn or two round the room with me. Lucas, I wish you'd sit down and play us a dance. Or, better still, let me sit down and play, and you and Miss Hammond take a few turns together. Mr. Pybus, you must dance with Mrs. Chalmers. A flyaway gallop, or a rattling polka. They're better than valses."

There was a remarkable expression upon old Pybus's enamelled countenance. So far as that goes, I expect there was on mine—but, as to that, no matter.

"Might I ask, once more, for an explanation of these very singular proceedings?"

"I warn you, Mr. Pybus, that if you do not dance with Mrs. Chalmers, you must be responsible for the consequences, both as they regard yourself and the lady."

Pybus's eyes wandered from Hughes to Mrs. Chalmers. The lady was making noise enough for ten. She did not strike the imagination as being a promising partner for a dance. So Pybus seemed to think. Hughes struck up, "You should see me dance the polka," playing it at the rate of about sixty miles an hour. Margaret looked at me.

"Are you and I to dance? Why dance?"

I shook my head.

"Hughes," I said, "I can't."

"You must, man, you must! Are you mad?"

"I can't."

I couldn't. A numbness seemed to be settling on my brain. My legs refused to support me. I sank into a chair. Margaret hesitated for just one second. I could see her trembling. Then she sat on the ground close to my feet. She leaned her arm upon my knee. Her face was turned towards mine.

"Nor can I. If we must die, George, let us die together; but not dancing."

"What on earth," inquired Pybus, "is all this talk of dying, Mr. Hughes? I insist upon an answer, sir."

In a sort of fury Hughes leaped from the music-stool.

"And I insist, Mr. Pybus, upon your dancing with Mrs. Chalmers. I warn you that if you don't you will be morally guilty, not only of murder, but of suicide." He turned to me. "As for you—are you a man? Do you think that it is your life only which is hanging in the balance? I tell you that the only hope for Miss Hammond is to keep her circulating. Do that, and I will answer for it with my own life, that all will yet be well."

"Come, while I can, let me keep you circulating, Maggie!"

It was not often that I called my "rare, pale Margaret" Maggie. But, at that master moment of our lives, I felt that the endearing name was best. She rose, my darling. I put my arm about her waist.

"George, whatever you think it best."

"That's better," said Hughes.

"Now let me see you go it. Give her fits, my boy."

Again he dashed into Mr. Grossmith's popular air. I never heard it played at such a rate before. Possibly with a view of raising our spirits, he shouted out the chorus in a tone of voice which must have been audible quite two streets away. It was deafening!

You should see me dance the polka,   You should see me cover the ground;   You should see my coat-tails flying—

My coat-tails were anything but flying. We made no attempt at keeping time with Hughes. Under the most favourable circumstances the thing would have been impossible. We moved, Margaret and I, as if we were treading a funeral measure. My legs were going at the knees. I felt her frail frame quivering in my arms.

"Now, then, Pybus," shouted Hughes, "off you go with Mrs. Chalmers. Don't ask her; make her. Pull her off the couch and jump her about!"

Pybus appeared to be endeavouring to persuade Mrs. Chalmers to join him in the mazy dance. The lady had suddenly become still, which, for some reasons, the chief one being the noise which Hughes was making, was perhaps as well.

"How can I pull her off the couch," answered Pybus, "when she's in a fit, or dead, or something?"

Up jumped Hughes.

"Keep going, you two! Don't stop for a single instant. Lucas, everything depends upon your keeping Miss Hammond circulating."

"I can't," I said.

"Nor can I," said Margaret.

The utterances were almost simultaneous. Simultaneously we sank into an ottoman.

"Mrs. Chalmers! Mrs. Chalmers!" shouted Hughes, "Pybus, help me to lift her off the couch. Now, then, you two, what have you stopped for?"

He turned to Margaret and me. Something in our faces or in our attitudes appeared to frighten him. He ran to the door yelling in a manner which absolutely frightened me.

"Brooks! Brooks! Oh, my God, why doesn't the doctor come?"

CHAPTER III

DOCTORS TO THE RESCUE!

Just as he reached the door it was opened. A very tall, and very stout, old gentleman entered. He had a black bag in his hand. But he did not seem to be the least in a hurry.

"Good evening. I trust there is nothing serious the matter."

I suppose that in the agitated state of his nervous system, the stranger's sudden appearance took Hughes by surprise. He stared at him as though he were a ghost.

"Are—are you the doctor?"

"I am the doctor—Dr. Goldsmith."

I had already recognised him as the doctor who lived at the corner of the square. Although I had not the pleasure of his personal acquaintance, I had more than once wondered why he did not try Banting. Leaving off sugar, and butter, and milk, and trying a piece of lemon in your tea, is an excellent method of reducing the flesh. He looked round the room, and bowed—a little vaguely. Then he said, addressing Hughes, whom he apparently took to be the master of the house, "Where is the patient?"

"They're—they're all patients."

This answer seemed to cause the doctor to experience a slight sense of mystification. He placed a pair of gold glasses upon the bridge of his nose. He cast another glance around the room.

"All patients?"

Pybus came forward. Pybus knows everyone.

"How are you, Dr. Goldsmith?"

"How are you, Mr. Pybus? Charmed to see you."

"Whether I am charmed to see you remains to be seen. May I ask—and don't think it's an impertinent question—what you have come for?"

"Come for? I—" The doctor threw a glance of interrogation towards Hughes. "I—someone came to my house and said that I was wanted for a case of—"

Old Pybus laid his hand upon the doctor's arm.

"Case of what?"

"A case of laudanum poisoning."

"Laudanum poisoning!"

"I understood that it was a—" The doctor ceased. Pybus's face had assumed a very singular hue. "I—I hope that I have said nothing—"

"No, you have said nothing. Laudanum poisoning?" He turned to Hughes. "So that is it." And then to me. "So that was 'Aunt Jane's Jalap.' It's—it's rather hard—that a man of my years—should—die of—jalap."

Pybus took a seat. The doctor stared at him.

"Mr. Pybus, I hope that nothing is the matter."

"Nothing, only—I'm the man—that's poisoned."

"You!"

"Me, Sam Pybus. I've been dining with a man, who asked me to meet—his girl—and smooth the tabby—and he gives me—jalap, which is another name for laudanum."

The doctor seemed bewildered.

"I am afraid I don't understand."

Hughes endeavoured to explain. He was suffering as much as either of us. The words fell from his stammering lips.

"What Mr. Pybus says is correct. There's been a mistake."

"Yes," said Pybus, "there's been a mistake."

"My friend, Lucas, thought he was giving his guests 'Aunt Jane's Jalap,' and instead of that he was giving them—I am afraid, through my carelessness—pure laudanum."

"Oh, it was through your carelessness, was it?" Pybus assumed towards Hughes a little air of ferocity. But it soon disappeared. "But what does it matter if I must die?"

"Pure laudanum!" said the doctor. "Of what strength?"

"The highest possible."

"In what quantity?"

"Enough to kill a dozen men. A bottleful."

"A bottleful of laudanum!"

The words were uttered by a newcomer—a little man who came running in as if he ran a race. It was Dunn, another doctor, who had recently started practice round the corner. In appearance he was a complete contrast to Goldsmith. He was a little, wiry, hungry-looking man, who seemed as though he never could keep still. He hurried past Pybus, patting him on the shoulder as he went. Had Pybus been more himself he would have resented the insult to the death.

"Come, my dear sir, keep yourself alive. That's the great secret; let us keep our spirits up!" he paused in front of Margaret. "Now, my dear young lady, don't we feel quite well? Just a little out of sorts. Come, wake up!"

He actually caught Margaret by the shoulder and shook her. I don't know what Margaret's feelings were, but if I myself had not been quite so prostrate, I fancy that I should have let him know that he presumed. Then he turned and shook me.

"Come, my dear sir, wake up, wake up, wake up! We must keep ourselves awake." He wheeled round; he marched to the couch. When he saw Mrs. Chalmers lying on it, still in a dead faint—so far as I know no one had moved a finger to bring her round—he shook his head.

"Serious; I am afraid it's very, very serious. But we will do our best; always do our best. Let all the servants in the house be summoned, and let assistance be given to carry the poor dear sufferers up to their beds."

The little man took command of everything. The servants were summoned and they came trooping in. Several other doctors came in also. There is no necessity to specify their number. Brooks liberally carried out the instructions Hughes had given him. He fetched as many as he could. There were not one or two, but several. I have their bills.

CHAPTER IV

THE MISTAKE EXPLAINED

I will not dwell upon the dreadful details of that night. There are scenes, not necessarily pathetic scenes, on which a curtain should be drawn. Through it all I never once lost consciousness. I wish I had. One need but allude to the stomach pump to draw up visions from the vasty deep. Over such agonies let a veil be drawn. This is not an episode of vivisection. And, afterwards, when—when a too eager medical man, thinking the process had not gone far enough—he meant well; it was his zeal; may he be forgiven—tried emetics, mustard and water, and other preparations from the medical pharmacop[oe]ia—do not let us touch upon these subjects. Never, when the sea was at its wildest, among passengers entirely unused to the mysteries of navigation, was ever seen the like. I still live, and I was through it all. It is wonderful what a vigorous constitution will endure.

Mrs. Chalmers was put into my bedroom. There was nothing particular of mine lying about, but I would rather they had put her somewhere else. Margaret had the best guest-room, Pybus the second best, and I was put into an apartment which had not been occupied for years. It was done in the confusion, I suppose. Looking back, I am surprised they did not overlook me altogether. I wish they had. And all through the night the issue was hanging in the balance. Hamlet's question was waiting for an answer. "To be, or not to be?" What their sufferings were—Margaret's, her aunt's, and Pybus's—I can imagine when I let memory hark back to my own. But none of them succumbed. And in the morning I, for one, was able to leave my room; in fact, I insisted on doing so. Had I remained any longer in that dreadful chamber I should certainly have died. Pale and ghastly, with my dressing-gown wrapped round my trembling limbs, I descended to my snuggery. I felt that I was but the wreck of what once I was. Hughes was there—the sight of me seemed to give him pain—well it might!—and Dr. Dunn, and Dr. Goldsmith, and a Dr. Casey. He was a tall, thin man, with a serious manner. I always think of Dr. Casey when I think of Mr. Stiggins. Dunn seemed in quite a cheerful frame of mind.

"Well, that's over. With a little care, Mr. Lucas, you'll forget all about it in a week."

Never! But I did not tell him so. And he went on:

"And this all comes of what I venture to call a trifling indiscretion. You think it's jalap, and it's laudanum."

"Laudanum is not a thing to trifle with," said Dr. Casey.

"It certainly isn't a thing to drink in pailfuls."

As he said this, Dr. Goldsmith rattled his keys and coppers.

"Nor is it to be recommended as a liqueur with dessert—eh, Mr. Lucas?" Dunn rubbed his hands, and grinned at me.

"The poor lady," said Dr. Casey, "whom I treated found it a very serious matter."

This was Mrs. Chalmers.

"The sweet young thing," said Goldsmith, "for whom I did my best, did not seem to think that the occasion was altogether a festive one," and this was how he spoke of her.

"I dare say, Mr. Lucas," sniggered Dunn, "that you have spent far more agreeable nights."

Dunn was the fiend who had pushed his zeal too far. And now he laughed at me!

"Dr. Lambert," observed Dr. Casey, "who treated the other gentleman, assured me that his patient asked him to put him out of his misery rather than push his treatment further."

That was Pybus. I could easily believe it. Death was preferable to Dunn's emetics.

"Now, where is the bottle which contained the cause of all the mischief?"

The fatal bottle had been brought into my snuggery for safety. It was handed to Dunn. He sniffed at it.

"Hum!" He sniffed again. "Hum!" He seemed surprised. "Rather—rather an odd smell for laudanum. Smell that!"

He handed it to Goldsmith.

"Very"—sniff!—"odd"—sniff!—"indeed"—sniff. "You are sure it is the bottle?"

There was not the slightest doubt about its being the bottle. It was passed to Casey. He had a smell.

"This isn't laudanum," he declared.

"Not laudanum!" Back it went to Dunn.

"It doesn't smell like laudanum."

"It isn't laudanum," said Goldsmith.

"Not a trace of it," said Casey.

NOT laudanum! I looked at Hughes. He looked at me. Then he staggered towards that fatal bottle.

"Let me—let me smell it."

They let him. An extraordinary change came over his countenance as he applied it to his nose. He staggered against the wall.

"Good—good heavens!"

What was it? Had he mistaken the poison? Was it strychnine, arsenic, prussic acid? Would the treatment have to be gone through all over again? For me, death rather than that.

"I see it all," cried Hughes, "I see the mistake I made. After all, it was not the bottle I supposed. I remember now that I placed that upon the shelf above."

"What is it?" I screamed.

"It's—it's what I thought it was."

"What you thought it was?"

"It's 'Aunt Jane's Jalap.'"

"'Aunt Jane's Jalap!'"

The words came from the three medical gentlemen in a sort of chorus. As for me, in spite of my piteous condition, I felt inclined to tear my hair—and Hughes's!

"I see, quite clearly, how the mistake arose. It was in this way. There were two sample bottles of the mixture, only in one of them the quantities were wrong. I placed it where I generally keep my laudanum—so that I shouldn't mistake it. And when I found it missing, of course I thought it was the laudanum which had gone."

"Was it—was it poison?"

"Not a bit of it, dear boy! The finest medicine in the world! Only in that particular bottle there was a little too much jalap, and, taking it on the top of such a dinner as you'd been eating, it a little upset you—that was all."

That was all?

I thought of how those doctors had spent the night in practising on us their dreadful arts, of their bills, and—that was all.

WILLYUM.

I had been seated in the next chair to hers for at least two minutes. I felt that it was time to introduce myself.

"It's a fine evening."

She turned, she looked me up and down, then she looked straight in front of her again.

"I don't know you."

But I was not to be crushed; there was something about the shape of her that which suggested sociability.

"That is my misfortune, rather than my fault."

"I don't know nothing at all about that. I do not speak to strangers as a rule. Sometimes there's never no knowing who they are."

I felt that I was getting on—so I went on.

"What do you think of the band?"

"It's not loud enough for me. I like a band as I can hear."

One suspected there might be occasions on which one could almost like a band which one could not hear, but I did not say so. That broke the ice, and the conversation drifting on to personal topics she explained to me that she had a young man, who, so to speak, was "resting," owing to what she called a "difference" which she had had with him. It struck me that the tale, as she told it, contained elements of tragedy.

"Bakers," she observed, "is what I like. I have a sister who likes butchers. To me there's always the smell of the meat about a butcher. But it's as you're made. The worst of bakers is, they're such a thirsty lot."

"Possibly," I suggested, "that is in a measure owing to the nature of their occupation."

"That may be, but still there is a limit, and when a man is always drinking, I think it's time for him to stop."

I thought so too, but she went on:

"My young man, his name is Willyum Evans, is a baker, and him and me have been walking out together four years come next month. So I said to him, 'Willyum, it's my day out, Tuesday. I shall expect you to take me somewhere.' So he said, 'I will.' So I said, 'Hyde Park Corner, half-past ten.' I was there as the clock was striking, and a fine scuffle I had to get there too; and, if you'll believe me, he kept me waiting two hours and three-quarters by the clock what's over the gatekeeper's lodge—which is longer than any gentleman ought to keep a lady waiting, I don't care who he is. So when he did come, I was a bit huffy.

"So I said, 'Well, Willyum, I hope I've put you to no hurry, and it's a pity you should have troubled yourself to come at this time of day, seeing as how I'm just off home.' So he said, and he wiped his lips, and I could see he had had a moistener, if not more, 'It's like this—I accidentally had an appointment, which was of the nature of business, and which I couldn't help; and that's how it is I'm a little behind!' 'I see,' I said, 'and it had something to do with pint pots, I have no doubt.' So he sat down on a seat, which was wet, owing to there being a drizzle on, and as it seemed silly for me to stand whilst he was sitting, I sat down likewise.

"So there we sat, neither of us saying nothing, till I began to feel a little damp, because I had my thin things on, and it was beginning to come down heavy. So I said, 'Well, Willyum, have you forgotten it's my day out? I thought you was going to take me somewhere.' He said, 'So I am.' So I said, 'Where are you going to take me to? It's getting on, and I'm likewise getting wet'—which I was. So he said, 'What do you say to Battersea Park?' So I said, 'I say nothing. And the idea, Willyum, of your talking about taking me to Battersea Park, when, as you very well know, it is raining cats and dogs, is not what I expected'—because, as he could very well see, I only had a parasol, which was red, and the rain was coming through, and the colour coming out. But he didn't care for the rain no more than nothing; because, as I tell you, he being a baker, to him it was a kind of a change.

"You must know that Willyum is that near about money that I never saw nothing like him; not that it's a bad thing in a man, though it may be carried too far and I must say I do think Willyum do carry it too far. He has never given me nothing which he didn't want me to pay for, not even half a pint of beer. So I was not surprised when he said, 'The fact is Matilda'—which is me—'I haven't got no money.' 'Well,' I said, 'that's a nice thing, to promise to take me out, and then to have no money.' So he said, 'If you was to pay the expenses for both the two of us, it might make things more pleasant.' So I said, 'No, I thank you,' because I had been had that way before, and more than once. So I got up, and I said, 'Well, Willyum, I will now wish you a good day; because I have been here since half-past ten, and it is now past two, and my clothes is sticking to me, and I don't care to stop no longer.' So he said, 'Now, Matilda, don't you get disagreeable'—which I was beginning to feel it, and so I own. 'We are both of us having a day out,' he said, 'and don't let no bad tempers spoil our pleasure. I may have some money somewhere, unbeknown to myself, so I will look and see; though I must say I do think it hard that all the expenses should be borne by me!'

"So he begins feeling in his pockets, and, presently, he gives a kind of a start, and he brings out half-a-crown. 'There,' he said, 'is half-a-crown; and if you put five shillings to it, it will make it seven and six!' 'No!' I said, 'I shall put no five shillings of mine to no half-crown of yours, and so the least said the soonest mended. And, if you don't mind, I will go and get myself something to eat, being hungry, and having, I am thankful to say, money of my own with which to pay for it.' Then he gives another kind of start, and he says, 'There! If I didn't make a pasty for you, last night, with my own hands, and I've been sitting on it all the time,' which he had, and anything like the mess he'd made of it you never saw. He held it out to me. 'No,' I said. 'I thank you. I am particular about my vittles, and I never eat no scraps, and, still less, things what have been sat down upon.' 'Well,' he said, 'it's a pity it should be wasted, I'll eat it myself.' Which he did, and me standing in the rain there looking on. That did put my back up. 'Mr. Evans,' I said, short and sharp, 'I wish you a good day. I am going.' So I goes. And he comes running after me, picking at the bits of pasty what was stuck to the paper; I must say this for Willyum, that it takes a deal to get his temper up. So I pulls up. 'Now, let us understand each other. Willyum, if you please, are you going to pay for something for me to eat, or are you not?' He gives himself a kind of a shake, so as to get his courage up, and he says, 'You shall have anything you like to eat, at my expense, Matilda, so long as the cost does not exceed'—then he hesitated—'ninepence.' Then he gave himself another kind of shake, which I took as a sign that his courage was running down, 'for both the two of us.'

"That made me fairly wild it really did. To think that he had promised to take me somewhere, and that I had been more than three hours there in the rain, and got wet through, and my things all spoiled—which it was a new dress I had on, what I had got special for the occasion, and it had only come home from the dressmaker's the day before—and the colour was coming out of my parasol—which was likewise new—and my hair all coming out of curl, and me feeling as limp as a rag, and starving hungry, and that he should want to put me off with fourpence-halfpenny worth of food, drawn from him as if it were his eye-tooth—it did make me feel really wild.

"I never said a word to him, but I walks right out of the park. He comes running after me, and he catches hold of my arm and he says, 'Now, Matilda, what did I say just now about letting no bad tempers spoil our pleasure?' I said, 'I don't know what your idea of pleasure is, but it isn't mine, and as I don't want to have no more to do with you, Mr. Evans, perhaps you will be so kind as to let me go.' But he holds on to me all the tighter, and he says, 'I tell you what, Matilda, a idea has just come into my head 'My brother, as you have heard me talk about, lives close by here, we will go and dine with him. He being a married man, and with a comfortable home, he will be glad to see us.'

"Well, I didn't know what to do, not liking to have no quarrel with him in the street, so off we starts for his brother's. He took me to a mews what led out of Park Lane, and, as we was turning the corner, he said, 'There's only this one thing about my brother, him and me has had a little difference of opinion, and he is not of a forgiving disposition.' So I said, 'Now, Willyum, what do you mean by that?' So he said, 'No. 32, on the other side, is where he lives, and if you was to go on and knock at the door, and ask for Mrs. Henry Evans, what is my brother's wife, so to speak, it might smooth the way.' So I said, 'I do not understand you. Just now you was saying as how your brother would be glad to see us. Are you now insinuating otherwise?' He catches a glimpse of my eye, and he sees the kind of mood I was in, and he plucks up, and he walks on, and he says, 'We will hope for the best. Do not let us spoil our day's pleasure by no disagreeable observations. There is never no knowing what might happen.' All of a sudden he cries out, 'There is my brother! Now, Matilda, don't you let him start hitting me.' And he jumps behind me, so as to get into the shadow, as it were. So I says, 'Willyum, whatever is the matter now? Your conduct do seem to me to be of the most extraordinary character.'

"And there was a great big giant of a man on the other side of the road, washing a carriage, with a bucket of water and I don't know what, and as I moves on one side he catches sight of Willyum, and anything like the way in which he started swearing you never heard. 'Hollo' he says, 'there's that putty-faced brother of mine. I've been looking for you for some time. Here's something for you, Willyum.' And before I had no idea of what he was going to do, he catches up the bucket of water and he throws it over Willyum, and some of it went over me. Oh, dear me, you never saw nothing like the mess that I was in! And he grabs hold of Willyum by the collar, and he says, 'Hang me if I don't wipe down the street with you!' And he shouts out, ''Enrietta, here's Brother Willyum. Haven't you got anything for him? You bet your life he's come for something.' And a window opens over the way, and a woman puts her head out, and she empties something out of a pail over Willyum, and again some of it went over me. Oh dear! oh dear! And that giant of a man he set about Willyum something cruel; and all the mews was in a uproar, and I hurried away as hard as ever I could, I was that frightened, and I got into a cab, just as I was—and you should have seen how the cabman stared, and drove right away to a sister of mine what lives at Camberwell, and I nearly cried my eyes out, and I've never spoken to Willyum nor set eyes on him since then, which it's a fortnight the day after to-morrow, and if you had been in my place, and had been treated as I was, would you have let things go on as usual, just as if there hadn't been no difference?"

No, I said, I should not. I should have insisted on their going on in quite a different kind of way.

And so I told her.

Last winter George Pownceby spent some weeks at the Empire Hotel. One morning he was coming along the corridor leading from the smoking-room when he met Mrs. Pratt. The lady stopped.

"What is that you have in your hand?" she asked.

Mr. Pownceby had in his hand a slim pamphlet, in a green paper cover. He held it up.

"I've got it!"

"No?"

"Yes!"

"Oh, I say!"

These remarks are not given here as examples of English conversation, but with a view of presenting the reader with an accurate report of what was spoken. There was a pause. Then the lady said, with great solemnity:—

"You don't mean to say that it has actually come?"

"I do!" Mr. Pownceby held out the slim pamphlet at arm's length in front of him. He pointed at it with the index-finger of his other hand: "'How to Hypnotise. A Practical Treatise. Hints to Amateurs. With full instructions for marvellous experiments. Price 7d. post free, eight stamps.'"

"Oh, Mr. Pownceby, I am so sorry."

"Sorry, Mrs. Pratt! Why, it was, at your instigation I plunged to the extent of those eight stamps."

"But you don't understand; my husband's coming; I have to meet him at the station at 12.32." Mr. Pownceby stroked his moustache; there was not much, but he was fond of stroking what there was of it. Mrs. Pratt's husband had been rather a joke. People who winter in hotels are, as a rule, quite prepared to be epigrammatic at the expense of a pretty married woman whose husband is not in evidence. And Mrs. Pratt's husband had not been in evidence—as yet.

"I don't quite follow you." Mr. Pownceby spoke with a little malice. "Whence your sorrow? Because your husband is coming by the 12.32?"

"Don't you see, I want to be the first to be experimented on. I've been waiting for that book two days, and now it just comes when I can't stay. Don't' you think there's time? Come into my sitting-room."

They went into her sitting-room. When they were there, the lady again assailed the gentleman with the inquiry:

"Don't you think there's time?"

"It depends. I think you're going too fast. To commence with, I've been looking through the thing in the smoking-room, and I believe it's a swindle."

"A swindle! Oh, don't say that."

"It's nothing but a hash of old mesmeric tricks I've seen performed at country fairs."

"But doesn't it tell you how to do them?"

"It pretends to. It gives some ridiculous directions—but I don't believe they can be done that way."

"Try!—do!—on me!"

Mr. Pownceby laughed. Mrs. Pratt amused him; and not for the first time either.

"To begin with, we have to sit face to face and stare at each other for ten minutes or a quarter of an hour."

"Come along! Let's begin."

The lady brought forward a couple of chairs and they sat down on them, face to face; and very close together. Opening the pamphlet, Mr. Pownceby searched for further instructions.

"You're not staring at me," remarked the lady.

"Half a minute; I'm looking for what comes next."

"What does it say? Read it aloud."

"After I've stared at you long enough—It doesn't sound civil, does it?"

"Never mind the civility; go on!"

"'After I've stared at you long enough, you begin to feel queer. Then'"—Mr. Pownceby read from the pamphlet, "'Place the thumb of your left hand on the subject's forehead'—you're the subject—'just above the nose, and level with the eyebrows.'" Mrs. Pratt placed her pretty little hand above her pretty little nose to point out the exact spot denoted. Mr. Pownceby read on. "'This is the locality of the Phrenological Organ of Individuality.'"

"Is it?" said Mrs. Pratt in an awe-struck whisper. The reader continued:

"'Rest the ends of your fingers on the top of the subject's head. At the same time take hold of the left hand with your right hand, applying the inside part of your thumb to the middle of the palm of the hand.' I'm punctuating this," interpolated Mr. Pownceby, "as I go on. The man who printed it seems to have had a fount of type containing no other stops but commas. 'The object of this is for the operator to get in contact with two very important nerves that pass in the palm of the hand which are called Ulnar and Median nerves'—I don't know if that's true, or what it means, but it says so here—'with your left hand, still keeping the thumb on the forehead between the eyes, and the fingers resting on the subject's head, which must be inclined slightly back. Say, "Look into my eyes." After gazing in his eyes intently for a few seconds, say in a loud, clear, firm tone of voice, "Close your eyes quite tight." Let him remain a few seconds like this,'—and the trick is done. There's a lot more nonsense to follow, but when you've remained for a few seconds like that you're supposed to be mesmerised, or hypnotised, or whatever they call the thing."

"Really! It sounds quite simple."

"It does—simple folly."

"Hush! You shouldn't speak like that. Perhaps, if you don't believe, you mayn't succeed."

"It says something to that effect in these precious pages."

"Then try to believe. Let us begin."

They began. The lady was preternaturally solemn, but the gentleman was tortured by a desire to smile. He felt that the lady might resent his laughter. Under these circumstances the ten minutes' stare was trying. Mrs. Pratt had sweet blue eyes, which were large and round—the sort of eyes which the average man would not object to stare at for ten minutes or even longer. As the appointed space of time drew to a conclusion even Mr. Pownceby became reconciled to his lot. He placed his left thumb on the lady's forehead above her nose.

"Is that level with my eyebrows?" she inquired. He reproved her.

"I don't think you ought to speak. You destroy the connection."

Mrs. Pratt was dumb. Mr. Pownceby proceeded in accordance with the directions contained in the pamphlet. He rested the tips of his fingers on the top of the lady's head. He took hold of her left hand with his right. He applied the "inside part" of his thumb to the centre of her palm. He said to her:

"Look into my eyes."

She looked into his eyes, her head inclined a little backwards. This part of the proceedings was, so far as the gentleman was concerned, on the whole agreeable. He gazed fixedly into her pretty eyes. Then he added, in a "loud, clear, firm tone of voice":

"Close your eyes quite tight."

She closed her eyes. There was a pause for a few seconds. Remembering the instructions contained in the pamphlet, he proceeded another step:

"You cannot open your eyes," he said. "Your eyes are fast, quite fast."

The pamphlet had it, "Should the subject be very sensitive he will be unable to open them." Apparently the subject, though in this case feminine, was very sensitive. At least Mrs. Pratt kept her eyes shut fast. Mr. Pownceby was a little startled. He removed his touch from her brow and released her hand.

"Mrs. Pratt, are you hypnotised already?" Mrs. Pratt was silent. "Mrs. Pratt, you don't mean you're really hypnotised?" Still silence. He leant forward and stared at the lady, not in the same way he had done before, but quite as fixedly. "By Jove! I believe she is!" He got up from the chair. He glanced at the pamphlet. He wanted to know how to reverse the process—how to bring the lady to again.

"This is a pretty state of things! The thing is not such a swindle as I thought it was. But it's all nonsense. She can't be magnetised, or mesmerised, or hypnotised, or whatever it is. If she is, the thing's as easy as winking. If I'd only known it I'd have been mesmerising people since the days of childhood. Mrs. Pratt!"

But Mrs. Pratt was silent. If she was not "hypnotised," then she was in some condition which was equally curious. She sat back in her chair, with her face turned up to the ceiling, in a state of the most complete quiescence. Something in her appearance struck Mr. Pownceby as even unpleasantly odd. He recommended searching down the page of the green covered pamphlet for the reversal process. It was beautifully simple.

"In order to release him," the pamphlet said—throughout the writer had taken it for granted that the "subject" would be masculine—"blow a sharp, cold wind from your mouth on his eyes, and say with authority, 'Now you can open them.' Repeat if necessary. It is important to recollect that a cold wind blown from the operator destroys the effect and demagnetises."

One could not but suspect that some subjects might not like this. But its simplicity was charming. If that was all that was necessary, then, so far as Mr. Pownceby was concerned, the whole science of hypnotism was already mastered.

He approached Mrs. Pratt. He bent over her, devoutly hoping that no one might enter the room as he was engaged in doing so. Quite a shock went through him as he advanced his face towards hers, the expression of her countenance was so very much like death. He blew a "cold wind" on her eyes—those pretty blue eyes, whose cerulean hue he had veiled.

"Now you can open them."

The words were spoken with as much "authority" as he could muster in the then agitated state of his mind; but Mrs. Pratt did not open them. The pamphlet said, "Repeat if necessary." Mr. Pownceby repeated. He blew, and he blew. He blew the "cold wind" all out of him, so that the beads of perspiration stood upon his brow, but still the "subject" gave no signs.

"Mrs. Pratt! Mrs. Pratt! I say, Mrs. Pratt, for heaven's sake do look at me!"

All signs of "authority" had gone from him now. But wind and voice alike were ineffectual. Apparently it was easier to hypnotise than to do the other thing. In his trouble Mr. Pownceby told himself that the writer of that pamphlet was—well, untrustworthy. Or else something had gone wrong in the working. But what could it be? He looked at his watch.

"Half-past twelve! I shall have her husband here directly. I imagine that he will make some observations if he finds his wife like this."

Such a contingency was only to be expected. When a man, after long absence from his wife, returns to find a stranger experimenting on her, and she in a "hypnotic" condition, from which the stranger cannot release her, his first feelings towards that stranger are not, in civilised countries, invariably friendly. Mr. Pownceby, when he had blown the "cold wind" all out of him, arrived at a resolution.

"I will tell Doris. I must get her to help me. It is quite certain that, whatever happens, I mustn't let that man come and find me alone with his wife."

It was only the dread of such a catastrophe that brought him to the "sticking-point" of his resolution. Miss Haseltine—christened Doris—was Mr. Pownceby's betrothed. She also was wintering in the hotel with her mamma. Mr. Pownceby was aware, even painfully aware, that the young lady's feelings towards Mrs. Pratt were not of the warmest possible kind. He was equally conscious that her impression was that his feelings were, if anything, too warm. He would rather anything had happened, almost, than that he should have been reduced to the necessity of acquainting Miss Haseltine with the situation he was in. But it was certainly impossible for him to allow the returning husband to come in and find him there, alone with his wife, and she apparently in a chronic hypnotic condition.

So he went in search of the young lady. Of course he found her where he would have least wished to find her—in the drawing-room with the ladies. He had to call her out, and at first she wouldn't come.

But as it would have been impossible for him to tell his tale in the presence of a dozen sharp-eared and sharp-tongued women, he protested that there was something of the utmost importance which he must say to her alone. "Well, what is it?" she asked, directly he had got her outside the door. He perceived that she was not in one of her sentimental moods. Perhaps something in his manner had roused her suspicions.

"Mrs. Pratt has fainted."

"Indeed? What has that to do with me? Let her faint. She looks to me as though she were the sort of person who could faint at pleasure."

"Doris, for goodness' sake hear me out; I want your help. It's through me she's fainted."

"Pray what do you mean?"

"It's—it's this confounded thing." Mr. Pownceby held out the slim, green-covered pamphlet. "You know I told you I'd written for that pamphlet, 'How to Hypnotise.' Well, the thing came this morning; here it is! I've been experimenting on her, and I've not only hypnotised her, but, by George, I can't get her round again."

"A pretty state of things, upon my word."

"Don't pitch into me now, Doris, don't. There she is in her sitting-room in a fit or something; I don't know what's the matter with her; and her husband's coming this morning."

"He is coming at last, is he?"

"I expect him every moment; he's due at 12.32."

"She seems to have told you all about it."

"She told me so much, at any rate. I know I've been an ass, I can see that now, but lend me a hand first, and let me have it afterwards. I was obliged to come to you. I couldn't let him find me alone with her in such a state as that. Come and see what you can do for her, there's a darling, do! After all, it's for me, you know, not her."

Miss Haseltine yielded so far as to advance with him along the corridor. There was a fresh arrival when they reached the hall—a gentleman. He was speaking to the young lady, who acted as book-keeper, through the office window.

"My name is Pratt—Gilead J. Pratt. I believe my wife is staying here."

Mr. Pownceby clutched Miss Haseltine's arm.

"It's he!" he whispered.

"There is a Mrs. Pratt staying here," replied the book-keeper. "Her sitting-room is No. 13."

The new arrival was about to be ushered into No. 13, when Mr. Pownceby interposed. He hurried across the hall and touched him on the shoulder. "Excuse me, may I speak to you? My name is Pownceby."

The new arrival turned and faced him. As he did so Mr. Pownceby perceived, a little dimly perhaps, what sort of a man he was. He was of medium height, slightly built, about forty years of age, very dark, with a clean-shaven face and a pair of keen black eyes, which looked at Mr. Pownceby as though they meant to pierce him.

"Delighted to hear you speak, or any man, even if his name's not Pownceby."

Directly the words were spoken Mr. Pownceby became conscious that the new arrival was an American.

"I believe you are Mr. Pratt—Mrs. Pratt's husband."

"I am—worse luck."

"Eh—she intended to meet you at 12.32."

"She did, did she? That's her all through. As she used to be. She never did get farther than intentions. It is about two years since I saw her, and I don't see her now. Have you a message to deliver? Does she desire that I should go away for another two years? If so, I'm willing."

As this was said out loud, without the slightest attempt at concealment, so that every word was audible, not only to Mr. Pownceby, to whom the remarks were addressed, but also to Miss Haseltine, and the book-keeper, and the porter, and the boots, and the waiter, and the chambermaid, and any other straggler who might happen to be within fifty yards or so, it would seem that in her husband Mrs. Pratt possessed a man of character. But Mr. Pownceby was not fond of such publicity.

"Can I say a word to you alone?"

"No, sir, you cannot. If you have a message from my wife, say it. If not, lead on to No. 13."

"The fact is, Mr. Pratt, eh—Mrs. Pratt is not—eh—quite well."

"Is that so? I'm glad to hear it. It's a comfort to know that only sickness would keep her from her husband; though it wouldn't need much of that to keep her from a chance of seeing me."

"The fact is, I wish, Mr. Pratt, you would let me speak to you alone."

"No, sir, I will not. If she's dead, don't spare my feelings. If she has left me for a better man, don't spare my feelings either."

"The fact is, she's in a hypnotic state."

"In a what state?"

"A hypnotic state."

"What state's that?"

"'Hypnotic' 's a new word—it's been brought in lately—it means 'mesmeric.'"

Mr. Pratt paused before replying. He looked Mr. Pownceby up and down.

"Look here, Mr. — I think you mentioned Pownceby; I don't know who you are, but you seem a friendly kind of man. Take my advice and get something off your chest. I see you've got it on."

Mr. Pownceby smiled, rather faintly. He did not lack presence of mind, as a rule, though just then the situation was as much as he could manage. He made a dash at it.

"I wish you would give me half a minute alone; but, since you will not, I must try to tell my story where we are. You see this book?" Mr. Pownceby held up the fatal treatise. "It contains instructions for the performance of mesmeric experiments. Mrs. Pratt insisted on my performing one of them on her. I succeeded in producing the mesmeric state, but I—I couldn't get her out of it."

There was a curious twinkle in Mr. Pratt's eyes.

"I don't catch on," he said.

"I say that I hypnotised her—that is, produced the mesmeric state, but that I—I couldn't get her out of it."

"Well?"

"She's in it now."

"In what?"

"The mesmeric state."

"Does she seem to like it?"

"That is more than I can say. I had just induced Miss Haseltine to come to my assistance when we were so fortunate as to encounter you."

"Then I am to understand that when she ought to have been at the depôt looking out for me, she was engaged in looking out for the mesmeric state along with you; is that so?"

"I'm afraid it is."

"Where is she?"

"In her sitting-room, No. 13."

"Lead on to No. 13."

The procession started. The waiter went first, Mr. Pratt next, and after him Miss Haseltine and Mr. Powenceby. Miss Haseltine's demeanour was severe. Either her severity or something else seemed to weigh upon her lover, who did not appear to be altogether at his ease. They reached No. 13. The waiter knocked. There was no reply. He knocked again; still no reply. Mr. Pratt turned towards Mr. Powenceby.

"I guess she's still in that state of yours. I think we'll all go in." He turned the handle of the door and entered. "I guess she's quitted."

The room was empty.

AND THE GENTLEMAN

It was undoubtedly the case, unless they were to suppose that she had hidden under the sofa, or behind the curtains. Mr. Powenceby looked about him, conscious of a slight feeling of bewilderment. There were the two chairs, exactly as he left them, but the one which Mrs. Pratt had occupied was vacant.

"It's very odd," he murmured.

"How?"

"She was certainly unconscious when I left her."

"Perhaps the knowledge that she was failing in her duty as a wife came to her in that mesmeric state; came to her so strongly that she started off to the depôt, just then and there, to look for me. If she's at the depôt now, in the state you say she was, I guess she'll soon be popular."

"Don't you think I'd better go and look for her?"

"I do not. If she's gone, she's gone, and if she comes back again she comes, but I'm not the man to put my friends out for a trifle. My friend, if you will allow me to call you so, give me your hand." Before Mr.

Pownceby was quite aware of it, Mr. Pratt had possession of his hand. "I thank you. You have placed me under an obligation to you this day. But it may be that I shall cry you evens yet. Let's liquor. Perhaps the young lady will pool in?" Miss Haseltine, however, making some inaudible remark having reference to her mamma, vanished out of sight. Mr. Pratt was not at all abashed. He addressed the waiters. "Champagne—a large bottle—and a bucket of ice."

Mr. Pownceby protested.

"You are very kind, but I don't drink at this hour of the day, and only so—"

Mr. Pratt cut him short.

"Fetch the drink." The waiter fled. "If, after performing those pleasing experiments on the wife, you refuse to drink with the husband, I shall take it quite unkindly."

"But don't you think some inquiries ought to be made for Mrs. Pratt?"

"I do not. What I do think is that I ought to cultivate your friendship now that I have the chance. A man who knows the wife so well should know something of the husband too."

The drink came. Mr. Pratt saw two bumpers filled. Mr. Pownceby, who was an abstemious man, had a difficulty in escaping being compelled to drain his draught.

"Bring another bottle when I ring," said Mr. Pratt as the waiter left the room.

The two gentlemen were left alone. Mr. Pownceby still did not feel quite easy in his mind. Champagne generally disagreed with him at any time, always in the morning. He had some glimmerings of an idea that, if he refused to drink, Mr. Pratt would seek in his refusal an occasion to quarrel. He had heard and read of some curious customs in the States; how, for instance, to refuse, under certain circumstances, to drink with a citizen of the Great Republic was to place on him an insult which could only be wiped out by blood—blood in which six-shooters played a part. He half suspected that Mr. Pratt was a citizen like that. Certainly he was unlike any American he had seen. His indifference to his wife's fate was almost brutal. Mr. Pownceby felt this, but he also felt that it was impossible for him to insist on making inquiries if the husband declined to sanction them. Nor was his uneasiness lessened by Mr. Pratt's appearance of entire ease. That gentleman leaned back in his chair—the one his wife had occupied—his summer coat unbuttoned, his hat tilted on to the back of his head.

"So you hypnotised my wife?" Mr. Pownceby smiled faintly; the subject was beginning to be unpleasant. "Hypnotise me."

Mr. Pownceby started.

"I suppose you're joking?"

"Why? My wife had an inquiring mind, why shouldn't I have too? Perhaps you prefer trying those sort of experiments on wives rather than on their husbands."

Mr. Pownceby was not quite sure if this remark was intended disagreeably. It made him wince.

"Perhaps you think I have been trying these experiments all my life. Until this pamphlet was brought by this morning's post I knew no more about hypnotism than you do. My first experiment was tried, at her own urgent request, upon your wife."

"I take after her; I'm fond of experiments too. That book must be a treasure. Oblige me with a glance at it."

Mr. Pownceby handed it to him. Mr. Pratt began reading at the end.

"There's a nice little bit as a finish." Mr. Pratt read it aloud: "'In conclusion, I would earnestly ask all my readers to remember that this valuable science should not be abused, especially in the case of females, and that, in all cases when making experiments, they should have friends or other persons present.' That's sound advice. Did you notice it?"

"I—I think it caught my eye!"

Mr. Pownceby seemed a little fidgety. Mr. Pratt turned to the beginning.

"I see it mentions that the subject is to stare at the operator, and the operator is to stare at the subject, for about ten minutes or a quarter of an hour. Did you work the thing like that?"

"I followed, to the best of my ability, the instructions contained in the pamphlet."

"Did you stare at my wife?"

"It sounds uncivil, but I'm afraid I did."

"For ten minutes or a quarter of an hour?"

"About that."

"And did my wife stare at you?"

Mr. Pownceby laughed. He was conscious that Mr. Pratt's line of examination was tending to place him in a false position.

"I perceive you've marked this work with your pencil where it says, 'Place the thumb of your left hand on the subject's forehead, just above the nose, and level with the eyebrows.' Did you place the thumb of your left hand on my wife's forehead just above the nose, level with the eyebrows?"

"Really, Mr. Pratt, I can only say that, with the view of making a little experiment, I followed, to the best of my ability, the instructions generally."

"You seem to have seen the thing well through. It says that you've next to rest the ends of your fingers on the top of the subject's head. Did you rest the ends of your fingers on the top of my wife's head?"

"You may take it for granted that I did whatever the book directs."

"May I? That's kind. You increase my sense of obligation. Then you're to say to the subject, 'Look into my eyes.' Did you ask my wife to look into your eyes?"

"I did—certainly."

"Certainly. Of course. You're thorough—like the book. The man who put this book together had seen it done before. Then you're to say, 'Close your eyes quite tight.' Did you tell my wife to close her eyes quite tight?"

"I did. It was at that point that she went off into the hypnotic state."

"Was it now? This is really interesting. And what did you do next?"

"I tried to bring her to."

"Now, hark at that! And after all the trouble you had taken to send her off. And did she come?"

"I am sorry to say, as I have already explained to you, that my efforts were not attended with success."

"That was mean of her—real mean. And I suppose that, when you were performing these little experiments of yours upon my wife, this room was filled with a large assemblage?"

"We were alone together. I wish, now, it had been otherwise."

"Why?"

"After the questions you have already put to me, that needs no answer."

"Think not? Well, let me fill up your glass for you, Mr. Pownceby."

"I am obliged to you, but must beg you to excuse me."

"Is that so? You don't show yourself so friendly towards me as towards my wife. Perhaps, Mr. Pownceby, you're not aware that for the last two years I've been trotting round the world picking up the pieces to throw into her lap. She's English, and I'm American. She's not at all times fond of me, and we sometimes differ; but I love her, in my way. So you may think that when the first thing I hear, when I come to catch a sight of her after a two years' parting, is this little tale of yours, I find it a pleasing tale entirely. I find it that, I do assure you. Now, the only thing I should like you to do would be to play those little tricks on me which you played upon my wife. I should like to be hypnotised, uncommonly."

"If I were to attempt to do so I don't think that I should succeed. But, in any case, after my experience of this morning, it will be a long time before I make any more experiments on any one."

"Is that so? Think it over, Mr. Pownceby, while I lock this door and slip the key into my pocket."

Mr. Pratt locked the door and "slipped," as he called it, the key into his pocket.

"Mr. Pratt, I insist upon your unlocking that door."

"Mr. Pownceby, I was raised out West, and I was raised fighting, and I learnt to smell a fight when it was coming, and there's as big a fight now coming as ever I yet smelt."

"Why do you use this language, sir, to me?"

"It's my ignorance, may be. But in those parts where I was raised, when one man played upon another man's wife the tricks you've played on mine, it generally ended up in fighting. You bet it's going to end in fighting now." Mr. Pownceby made a movement towards the bell. Mr. Pratt sprang in front of him. "You can ring the bell, sir, afterwards; but first you'll listen to me. They'll have to break the door down to get into this room, and that'll be a scandal; and while they're breaking it down I'll be whipping you. You'd better, take it fighting. I've got a shooter." Putting his hand to his pistol-pocket, Mr. Pratt flashed the barrel of a revolver in Mr. Pownceby's face. "But I know your English notions, and I don't want to use it in a little affair like this. Let's strip to the waist, and clear the furniture out of the middle of the room, and have a little prize-fight all to ourselves."

"Do you take me for a madman, Mr. Pratt? If you don't immediately unlock the door I shall summon assistance, and if you use any violence towards me, I shall give you into the charge of the police."

"Is that your line? That's mine!"

Dropping the hand which held the revolver, Mr. Pratt delivered with his left. Delivered so neatly, in the centre of Mr. Pownceby's forehead, that that gentleman was hurled backwards on to the floor.

"If you like you can take it lying down, and you can summon assistance while you are taking it; but you'll take it somehow—that you bet."

Mr. Pownceby, lying on the floor, looked up at Mr. Pratt standing over him.

"Let me get up." He got up. The blow had cut the skin, and the blood was trickling through. With his handkerchief he staunched the flow. "In America, Mr. Pratt, they may think the sort of thing that you propose heroic. In England they consider a row of any sort ridiculous."

"Consider! It isn't what they consider I'm thinking of, it's how you're going to take it."

Mr. Pownceby fixed his glance on Mr. Pratt's keen black eyes. He smiled.

"Take it? I'll take it fighting, like the converter of Colonel Quagg!"

"I thought you would. I smelt it coming on."

As he spoke Mr. Pratt placed his revolver on the mantelshelf. Mr. Pownceby was still smiling.

"Do you propose to settle it now?"

"I do. I propose to settle it before you leave this room."

"In that case don't you think we'd better pull the blind down, or people walking on the terrace will be able to see the fun? If we are going to make asses of ourselves, we may as well do it, as far as possible, in private."

Mr. Pratt pulled the blind down. The sun was shining outside. The room was still quite light.

"I guess," said Mr. Pratt, "we had better clear the furniture out of the middle of the room."

Mr. Pownceby assisted him in doing so, what little there was to clear. The bottle of champagne and the two glasses they placed with the revolver on the mantelshelf. They then proceeded to strip. As they were doing so Mr. Pownceby asked a question.

"How shall we manage about time?"

"We will call time when we feel we want it. You understand, this is not only a fight; it's a whipping. I'm whipping you."

Mr. Pownceby smiled as he answered: "I understand exactly."

When they were in position there was not much, so far as appearance went, for a lover of the "fancy" to choose between the two. Now that they were peeled, both seemed thoroughly fit—as fit almost as though they had been trained. Mr. Pownceby was fair, Mr. Pratt was dark; that was about the only difference. Both would have turned the scale at something near eleven stone, and both measured something under five foot eight. Nor did it take long to show that both could use their hands. There was none of that waiting for each other which so often tries the patience of the spectators round a ring. Mr. Pratt came at once to business; with, perhaps, rather too much self-confidence. He was apparently under the impression that it was going to be a case of whipping his opponent from the first; which was the reason, doubtless, that Mr. Pownceby succeeded in returning the compliment which had been paid himself, and landing Mr. Pratt upon his back. That gentleman seemed surprised.

"I say," he asked, lying where he had fallen, "what's this?"

Mr. Pownceby replied politely: "I hope I haven't hurt you?"

"You haven't hurt me—much. You've surprised me—more. I reckon we'll continue."

The proceedings recommenced. But this time Mr. Pratt had changed his tactics. Instead of coming up with the apparent intention of wiping his opponent off the face of the earth with a single blow, he played his game more cautiously. He fenced; but, becoming tired of this, and feeling possibly that the whipping was not proceeding fast enough, he led off with his right, and followed on with his left, and Mr. Pownceby countered and returned—returned with such effect that for half a minute Mr. Pratt was dancing about while Mr. Pownceby was performing on him much in the fashion which the regimental drummer beats to quarters on his drum.

"Time!" he cried.

The round was over. A pause ensued, during which his feelings were plainly too deep for words.

"Have you ever had a whipping before?" he asked.

Mr. Pownceby smiled; it was evident that his smile was a smile of enjoyment at last.

"One or two," he said.

"Like this?"

"Not exactly. In England we don't, as a rule, indulge in this form of amusement in the private sitting-room of an hotel."

"Don't you? Well, it's as well. I smelt that a big fight was coming, and it's come. I'm going to enjoy myself entirely. You've closed up one of my eyes, I should say, from the feel of it, for ever. You've broken the bridge of my nose; what there'll be to pay for the blood upon the carpet—there's a quart gone from me already—is more than I quite care to think. Before I've finished whipping you I reckon I'll be slain."

"Come, Mr. Pratt, don't you think this foolish business had better cease? If you require an apology I am willing to tender one in any form you like. What passed between your wife and myself was simply in the nature of a little scientific experiment."

"It'll be in the nature of a little scientific experiment what's going to pass between us too. I'm fond of experiments as well as you. Time!"

Mr. Pratt fell into position. He struck at Mr. Pownceby. Mr. Pownceby laughed as he warded off the blow.

"Come, Mr. Pratt, why will you persist in this absurdity?"

"I'm going to whip you, sir."

"In that case you really must excuse me for putting on the steam. If a waiter or someone were to come and find me engaged like this, I should never hear the last of it as long as I lived. Here goes!"

It went. He had been warding off Mr. Pratt's blows while he was speaking. When he ceased the battle really joined. Mr. Pratt's guards were nowhere. In spite of all that he could do to save himself, his antagonist proceeded to administer severe punishment in thoroughly workmanlike style. The blows rang out upon his head and body. Mr. Pownceby wound up with one under the chin which lifted him off his feet and laid him on his back. He lay where he fell. The blow had knocked him senseless. Mr. Pownceby proceeded to revive him with the remains of the champagne.

"This," he murmured, opening his eyes and looking up, "is nice."

Mr. Pownceby propped him up upon a chair.

"You compelled me to rush the thing; but I hope I haven't hurt you much."

"Well," said Mr. Pratt, "you haven't killed me—quite. I never enjoyed whipping a man so much before. Say, stranger, is this the first little fight you've had?"

"I've sparred for the amateur championship, and won it twice. I'm going in for it again next week."

"You might have mentioned that before the game began."

"If the inherent absurdity of your proposal could not deter you, I doubt if any information I might have imparted would have been of much avail."

"There's something in that. Time!"

Mr. Pratt rose from his chair. He stood on his feet—rather doubtfully.

"What do you mean?" asked Mr. Pownceby.

"I'm going on whipping you."

"Look here, Mr. Pratt, each time you stand up I shall simply knock you down again. Of course you can go on with that sort of thing as long as you like."

"That is so; I can. And that's a sort of thing of which one doesn't care to get more than enough."

Mr. Pratt rested his hand on the back of a chair. It seemed as though, without some support of that kind, he could not stand. Mr. Pownceby advanced to him.

"Mr. Pratt, give me your hand."

Mr. Pratt gave it to him, it would seem, mechanically. The two men stood looking at each other in silence—the one almost without a scratch, the other a battered ruin. While they were so engaged the latch of the French window was opened from without, the blind was thrust aside, and a lady entered. It was Mrs. Pratt. When she saw what met her eyes she stared, which, as a breach of good manners, was, under the circumstances, excusable.

"Mr. Pownceby! Gilead! What have you been doing?"

"I've been whipping him," said Mr. Pratt. "I must be off my ordinary, for I never whipped a man that way before."

Mr. Pownceby slipped on his jacket. He helped Mr. Pratt to put on his.

"It's my fault, Mrs. Pratt. When I told your husband of our little experiment and that I found myself unable to release you from the hypnotic state which I had induced he thought I must have done you a serious injury, and that he naturally resented."

Mrs. Pratt looked at Mr. Pownceby. There was a twinkle of intelligence in her sweet blue eyes.

"I see. Miss Haseltine is looking for you. You'll find her in the drawing-room."

"Thank you," said Mr. Pownceby. "I—I'll go and look for her."

As he sneaked out of the room, with his shirt and waistcoat under his arm, devoutly hoping that no one might encounter him on his journey to his own apartment, he heard Mrs. Pratt make this remark to her husband—the first after two years absence:

"So, Gilead, you've been at it again."

He heard Mr. Pratt reply:

"I have. I was raised fighting, and I reckon that fighting I shall die. If I have to whip that Pownceby again it is a certainty I shall."

AN OLD-FASHIONED CHRISTMAS

CHAPTER I

THE PROMISE

"An old-fashioned Christmas.—A lively family will accept a gentleman as paying guest to join them in spending an old-fashioned Christmas in the heart of the country."

That was the advertisement. It had its points. I was not sure what, in this case, an old-fashioned Christmas might happen to mean. I imagine there were several kinds of "old-fashioned" Christmases; but it could hardly be worse than a chop in my chambers, or—horror of horrors!—at the club; or my cousin Lucy's notion of what she calls the "festive season." Festive? Yes! She and her husband, who suffers from melancholia, and all the other complaints which flesh is heir to, and I, dragging through what I call a patent-medicine dinner, and talking of everybody who is dead and gone, or else going, and of nothing else.

So I wrote to the advertiser. The reply was written in a sprawling feminine hand. It was a little vague. It appeared that the terms would be five guineas; but there was no mention of the length of time which that fee would cover. I might arrive, it seemed, on Christmas Eve, but there was no hint as to when I was to go, if ever. The whole thing was a trifle odd. There was nothing said about the sort of accommodation which would be provided, nothing about the kind of establishment which was maintained, or the table which was kept. No references were offered or asked for. It was merely stated that "we're a very lively family, and that if you're lively yourself you'll get on uncommonly well." The letter was signed "Madge Wilson."

Now it is a remarkable thing that I have always had an extraordinary predilection for the name Madge. I do not know why. I have never known a Madge. And yet, from my boyhood upward, I have desired to meet one. Here was an opportunity offered. She was apparently the careworn mother of a "lively family." Under such circumstances she was hardly likely to be "lively" herself, but her name was Madge, and it was the accident of her Christian name which decided me to go.

I had no illusions. No doubt the five guineas were badly wanted; even a "lively family" would be hardly likely to advertise for a perfect stranger to spend Christmas with them if they were not. I did not expect a princely entertainment. Still I felt that it could hardly be worse than a chop or cousin Lucy; the subjects of her conversation I never cared about when they were alive, and I certainly do not want to talk about them now they are dead. As for the "pills" and "drops" with which her husband doses himself between the courses, it makes me ill even to think of them.

On Christmas Eve the weather was abominable. All night it had been blowing and raining. In the morning it began to freeze. By the time the streets were like so many skating rinks it commenced to snow. And it kept on snowing; that turned out to be quite a record in the way of snow-storms. Hardly the sort of weather to start for an unknown destination "in the heart of the country." But, at the last moment, I did not like to back out. I said I would go, and I meant to go.

I had been idiot enough to load myself with a lot of Christmas presents, without the faintest notion why. I had not given a Christmas present for years—there had been no one to give them to. Lucy cannot bear such trifling, and her husband's only notion of a present at any time was a gallon jar of somebody's Stomach Stirrer. I am no dealer in poisons.

I knew nothing of the people I was going to. The youngest member of the family might be twenty, or the oldest ten. No doubt the things I had bought would be laughed at, probably I should never venture to offer them. Still, if you have not tried your hand at that kind of thing for ever so long, the mere act of purchasing is a pleasure. That is a fact.

I had never enjoyed "shopping" so much since I was a boy. I felt quite lively myself as I mingled with the Christmas crowd, looking for things which might not turn out to be absolutely preposterous. I even bought something for Madge—I mean Mrs. Wilson. Of course, I knew that I had no right to do anything of the kind, and was aware that the chances were a hundred to one against my ever presuming to hint at its existence. I was actually ass enough to buy something for her husband—two things, indeed; alternatives, as it were—a box of cigars, if he turned out to be a smoker, and a case of whiskey if he didn't. I hoped to goodness that he would not prove to be a hypochondriac, like Lucy's husband. I would not give him pills. What the "lively family" would think of a perfect stranger arriving burdened with rubbish, as if he had known them all their lives, I did not dare to think. No doubt they would set him down as a lunatic right away.

It was a horrible journey. The trains were late, and, of course, overcrowded; there was enough luggage in our compartment to have filled it, and still there was one more passenger than there ought to have been; an ill-conditioned old fellow who wanted my hat-box put into the van because it happened to tumble off the rack on to his head. I pointed out to him that the rack was specially constructed for light luggage, that a hat-box was light luggage, and that if the train jolted, he ought to blame the company, not me. He was impervious to reason. His wrangling and jangling so upset me, that I went past the station at which I ought to have changed. Then I had to wait three-quarters of an hour for a train to take me back again, only to find that I had missed the one I intended to catch. So I had to cool my heels for two hours and a half in a wretched cowshed amidst a bitter, whirling snowstorm. It is some satisfaction for me to be able to reflect that I made it warm for the officials, however cold I might have been myself.

When the train did start, some forty minutes after scheduled time, it jolted along in a laborious fashion at the rate of about six miles an hour, stopping at every roadside hovel. I counted seven in a distance, I am convinced, of less than twenty miles. When at last I reached Crofton, my journey's end, it turned out that the station staff consisted of a half-witted individual, who was stationmaster, porter, and clerk combined, and a hulking lad who did whatever else there was to do. No one had come to meet me, the village was "about half a mile," and Hangar Dene, the house for which my steps were bent, "about four miles by the road"—how far it was across ploughed fields my informant did not mention.

There was a trap at the "Boy and Blunderbuss," but that required fetching. Finally the hulking lad was dispatched. It took him some time, considering the distance was only "about half a mile." When the trap did appear it looked to me uncommonly like an open spring cart. In it I was deposited, with my luggage. The snow was still descending in whirling clouds. Never shall I forget the drive, in that miserable cart, through the storm and those pitch black country lanes. We had been jogging along some time before the driver opened his mouth.

"Be you going to stop with they Wilsons?"

"I am."

"Ah!"

There was something in the tone of his "Ah!" which whetted my curiosity, near the end of my tether though I was.

"Why do you ask?"

"It be about time as someone were to stay with them as were a bit capable like."

I did not know what he meant. I did not ask. I was beyond it. I was chilled to the bone, wet, tired, hungry. I had long been wishing that an old-fashioned Christmas had been completely extinct before I had thought of adventuring in quest of one. Better cousin Lucy's notion of the "festive season."

We passed through a gate, which I had to get down to open, along some sort of avenue. Suddenly the cart pulled up.

"Here we be."

That might be so. It was a pity he did not add where "here" was. There was a great shadow, which possibly did duty for a house, but, if so, there was not a light in any of the windows, and there was nothing visible in the shape of a door. The whereabouts of this, however, the driver presently made clear.

"There be the door in front of you; you go up three steps, if you can find 'em. There's a knocker, if none of 'em haven't twisted it off. If they have, there's a bell on your right, if it isn't broken."

There appeared to be no knocker, though whether it had been "twisted" off was more than I could say. But there was a bell, which creaked with rust, though it was not broken. I heard it tinkle in the distance. No answer; though I allowed a more than decent interval.

"Better ring again," suggested the driver. "Hard. Maybe they're up to some of their games, and wants rousing."

Was there a chuckle in the fellow's voice? I rang again, and again with all the force I could. The bell reverberated through what seemed like an empty house.

"Is there no one in the place?"

"They're there right enough. Where's another thing. Maybe on the roof; or in the cellar. If they know you're coming perhaps they hear and don't choose to answer. Better ring again."

I sounded another peal. Presently feet were heard advancing along the passage—several pairs it seemed—and a light gleamed through the window over the door. A voice inquired: "Who's there?"

"Mr. Christopher, from London."

The information was greeted with what sounded uncommonly like a chorus of laughter. There was a rush of retreating feet, an expostulating voice, then darkness again, and silence.

"Who lives here? Are the people mad?"

"Well—thereabouts."

Once more I suspected the driver of a chuckle. My temper was rising. I had not come all that way, and subjected myself to so much discomfort, to be played tricks with. I tolled the bell again. After a few seconds' interval the pit-pat of what was obviously one pair of feet came towards the door. Again a light gleamed through the pane. A key was turned, a chain unfastened, bolts withdrawn; it seemed as if some one had to drag a chair forward before one of these latter could be reached. After a vast amount of unfastening, the door was opened, and on the threshold there stood a girl, with a lighted candle in her hand. The storm rushed in; she put up her hand to shield the light from danger.

"Can I see Mrs. Wilson? I'm expected. I'm Mr. Christopher, from London."

"Oh!"

That was all she said. I looked at her; she at me. The driver's voice came from the background.

"I drove him over from the station, Miss. There be a lot of luggage. He do say he's come to stay with you."

"Is that you, Tidy? I'm afraid I can offer you nothing to drink. We've lost the key of the cellar, and there's nothing out, except water, and I don't think you'd care for that."

"I can't say rightly as how I should, Miss. Next time will do. Be it all right?"

The girl continued to regard me.

"Perhaps you had better come inside."

"I think I had."

I went inside; it was time.

"Have you any luggage?" I admitted that I had. "Perhaps it had better be brought in."

"Perhaps it had."

"Do you think that you could manage, Tidy?"

"The mare, she'll stand still enough. I should think I could, miss."

By degrees my belongings were borne into the hall, hidden under an envelope of snow. The girl seemed surprised at their number. The driver was paid, the cart disappeared, the door was shut; the girl and I were alone together.

"We didn't expect that you would come."

"Not expect me? But it was all arranged; I wrote to say that I would come. Did you not receive my letter?"

"We thought that you were joking."

"Joking! Why should you imagine that?"

"We were joking."

"You were? Then I am to gather that I have been made the subject of a practical joke, and that I am an intruder here?"

"Well, it's quite true that we did not think you were in earnest. You see, it's this way, we're alone."

"Alone? Who are 'we'?"

"Well, it will take a good while to explain, and you look tired and cold."

"I am both."

"Perhaps you're hungry?"

"I am."

"I don't know what you can have to eat, unless it's to-morrow's dinner."

"To-morrow's dinner!" I stared. "Can I see Mrs. Wilson?"

"Mrs. Wilson? That's mamma. She's dead."

"I beg your pardon. Can I see your father?"

"Oh, father's been dead for years."

"Then to whom have I the pleasure of speaking?"

"I'm Madge. I'm mother now."

"You are—mother now?"

"The trouble will be about where you are to sleep—unless it's with the boys. The rooms are all anyhow, and I'm sure I don't know where the beds are."

"I suppose there are servants in the house?"

She shook her head.

"No. The boys thought that they were nuisances so we got rid of them. The last went yesterday. She wouldn't do any work, so we thought she'd better go."

"Under those circumstances I think it probable that you were right. Then am I to understand that there are children?"

"Rather!"

As she spoke there came a burst of laughter from the other end of the passage. I spun round. No one was in sight. She explained.

"They're waiting round the corner. Perhaps we'd better have them here. You people, you'd better come and let me introduce you to Mr. Christopher."

A procession began to appear from round the corner of boys and girls. In front was a girl of about sixteen. She advanced with outstretched hand and an air of self-possession which took me at a disadvantage.

"I'm Bessie. I'm sorry we kept you waiting at the door, but the fact is that we thought it was Eliza's brother who had come to insult us again."

"Pray, don't mention it. I am glad that it was not Eliza's brother."

"So am I. He is a dreadful man."

I shook hands with the rest of them. There were six more, four boys and two girls. They formed a considerable congregation as they stood eyeing me with inquiring glances. Madge was the first to speak.

"I wondered all along if he would take it as a joke or not, and you see he hasn't. I thought all the time that it was a risky thing to do."

"I like that! You keep your thoughts to yourself then. It was you proposed it. You said you'd been reading about something of the kind in a story, and you voted for our advertising ourselves for a lark."

The speaker was the biggest boy, a good-looking youngster, with sallow cheeks and shrewd black eyes.

"But, Rupert, I never meant it to go so far as this."

"How far did you mean it to go then? It was your idea all through. You sent in the advertisement, you wrote the letters, and now he's here. If you didn't mean it, why didn't you stop his coming?"

"Rupert!"

The girls cheeks were crimson. Bessie interposed.

"The thing is that as he is here it's no good worrying about whose fault it is. We shall simply have to make the best of it." Then, to me, "I suppose you really have come to stay?"

"I confess that I had some notion of the kind—to spend an old-fashioned Christmas."

At this there was laughter, chiefly from the boys. Rupert exclaimed:

"A nice sort of old-fashioned Christmas you'll find it will be. You'll be sorry you came before it's through."

"I am not so sure of that."

There appeared to be something in my tone which caused a touch of silence to descend upon the group. They regarded each other doubtfully, as if in my words a reproof was implied. Bessie was again the spokeswoman.

"Of course, now that you have come, we mean to be nice to you, that is as nice as we can. Because the thing is that we are not in a condition to receive visitors. Do we look as if we were?"

To be frank, they did not. Even Madge was a little unkempt, while the boys were in what I believe is the average state of the average boy.

"And," murmured Madge, "where is Mr. Christopher to sleep?"

"What is he to eat?" inquired Bessie. She glanced at my packages. "I suppose you have brought nothing with you?"

"I'm afraid I haven't. I had hoped to have found something ready for me on my arrival."

Again they peeped at each other, as if ashamed. Madge repeated her former suggestion.

"There's to-morrow's dinner."

"Oh, hang it!" exclaimed Rupert. "It's not so bad as that. There's a ham."

"Uncooked."

"You can cut a steak off, or whatever you call it, and have it broiled."

A meal was got ready, in the preparation of which every member of the family took a hand. And a room was found for me, in which was a blazing fire and traces of recent feminine occupation. I suspected that Madge had yielded her own apartment as a shelter for the stranger. By the time I had washed and changed my clothes, the impromptu dinner, or supper, or whatever it was, was ready.

A curious repast it proved to be; composed of oddly contrasted dishes, cooked—and sometimes uncooked—in original fashion. But hunger, that piquant sauce, gave it a relish of its own. At first no one seemed disposed to join me. By degrees, however, one after another found a knife and fork, until all the eight were seated with me round the board, eating, some of them, as if for dear life.

"The fact is," explained Rupert, "we're a rum lot. We hardly ever sit down together. We don't have regular meals, but whenever anyone feels peckish, he goes and gets what there is, and cooks it and eats it on his own."

"It's not quite so bad as that," protested Madge, "though it's pretty bad."

It did seem pretty bad, from the conventional point of view. From their conversation, which was candour itself, I gleaned details which threw light upon the peculiar position of affairs. It seemed that their father had been dead some seven years. Their mother, who had been always delicate, had allowed them to run nearly wild. Since she died, some ten months back, they appeared to have run quite wild. The house, with some six hundred acres of land, was theirs, and an income, as to whose exact amount no one seemed quite clear.

"It's about eight hundred a year," said Rupert.

"I don't think it's quite so much," doubted Madge.

"I'm sure it's more," declared Bessie. "I believe we're being robbed."

I thought it extremely probable. They must have had peculiar parents. Their father had left everything absolutely to their mother, and the mother, in her turn, everything in trust to Madge, to be shared equally among them all. Madge was an odd trustee. In her hands the household had become a republic, in which every one did exactly as he or she pleased. The result was chaos. No one wanted to go to school, so no one went. The servants, finding themselves provided with eight masters and mistresses, followed their example, and did as they liked. Consequently, after sundry battles royal—lively episodes some of them had evidently been—one after the other had been got rid of, until, now, not one remained. Plainly the house must be going to rack and ruin.

"But have you no relations?" I inquired.

Rupert answered.

"We've got some cousins, or uncles, or something of the kind in Australia, where, so far as I'm concerned, I hope they'll stop."

When I was in my room, which I feared was Madge's, I told myself that it was a queer establishment on which I had lighted. Yet I could not honestly affirm that I was sorry I had come. I had lived such an uneventful and such a solitary life, and had so often longed for someone in whom to take an interest—who would not talk medicine chest!—that to be plunged, all at once, into the centre of this troop of boys and girls was an accident which, if only because of its novelty, I found amusing. And then it was so odd that I should have come across a Madge at last!

In the morning I was roused by noises, the cause of which, at first, I could not understand. By degrees the explanation dawned on me; the family was putting the house to rights. A somewhat noisy process it seemed. Someone was singing, someone else was shouting, and two or three others were engaged in a heated argument. In such loud tones was it conducted that the gist of the matter travelled up to me.

"How do you think I'm going to get this fire to burn if you beastly kids keep messing it about? It's no good banging at it with the poker till it's alight."

The voice was unmistakably Rupert's. There was the sound of a scuffle, cries of indignation, then a girlish voice pouring oil upon the troubled waters. Presently there was a rattle and clatter, as if someone had fallen from the top of the house to the bottom. I rushed to my bedroom door.

"What on earth has happened?"

A small boy was outside—Peter. He explained,

"Oh, it's only the broom and dustpan gone tobogganing down the stairs. It's Bessie's fault; she shouldn't leave them on the landing."

Bessie, appearing from a room opposite, disclaimed responsibility.

"I told you to look out where you were going, but you never do. I'd only put them down for a second, while I went in to empty a jug of water on to Jack, who won't get out of bed, and there are all the boots for him to clean."

Injured tones came through the open portal.

"You wait, that's all! I'll soak your bed tonight—I'll drown it. I don't want to clean your dirty boots, I'm not a shoe-black."

The breakfast was a failure. To begin with, it was inordinately late. It seemed that a bath was not obtainable. I had been promised some hot water, but as I waited and waited and none arrived, I proceeded to break the ice in my jug—it was a bitterly cold morning, nice "old-fashioned" weather—and to wash in the half-frozen contents. As I am not accustomed to perform my ablutions in partially dissolved ice, I fear that the process did not improve my temper.

It was past eleven when I got down, feeling not exactly in a "Christmassy" frame of mind. Everything, and everyone, seemed at sixes and sevens. It was after noon when breakfast appeared. The principal dish consisted of eggs and bacon; but as the bacon was fried to cinders, and the eggs all broken, it was not so popular as it might have been, Madge was moved to melancholy.

"Something will have to be done! We can't go on like this! We must have someone in to help us!"

Bessie was sarcastic.

"You might give Eliza another trial. She told you, if you didn't like the way she burned the bacon, to burn it yourself, and as you've followed her advice, she might be able to give you other useful hints on similar lines."

Rupert indulged himself in the same vein.

"Then there's Eliza's brother. He threatened to knock your blooming head off for saying Eliza was dishonest, just because she collared everything she laid her hands on; he might turn out a useful sort of creature to have about the place."

"It's all very well for you to laugh, but it's beyond a jest. I don't know how we're going to cook the dinner."

"Can I be of any assistance?" I inquired. "First of all, what is there to cook?"

It seemed that there were a good many things to cook. A turkey, a goose, beef, plum pudding, mince pies, custard, sardines—it seemed that Molly, the third girl, as she phrased it, could "live on sardines," and esteemed no dinner a decent dinner at which they did not appear—together with a list of etceteras half as long as my arm.

"One thing is clear; you can't cook all those things to-day."

"We can't cook anything."

This was Rupert. He was tilting his chair back, and had his face turned towards the ceiling.

"Why not?"

"Because there's no coal."

"No coal?"

"There's about half a scuttle full of dust. If you can make it burn you'll be clever."

What Rupert said was correct. Madge confessed, with crimson cheeks, that she had meant, over and over again, to order some coal, but had continually forgotten it, until finally Christmas Day had found them with an empty cellar. There was plenty of wood, but it was not so dry as it might have been, and anyhow, the grate was not constructed to burn wood.

"You might try smoked beef," suggested Rupert. "When that wood goes at all it smokes like one o'clock. If you hung the beef up over it, it would be smoked enough for anyone by the time that it was done."

I began to rub my chin. Considering the breakfast we had had, from my point of view the situation commenced, for the first time, to look really grave, I wondered if it would not be possible to take the whole eight somewhere where something really eatable could be got. But, when I broached the subject, I learned that the thing could not be done. The nearest hostelry was the "Boy and Blunderbuss," and it was certain that nothing eatable could be had there, even if accommodation could be found for us at all. Nothing in the shape of a possible house of public entertainment was to be found closer than the market town, eight miles off; it was unlikely that even there a Christmas dinner for nine could be provided at a moment's notice. Evidently the only thing to do was to make the best of things.

When the meeting broke up Madge came and said a few words to me alone.

"I really think you had better not stay."

"Does that mean that you had rather I went?"

"No; not exactly that."

"Then nearly that?"

"No; not a bit that. Only you must see for yourself how awfully uncomfortable you'll be here, and what a horrid house this is."

"My dear Madge"—everybody called her Madge, so I did—"even if I wanted to go, which I don't—and I would remind you that you contracted to give me an old-fashioned Christmas—I don't see where there is that I could go."

"Of course, there's that. I don't see, either. So I suppose you'll have to stay. But I hope you won't think that I meant you to come to a place like this—really, you know."

"I'm sorry; I had hoped you had."

"That's not what I mean. I mean that if I had thought that you were coming, I would have seen that things were different."

"How different? I assure you that things as they are have a charm of their own."

"That's what you say. You don't suppose that I'm so silly as not to know you're laughing at me? But as I was the whole cause of your coming, I hope you won't hate the others because of me."

She marched off, brushing back, with an impatient gesture, some rebellious locks which had strayed upon her forehead.

That Christmas dinner was a success—positively. Of a kind—let that be clearly understood. I am not inferring that it was a success from the point of view of a "chef de cuisine." Not at all; how could it be?

Quite the other way. By dint of ransacking all the rooms, and emptying all the scuttles, we collected a certain amount of coal, with which, after adding a fair proportion of wood, we managed. Not brilliantly, but after a fashion. I can only say, personally, I had not enjoyed myself so much for years. I really felt as if I were young again; I am not sure that I am not younger than I thought I was. I must look the matter up. And, after all, even if one be, say forty, one need not be absolutely an ancient. Madge herself said that I had been like a right hand to her; she did not know what she would have done without me.

Looking back, I cannot but think that if we had attempted to prepare fewer dishes, something might have been properly cooked. It was a mistake to stuff the turkey with sage and onions; but as Bessie did not discover that she had been manipulating the wrong bird until the process of stuffing had been completed, it was felt that it might be just as well to let it rest. Unfortunately, it turned out that some thyme, parsley, mint, and other things had got mixed with the sage, which gave the creature quite a peculiar flavour; but as it came to table nearly raw, and as tough as hickory, it really did not matter.

My experience of that day teaches me that it is not easy to roast a large goose on a small oil stove. The dropping fat caused the flame to give out a strong smelling and most unpleasant smoke. Rupert, who had charge of the operation, affirmed that it would be all right in the end. But, by the time the thing was served, it was as black as my hat. Rupert said that it was merely brown; but the brown was of a sooty hue, and it reeked of paraffin. We had to have it deposited in the ashbin. I daresay that the beef would not have been bad if someone had occasionally turned it, and if the fire would have burned clear. As it was, it was charred on one side and raw on the other, and smoked all over. The way in which the odour and taste of smoke permeated everything was amazing. The plum-pudding, came to the table in the form of soup, and the mince pies were nauseous. Something had got into the crust, or mincemeat, or something, which there, at any rate, was out of place.

Luckily we came upon a tin of corned beef in a cupboard, and with the aid of some bread and cheese, and other odds and ends, we made a sort of picnic. Incredible though it may seem, I enjoyed it. If there was anywhere a merrier party than we were, I should like to know where it was to be found. It must have been a merry one. When I produced the presents, in which a happy inspiration had urged me to invest, "the enthusiasm reached a climax"—I believe that is the proper form of words which I ought to use. As I watched the pleasure of those youngsters, I felt as if I were myself a boy again.

That was my first introduction to "a lively family." They came up to the description they had given of themselves. I speak from knowledge, for they have been my acquaintances now some time. More than acquaintances, friends; the dearest friends I have. At their request, I took their affairs in hand, Madge informally passing her trusteeship on to me. Things are very different with them now. The house is spick and span. There is an excellent staff of servants. Hangar Dene is as comfortable a home as there is in England. I have spent many a happy Christmas under its hospitable roof since then.

The boys are out in the world, after passing with honour through school and college. The girls are going out into the world also. Bessie is actually married. Madge is married too. She is Mrs. Christopher. That is the part of it all which I find is hardest to understand—to have told myself my whole life long that the name of my ideal woman would be Madge, and to have won that woman for my own at last! That is greater fortune than falls to the lot of most men. I thought that I was beyond that kind of thing; that I was too old. But Madge seemed to think that I was young enough. And she thinks so still.

And now there is a little Madge, who is big enough to play havoc with the sheets of paper on which I have been scribbling, to whom, one day, this tale will have to be told.

CHAPTER I

DESPOILED

"It would seem, Greenall, as if you couldn't even shoot."

"It would seem like it, wouldn't it."

As I sauntered back to the hotel I was conscious of a slight feeling of exacerbation. As if I had been "got at," "had." No man likes to feel that he is a laughing-stock. I felt that I had been made a laughing-stock just then; that, indeed, the process of manufacture had been going on ever since I showed my face in Ahmednugger. The men I had met were nice enough—in their way. Indeed, they were almost too nice— also in their way. They appeared to have so little to do, in the way of actual work, that they had made it the business of their lives to perfect themselves in what are usually regarded, say, as accomplishments. I was, and am, a plain civilian. I have worked for, and earned, my little pile, such as it is, and until I set out upon that pleasure tour in the East, it had never occurred to me that a man could be regarded as an uneducated idiot if he could not, say, run into double figures every time he took up his cue at billiards. A suspicion that a man might be so regarded had been dawning upon me ever since I arrived in India; but until I came to Ahmednugger I had never quite realised how shockingly my education had been neglected on exactly those points on which it ought to have been most carefully attended to. The men of Ahmednugger were the most sporting individuals I had ever yet encountered. Possibly I have not moved much among the congregations of the sporting men, but I certainly have seen something of men of business. These men of Ahmednugger were not only the keenest sportsmen I had encountered, they were the keenest men of business, too. And talk of the rigour of a competitive examination! They formed themselves into an examining board, which very soon took the "stiffening" out of me. They insisted on putting me through my paces before I had been a week in the place. They examined me in every game of cards which has been invented—and found me wanting in them all. They examined me as a rider, as a driver, as a shootist, as a cueist, in fact, in a range of subjects which I will not even venture to enumerate. They refused me one solitary "pass." They "plucked" me in them all. It did not add to my sense of satisfaction, that I found my ignorance expensive.

The joke of the thing was, that before I came to India I had rather fancied myself as an amateur sportsman. I flattered myself that I had a decent seat in a saddle, whether across country or on the flat. I thought that I made a tolerable fourth at whist; that I had some notion, at any rate, of English billiards, and of a hazard off the red. I certainly was under the impression that I could see with tolerable accuracy along the barrel of a gun. But these vain delusions were scattered, at once and for ever, by the men of Ahmednugger. My all-round, purblind, insensate ignorance had been so convincingly displayed, that, as I have said, I was the laughing-stock of all the place.

My latest performance in the exhibition line had been in a match with young Tebb, the youngest and the latest joined of the subalterns. Young Tebb had lured me on to skittles. Mr. Tebb—who would have been more correctly designated as "Master" Tebb—was an awkward hobbledehoy, who, at any other place than Ahmednugger, I should have looked down upon with the most supreme contempt. When he challenged me to see who could smash most glass balls with a rifle bullet, he or I, I rashly took his challenge up. I flattered myself that, at last, I had a "soft thing" on. I had, myself, been found a "soft thing" so many times, that I looked forward to a little change. I had no notion (it was rather late at night when the challenge was thrown down, and taken up) how difficult it really was to hit a glass ball with a rifle bullet. I had never fired at a glass ball, nor had I ever seen anyone else do so. But I conceived, that at any rate, young Tebb would find at least as much difficulty in the thing as I should.

We were each to fire at fifty glass balls, which were to be sent up into the air out of a trap. We were, of course, to fire at them while they were in the air. Out of my fifty I smashed one. Out of his fifty young Tebb smashed forty-nine. It was the most mirth-provoking exhibition that was ever seen. Of course, the young scoundrel had been doing nothing else but fire at glass balls his whole life long. It was when I handed over the two hundred rupees which I had staked and lost, that Mr. Tebb made his remark to the effect that "I couldn't even shoot."

When I returned to the hotel, a man was standing in the doorway. He addressed me as I came up the steps.

"It strikes me that you and I might shake hands, sir."

I asked him what he meant.

"I've made myself one kind of ass, and you've made yourself another kind. We'd be a pair of beauties."

I did not like being addressed in this manner, especially by a stranger, and especially by a stranger like this stranger. He was a short, undersized man, with a vacuous expression of countenance. His attire suggested seediness. Perceiving that I did not appreciate his manner, he explained.

"No offence intended, sir. But I just now saw you playing pantaloon to that youngster's clown, and I thought that he made the end of the poker rather hot. As for me, I'm an ass all over. My name's Johns. I came to this place to shear the sheep. There's been some shearing, but it's the sheep that's done it. They've about sheared me. I happened to have a trifle of money, so I came to these parts to see if I could do a bit of bookmaking. I've done a bit. The gentlemen in these parts have also done a bit. They've got hold of pretty well every blessed mag I had."

I did not encourage Mr. Johns; quite the contrary. I had heard of him before. The regimental races had recently been held; a bookmaker had appeared upon the scene—Mr. Johns. Nearly every man in the place had had bets with him, and to nearly every man in the place he had lost his money. With a vengeance had the Philistine been spoiled.

CHAPTER II

THE GAME

Later in the day on which I had shot off that match with Mr. Tebb I encountered Mr. Johns again. I was in the billiard-room of what was called "the club." As regards membership, it was very free-and-easy "club" indeed. A local celebrity was taking the floor. The room was tolerably full. On one of the side seats was Mr. Johns.

The local celebrity was a Mr. Colson. Mr. Colson was stud groom to the Rajah of Ahmednugger. He was also, and at the same time, one of the most obnoxious persons I have, in the course of my career, had the pleasure of meeting. There never was such a loud-voiced braggart. It set one's nerves on edge to hear him. To listen to him, there was nothing he could not do. The misfortune was, that some of the things which he said he could do, he could do, and do well. I had found that out to my cost, soon after my arrival in Ahmednugger. And, in consequence, he had sat on me heavily ever since. He was a horrible man.

That evening Mr. Colson was holding forth in his usual style, on the subject of billiards. I should mention that, at the period of which I am writing, Mr. John Roberts, the famous player, was on a tour in India.

"I saw John Roberts at Calcutta," observed Mr. Colson, "and he saw me. He also saw me play. When he saw me play, he said he doubted if he could give me fifteen in a hundred. I told him that I should like to see him do it. But he wouldn't take it on."

"Is that so?" asked Mr. Johns.

"That is so. I should like to see him give me ten in a hundred, either John Roberts or any man now living."

"I should like to have a game with you, Mr. Colson."

"You would?" Mr. Colson looked at Mr. Johns. He looked him up and down. Mr. Colson was large and florid. Mr. Johns was small and underfed. Mr. Colson was, at least, expensively attired. About Mr. John's costume there was certainly no suspicion of expense. "I don't mind having you a hundred up, my lad. How many shall I give you?"

"I am no player, Mr. Colson, but I'd like to play you even, if only for the sake of saying that I'd had the cheek to do it."

"You shall have that pleasure. And how much would you like to have on—if only for the sake of saying that you had the cheek to have it on?"

And Mr. Colson winked at the company in general.

"Well, Mr. Colson, you and the other gentlemen have won all my money; but, I daresay, I might manage ten rupees."

"Put 'em up, my lad. Here's my ten. We'll play for the twenty."

They played for the twenty. And, to my satisfaction, and I believe to the satisfaction of most of the others who were in the room, it was Mr. Johns who won. I am bound to say that it seemed to me to be rather a fluky win. Mr. Colson, whose disgust was amusing, had no doubt whatever about the fluke.

"Never saw anything like it, never! The balls never broke for me, not once! As for you; why, you did nothing else but fluke."

"Do you think so? I'll play you again double or quits, and I'll give ten in the hundred, Mr. Colson."

Mr. Colson seemed amazed. In fact, I have no doubt he was amazed.

"I like your modesty! You'll give me ten! Here's my twenty. I'll take you on."

Mr. Colson took him on. And, by way of fair exchange, Mr. Johns took him off. That is to say, he took off the stakes and the game. He did it rather neatly: just running in as Mr. Colson looked like winning. Mr. Colson was adjectival.

"Never saw anything like it—never, in all my born days! Never saw anything like my somethinged, somethinged, somethinged luck! And as for your fluking—why, it just beats anything."

"Think so? I'll play you again, Mr. Colson, and again double or quits; and this time I'll give you twenty in a hundred."

"You'll give me—you'll give me—twenty in a hundred? You will? Come on! That'll be forty rupees a side—here's mine! Macbee, put me on twenty, and we'll see what I can do."

We did see what he could do. We also saw that Mr. Johns seemed able to do a little better. Once more he won the game. I am sure that we were all enjoying ourselves very much—much more than we had had any reason to anticipate. As for Mr. Colson, he went purple. He showered on Mr. Johns a volley of that sort of language which I had found pretty fashionable at Ahmednugger. Mr. Johns listened to him in silence, while he pocketed the spoils. Then he had his say.

"You say I fluke? Why, my dear sir, you've no idea what a fluke is. You've no idea of any sort about billiards. You can no more play billiards than you can play the gentleman—you can't! You're the sort of person whom it is just as well, once in a way, to expose. You're a humbug, Mr. Colson, you're a humbug. As for John Roberts doubting if he could give you fifteen in a hundred—why, he could give you ninety-nine in a hundred, and beat you single-handed. I tell you what I will do, Mr. Colson. I will play you five hundred up, for five hundred rupees a side. I will give you four hundred start, and I will lay two to one against you with any gentleman who cares to back you. I don't think that's an unfair offer, Mr. Colson."

It struck me as, at any rate, a rash offer. Mr. Colson was not such a tyro as Mr. Johns made out. He had made mincemeat of me—I do know that. Yet the offer did not seem to be made in any spirit of braggadocio. I fancy that the quiet, matter-of-fact manner in which it was made impressed Mr. Colson more than he altogether cared to own. My impression it that, if he had had his own way, he would have changed the subject. But the odds offered him were such, and the challenge was made in such a public manner, that he probably felt that, if he wished to preserve a rag of reputation, now or never was the time to show the stuff that he was made of. Anyhow, the offer was accepted, and the terms of the match were definitely arranged before the parties left the room.

As I was retiring to rest, some one tapped at my bed-room door. In response to my invitation to enter, Mr. Johns came in. Without any preamble, he plunged at once into the purport of his presence in my chamber at that hour of the night, or, rather, morning.

"I have come, Mr. Greenall, to ask you to lend me five hundred rupees."

I turned. I looked at him. He met my glance without showing any signs of discomposure.

"You have come to—what?"

He repeated his remark—quite as though it were a matter of course.

"To ask if you will lend me five hundred rupees."

"I don't know if you are in earnest, Mr. Johns. If you are, I would remark, first, that I am not a money lender; and, second, that you are a complete stranger to me."

"I want the money to stake in my match with Mr. Colson."

"Indeed. Is that so? Then that is an added reason why I should decline to lend it to you. In my opinion, Mr. Johns, your chances of success in that match are, to say the least of it, remote."

"Look here, Mr. Greenall, I'm the last man in the world to wish to make myself offensive, but if we can understand each other I think that you and I might do each other a good turn. I know all about how you've been treated by the fellows here. I know how they've all been taking pop shots at you. From what I hear they've made you look like the biggest all-round muff that ever left his mammy. I daresay it's cost you something, too."

I did not altogether appreciate this gentleman's free-and-easy style of conversation. But to a certain extent I, so to speak, dissembled.

"I do not know what warrant you have, Mr. Johns, for your remarks; and, in any case, I fail to see what business it is of yours."

"It's this way; if you like, you can be even with all the lot of them—and more than even."

"How? By lending you five hundred rupees, and letting you have, as you put it, a pop-shot at me with the rest of them. Thank you, Mr. Johns. By the way, I fancy I have heard of some person or persons taking pop-shots at you. I think I did hear that you came here to make a fortune. Did you make it, Mr. Johns?"

"No, I didn't—hang 'em! I'm like you, I owe them one. And I mean to pay them, with compound interest. And, if you like to say the word, I'll pay them that little lot you owe them too. Look here, Mr. Greenall, I don't mind owning that a keener lot of gentlemen than the gentlemen here I don't think I ever had to do with. I won't say they robbed me, but they certainly cut me up into very nice little pieces, and they handed me round. I've seldom seen any thing of the kind which was better done. But never mind—my turn's coming! I'm not fond of bragging—quite the other way. If it wasn't that I was in a hole, I wouldn't say a word. But it is the simple truth that, at all the things at which these fellows think they're dabsters, I'm as far ahead of them as they're ahead of you,—no offence intended. You can take my word for it that I know what I'm talking about. It doesn't follow because, just once in a way, they happened to muck up my book, that I'm a flat. As for being able to give Colson four hundred out of five hundred at billiards,—if I choose, and I shall choose, he's simply bound to lose. I don't mean to say that I'm a John Roberts, because I'm not. But I do know how to play, and that in a sense which Colson hasn't even begun to understand. I've heard that Mr. Colson hasn't behaved over well to you. I thought that you'd like to see him taken down a peg or two."

I should. I should have liked to have seen more than one of them taken down a peg or two, though I said nothing of that to Mr. Johns.

"How came you to match yourself, Mr. Johns, when you were aware that you were not in possession of the required stakes?"

"I took it for granted that I should get the stakes from you."

Mr. Johns was frank, at any rate.

"From me? What claim did you suppose yourself to have on me?"

"No claim; but you see, sir, they've had me, and they've had you. They've had both of us, in fact, pretty smartly. And I thought that you might like to be even with some of them, by deputy."

By deputy. If it was workable, that was not a bad idea. I felt that I should like to be even with some of them, beginning, say, with Mr. Colson—how that man had squelched me beneath his elephantine foot! the brute!—even, as it were, by deputy.

"What guarantee have I that you will not lose my money, as you already have lost your own?"

"If we get up early, we shall have the billiard room all to ourselves. If you like, I will give you some idea of what I can do upon a billiard table."

We did get up early. We did have the billiard room all to ourselves. And Mr. Johns did give me some idea of what he could do upon a billiard table. For one thing, he got "on the spot," and he stopped there. He continued to put the red down, without once missing, until the marker appeared. When the marker did appear, we thought that perhaps the proceedings had better cease. If I can trust my memory, before the proceedings ceased, Mr. Johns had put the red down something like two hundred times in succession. I thought that was good enough, even for Mr. Colson. I agreed to advance the necessary number of rupees.

The match came off. It was a beautiful match. The room was crowded to overflowing. Mr. Johns had managed to back himself to a very fair amount. Even I, in my small way, had managed to back him too. But there was not so much readiness shown to support the local champion as I had expected. They were keen, were the men of Ahmednugger. I fancy that already they had begun to smell a rat. And not only so; they were always willing to "make a bet." But on that particular occasion they were almost equally willing to see Mr. Colson come to grief. I think that, in those parts, Mr. Colson was not so popular as he deserved to be. I verily believe that there were some who objected to him almost as much as I did.

Poor Mr. Colson! He was painfully nervous. His nervousness prevented his showing even his usual form. He had made fifteen, when Mr. Johns, getting on the spot, stayed there. He ran out without once putting down his cue. Nothing like it had ever been seen before in Ahmednugger. When the marker notified the fact that Mr. Johns had completed his fifth hundred, Mr. Colson was, for a moment, speechless. He seemed unable to realize that the thing was so.

"It's a—something swindle!"

"I beg your pardon, Mr. Colson—it's a what?"

Mr. Colson's tone was loud and threatening. Mr. Johns' tone was quiet, and almost indifferent. Yet Mr. Colson did not seem to altogether like it. He began to bluster. "You did not tell me that you were a professional."

"No; I did not tell you that I was a professional."

"You didn't play the other night as you have played to-day. It looks to me uncommonly like a put-up thing."

"It looks to you like a put-up thing, does it, Mr. Colson. Well, I'll give you a chance of showing your professional side. I believe you can drive?"

"Drive!" Mr. Colson looked at the little man as if he would like to eat him. "I'm the finest whip in India."

"Indeed! Is that so? Well, I'll drive you either four, or eight, in hand, for a thousand rupees a side, although you are the finest whip in India."

Mr. Colson snapped at his offer, before it was fairly out of his mouth, and I felt that Mr. Johns was going a little too far. It was one thing to match him at billiards, another thing to match him at driving. There Mr. Colson was on his native heath. When I was alone with Mr. Johns I told him so.

"I don't know if you are aware, Mr. Johns, that Mr. Colson really is a first-rate whip. I am informed that it was his magnificent driving which first attracted the Rajah's attention."

Mr. Johns did not exhibit much appearance of concern.

"I guess I'll fix him, anyhow. I haven't driven a stage over some of the worst country in the western states of America for nothing. I'll back myself to drive a coach-and-four along a wall just wide enough to hold the wheels—and I'll take you as a passenger, if you like to come."

"Thank you, Mr. Johns, my tastes do not incline that way."

"Don't you worry, Mr. Greenall. I mean to take on the whole lot of 'em, one after the other, and show 'em a thing or two all round. These gentlemen here fancy they know a little, but we'll be more than even with them before we've done."

The driving match came off. I do not know how they manage similar affairs in England. I have sometimes wondered. But I am under the impression that they are not managed on the lines on which they managed that driving match in Ahmednugger.

The way in which they managed it there was this. Mr. Colson was to drive upon the Monday, Mr. Johns upon the Wednesday. Each was to drive the same team—eight-in-hand. The horses, by-the-way, came out of the Rajah's stables. The course was to be up and down the streets of Ahmednugger, and then for a certain distance outside the city. The judges occupied the front of the coach. I had a seat among the insignificant people at the back. On the whole, I was content to sit behind. The proceedings, in the streets of Ahmednugger, were distinctly exciting—almost too exciting, I felt, for me. Those streets were very narrow, and they were blocked with traffic, be it understood. Mr. Colson and Mr. Johns, each with his eight horses, and a coach load of passengers, went down those streets at full speed, as if they had been fifty yards wide, and as if there had not been a soul in sight. What damages were done, and what was the list of the killed and wounded, I have never been informed. I never quite realized what it meant to belong to a subject race, till then. It appeared to me that, in the eyes of my companions, a native had, as a matter of course, no rights at all. We drove over whole streets full of them, in style. My heart was in my mouth most of the time. We dashed round impossible corners, shaking native tenements to their foundations. But we kept ourselves alive somehow. The peaceful pedestrians were slain. I am no judge of coachmanship—of such coachmanship as that, at any rate. Those who were judges, without a dissentient voice, awarded the palm to Mr. Johns and, in consequence it was said, Mr. Colson entered himself as a candidate for delirium tremens. He was a dreadful man.

It seemed as if Mr. Johns was prepared to match himself against the men of Ahmednugger at exactly those things at which each man fancied he was strongest. That is what he did do. He challenged any one to meet him at driving, or at billiards. And, when his challenge—for what seemed to me to be sufficient reasons—met with no response, he challenged any one to ride him. That challenge was taken up. But he beat all takers. He had a way with a horse which seemed little else than magical. A horse would jump six feet for him, when, apparently, it would not jump six inches for any other man in Ahmednugger. I don't know how it was, but so it was. I know nothing of Mr. Johns, beyond what I am writing. I never heard his story, nor how it was that a man of genius—he was a man of genius—came to find himself a broken-down small bookmaker in that little town "up country." Perhaps he was another exemplification of the fact that only mediocrity succeeds.

I know that I was more than even with the men of Ahmednugger—by deputy. The band played to them, as it had played to me. He made them face the music, and there was not one of them who did not leave his scalp upon the ground. My belt was adorned with trophies—by deputy. When Mr. Johns had beaten the men of Ahmednugger—as they had beaten me—at riding, and at driving, and at billiards, he took them on at shooting. And, so to speak, he shot their heads off. He showed them that, in the presence of this man, they were as nothing, and less than nothing. He even challenged Mr. Tebb to smash glass balls. He fixed the point from which they were to fire at an abnormal distance, and, if I remember rightly, he beat Mr. Tebb by about a score. After he had annihilated that presumptuous young vagabond, Mr. Johns informed me that shooting at glass balls really was not shooting. I was quite prepared to admit it. He said that it was only a trick. When you had once mastered the trick, it was impossible to miss. Perhaps. I have never fired at glass balls since then, so I have no reason to suppose that I have mastered the trick.

When I do again fire at glass balls I am inclined to think that I shall not experience the slightest difficulty in missing every one of them.

CHAPTER IV

EVENS

When Mr. Johns had beaten the men of Ahmednugger at almost everything at which they could be beaten, he began to amuse himself by taking a hand in various little games at cards. It was remarked that, to say the least of it, his luck was wonderful. There was scarcely a man in Ahmednugger who had not been compelled by Mr. Johns to take a lower seat; to take a lower seat, too, just where he felt that his claim was strongest to take the highest one. Naturally, here and there, a man resented it. An even stronger spirit of resentment was evinced when the men of Ahmednugger found that their money was going in search of their vanished reputations. There were some disagreeable little scenes. Then there was a royal row; it was at the club. Mr. Johns had been carrying everything in front of him. Things were said; then other things were said Then Mr. Johns laid down his cards; he faced the company.

"Gentlemen, I wish to inform you that you are, individually and collectively, a set of curs."

There were sounds which suggested neither the ways of pleasantness nor the paths of peace.

"Softly. Postpone the fighting for one minute. I would remind you that, when Mr. Greenall appeared in Ahmednugger, you all, with one accord, took shots at him. You used him as if he had been a variety of old Aunt Sally. When I made my appearance, you put your heads together, and you bested me. You see, we were strangers, and you took us in. Neither Mr. Greenall nor I quite liked this sort of thing, so we put our heads together, and, in our turn, we've bested you. We've used you as old Aunt Sallies. We've made you all sit up. We've made you all sing small. Even at games of mingled chance and skill, I've beaten you. Instead of taking your punishment like men, you begin to whimper. Therefore, gentlemen, I repeat that you are, individually and collectively, a set of curs."

Colonel Smith interposed so soon as Mr. Johns ceased speaking. I fancy that the Colonel had only just entered the room.

"Mr. Johns, you very much forget yourself."

"On the contrary, Colonel, I am remembering myself. It is the gentlemen you have the honour to command, who forget themselves. Should there be any one present who resents the words which I have used, I shall be happy to meet that person, either with the gloves, or without them, or with any weapon he may choose—for the honour of Ahmednugger."

There was silence—grim silence. Probably there was more than one there who would have liked to have ground Mr. Johns between the upper and the nether millstones. But, after all, they were gentlemen—in their way. Bean stood up, the adjutant of the —th. He was a big fellow, head and shoulders taller than the audacious little challenger. He went round to where Mr. Johns was sitting.

"Mr. Johns, you will either apologise for the words which you have just now used, or take a thrashing."

"I will take a thrashing," said Mr. Johns.

He took it. What is more, he took it there and then. The meeting was immediately adjourned; and in the moonlight, the little argument came off. The proceedings were a trifle irregular; perhaps over here we should deem them so. I am not prepared to say that any dignitaries were actually present. Still there was a goodly gathering. The two men "peeled." In a very short space of time the little man had knocked the big man senseless. This is not a fairy tale. It is a simple record of a sober matter-of-fact. It almost seems as if Mr. Johns was a lineal descendant of the Admirable Crichton. Looking back, I really fancy that he must have been.

When Mr. Bean's satisfaction had been signified in what, I believe, is the usual manner, Mr. Johns addressed the lookers-on:

"Is there any other gentleman present who would like to thrash me—for the honour of Ahmednugger?"

Someone came out of the shadow—someone who, in those parts, was a very great man indeed.

"Mr. Johns, you will be so good as to leave Ahmednugger within four-and-twenty-hours."

Mr. Johns looked the great man up and down. He seemed to be in no way awed, even though he stood there in the moonlight without his shirt.

"I am at a loss, sir, to understand by what authority you address yourself to me in such a manner. I am in no way answerable for my movements to you. I have not broken the law. I have not even broken the peace. As it happens, I do intend to leave Ahmednugger, and in less than four-and-twenty hours. Not in deference to your orders, but simply because I have had enough of Ahmednugger, having taught your compatriots hereabouts what, it strikes me, was a much-needed lesson—the next time they encounter strangers, except in the scriptural sense—not to take them in."

The next day Mr. Johns did leave Ahmednugger. And I went too. He went his way, I went mine. I have neither seen nor heard of him since. But, as I continued on my journeyings, I felt that after all I had been even, and more than even, with the men of Ahmednugger—by deputy.

MR. WHITING AND MARY ANN.

I did not mean to kiss her; it was a pure accident. Her face was close to mine, or my face was close to hers, and then her lips came into contact with my lips, or my lips came into contact with her lips—I don't know which it was—and then at that moment her mother came into the room, and she said, "Mr. Whiting, may I ask what is the meaning of this?" I said it meant nothing—nothing! Absolutely nothing! Only I found it difficult to explain, and when I did explain she would not understand. Her manner was not at all the sort of thing I care for. The result is that I am engaged to Mary Ann Snelling without being conscious of having entertained any intention of the kind.

Not that I have a word to say against Mary Ann, except that I never knew a girl with quite so many relations. To begin with she had six brothers and five sisters, and she is the eldest of the batch, and there's not one of the brothers whom I feel drawn to. Her father is a most remarkable person, to say the least.

After they had arranged between them that I was engaged to Mary Ann (I was really not allowed to have a voice in the matter) her father remarked, with a pointed air, which I cannot but think, under the circumstances, was unusual, that he thought it was about time that I did come to the scratch, and that if I had kept on dilly-dallying much longer he would have had a word to say to me of a kind. I do not know what he meant, and would rather not attempt to imagine. But it is quite plain to me that all the arrangements for my wedding are going to be made by the Snellings.

I do not know when it is going to be, but it will be either next week or the week after, certainly at the earliest possible moment, and I shouldn't be at all surprised to learn that all Mary Ann's "things" had been already bought, and perhaps some of them marked.

We are to live in a house which belongs to a cousin of Mr. Snelling; it is to be furnished by a brother of Mrs. Snelling, the house linen is to be supplied by the father of the young man to whom Jane Matilda is engaged, and the ironmongery by the uncle to whom George Frederic is apprenticed. All, apparently, that is left for me to do, is to pay for everything. It is most delightful. It might just as well be some one else's wedding, so unimportant is the part which I am set to play in it.

And it is all the result of an accident. I deny that for the last six months I have been using Mr. Snelling's home as if it were a boarding-house. Nothing of the kind. The mere suggestion is absurd. It is true that I have dropped in to dinner now and then, or to spend the evening, or for an afternoon call, or for an hour or two in the morning; but that has been simply and solely because the Snelling family have evinced so marked a desire for my society. The alteration which has taken place in their demeanour since my accident with Mary Ann is, therefore, all the more amazing. For instance, look at their behaviour in the matter of the ring.

The accident in question occurred upon the Sunday evening. I had been with Mary Ann to church, and had seen her home, and had had a little supper, and it was after supper that it happened. I did not go and purchase the engagement ring the first thing on the Monday morning, I own it. Certainly not. Nor did I take any steps in that direction during the whole of that week. I was not pressed for time.

Besides, I was turning things over in my mind. But that was no reason why, the Monday week following, four of her brothers should have called on me on their way to the office, when I was scarcely out of bed, and actually breakfasting, and assailed me in the way in which they did.

There was William Henry, John Frank, Ferdinand Augustus, and Stephen Arthur. Each of them twice my size and all of them frightfully ignorant and wholly regardless of the sensitive little points of those with whom they came in contact. There is no circumlocution about them. They go straight at what they want; and were scarcely inside my door before they blurted out the purport of their coming. It was Frederick Augustus; if the thing is possible he is, if anything, more direct even than the rest of his family.

"Look here, Whiting, how about Mary Ann's ring? The girl is fretting, but you don't seem to notice it. And as you don't appear to know what is the proper thing to do in a case of this kind, and don't understand that the ring ought to be bought straight away, we've bought it for you."

I gasped—positively gasped.

"Am I to understand that you've purchased my engagement ring?"

"That's it; on your account. From a cousin of ours who's in that line."

I never saw people like the Snellings for possessing relatives in all sorts of "lines." No matter what you want, or do not want, and never will want, they are sure to have some relative who has dealt in it, his or her whole life long.

They produced the ring, and told me what I had to pay for it. A handsome price it was. I was persuaded that somebody besides that cousin got a profit out of Mary Ann's engagement ring. But I handed over the amount. I did not want any unpleasantness; and I am quite sure there would have been unpleasantness had I demurred.

Later in the day I took it with me when I went to call on Mary Ann. She appeared to be surprised almost into speechlessness when I presented it to her. Her head dropped on my shoulder, and she kissed me under the chin, observing, "You dear old Sam." The moments when I am alone with Mary Ann are alleviations for those more frequent moments when I am not alone with Mary Ann. Still I noticed that the ring fitted her perfectly, and I could not but wonder if she had tried it on before.

At the same time I am beginning to be comforted by a suspicion that Mary Ann is on my side; on my side, that is, as against the rest of her family. There has been a difference of opinion as to where we are to spend our honeymoon. It is from her action in that matter that my suspicion springs.

The Snellings have an aunt who lives in an out-of-the-way hole at the other end of nowhere. The woman's name is Brady. There she owns a cottage, or it may be a pigstye for all I know. When she heard of my engagement with Mary Ann, she wrote and suggested that we should spend our honeymoon in her cottage, or pigstye, and that I should pay her rent for it. The matter was talked about at dinner. Mary Ann was silent for some time; then she quietly remarked:

"Don't trouble yourselves to discuss Aunt Brady's proposal. I shall do nothing of the kind."

This observation was followed by perfect silence. The members of the family looked at one another. But, after a very considerable pause, her mother said, with quite unusual mildness, "Very well, my dear. Then, it's settled."

After dinner I took advantage of an opportunity which offered to thank Mary Ann for her action in the matter, because, of course, I had no wish to spend my honeymoon in a place of which I knew nothing, to oblige an aunt of whom I knew still less. Mary Ann beamed at me, and she said, "You dear old man!" Presently she continued:

"Do you know that in marrying me you are doing the best thing for yourself that you ever did in all your life?"

I endeavoured to explain to her that I felt sure of it; but I fear that my explanation was a little stumbling. But she went on with the most perfect fluency. There were no signs of faltering about her flow of language.

"You want someone who can look after you; and you could not, by any chance, have chosen a person who will look after you better than I shall."

Such an assurance was most satisfactory. We had a long confidential chat on matters of business. I found that as a woman of business she was beyond all my expectations.

I told her exactly what my income was; and the source from which it came, and all about it. She drew up a plan on which we were to lay it out. It was an admirable plan. I had never had one, but I saw clearly that in that way the money would go twice as far.

It turned out that she had a little money of her own; about a hundred and thirty pounds a year. And, of course, I had my expectations, and she had hers. It was plain that together we should manage most comfortably. Delightfully, in fact. On the subject of wedding presents, too, her ideas were the most lucid I ever yet encountered. It was wonderful to listen to her—really wonderful.

"I shall make papa give me five hundred pounds, at least. 'A bird in the hand is worth two in a bush'— and it will be something to have by us."

I quite agreed with her remarks about the bird in the hand; and it certainly will be something to have by us.

"I know what mamma can afford to give, and I will see she gives it. And I will see that there is no shirking about the boys—or about the girls either. I will take care that my relations do their duty. I have drawn up a list of all the people who ought to give us a present, and I shall tell them what they ought to give— it won't be my fault if I don't get it. Of course there are some people with whom you can't be perfectly plain, but I shall be as plain as I can; there's a way and a manner of doing that kind of thing. I have no intention of being presented with an endless collection of duplicates, or a lot of useless rubbish which I don't know what to do with. If you take my advice you will follow in my footsteps."

I endeavoured to. At least I drew up a list of people who ought to meet the occasion, and I tried in more than one instance to drop a hint of what, as I felt, they ought to meet it with.

But I am bound to admit that so far my success has been as nothing compared with hers. Hers has been prodigious. It is certain that we have a large collection of really valuable property about the house—the wedding presents to Mary Ann. She has a knack of getting people to do what she wishes and to give her what she wants, which is a little short of miraculous.

A singular feature about the situation is that people are actually beginning to pity me—to sympathise with me for being about to marry Mary Ann. I notice that they are generally persons who have already tendered their offerings. The fact of having given Mary Ann a wedding present seems to fill them with a feeling of rancorous acidity which, to me, is inexplicable. My belief is that they have been induced to spend at least twice as much as they intended, and that they resent it. Such is the selfishness of human nature. But why, on that account, they should pity me, I altogether fail to understand.

"We have all been giving Mary Ann presents, and I suppose you, Mr. Whiting, have been giving her something too." That was what Mrs. Macpherson said to me only the other day. I have given Mary Ann two or three trifles, and I said so. "And what," inquired Mrs. Macpherson, "has Mary Ann given you?"

"Her love."

Someone sniggered. I cannot pretend to explain why, except on the supposition that romance is dead; at least in that circle of society in which the Snellings move. But that is not the only society the world contains.

As a matter of fact, Mary Ann has given me a pair of slippers, worked by her own hands. It is true that they are a trifle large for me, and that I shall never be able to keep them on my feet except when I am sitting still. But Mary Ann does not seem to think that that matters, so why should I? Her youngest sister, Clara Louisa, has quite gratuitously informed me that she has had them by her for some considerable time, and that, not to put too fine a point on it, they were originally designed for another individual altogether—a Mr. Pilbeam. But even supposing that what Clara Louisa says is true—of which I have no evidence—I have, surely, cause to congratulate myself on standing literally in Mr. Pilbeam's shoes, even if they are a little spacious.

On the whole I do not know that I regret that accident I had with Mary Ann. It is true that there are times when I am a little disposed to wish that she were not quite so good a manager; now and then every man likes to call his soul his own. On the other hand, she is well qualified to protect me from the rest of the family. She will keep them at bay. Because it is beginning to dawn on me that, singlehanded, she is more than a match for them all. Which is just as well. If she had been like me they would have rent us limb from limb. As it is, unless I am mistaken, some of the rending will be on our side. And they know it!

P.S.—The cards are out for the wedding. It is to take place on Tuesday fortnight. We are going for our honeymoon to Italy and the South of France. A second cousin of Mary Ann's is in the Cook's Tours line. He has given us free passes all the way to the end of our journey, and all the way back again; and coupons for free board and lodging at the hotel. It's a wedding present. So that, as Mary Ann says, our honeymoon need cost us practically nothing. Besides which we can always sell the coupons and railway passes which we don't use.

Nothing could be more delightful.

A SUBSTITUTE

THE STORY OF MY LAST CRICKET-MATCH

CHAPTER I

I AM APPOINTED CAPTAIN

I have some idea of cricket—not much, perhaps, but I certainly have some. I was not in the 'Varsity team, nor near it; but I played in the Freshman's match, and provided myself with spectacles. I was nearly in the school team once. That was when I carried my bat for forty-five. I must own that my performance was a surprise to everyone—and to myself among the rest. But as I never repeated it—or anything like it—they left me, very wisely, out of the eleven.

Thus it will be seen that, from a cricketing point of view, I did not, even in my best days, come up to first-rate form; and my best days were, reckoning from last summer, quite fifteen years ago. During those fifteen years I do not remember once handling a bat, far less hitting at a cricket-ball with one; and yet, in this state of unpreparedness, I had the presumption last summer to captain a team, and to lead them on—well, not to victory but to disgrace. It's a fact. The match was Storwell v. Latchmere. Storwell was my team; and as I do not think a more remarkable match was ever known in the whole annals of cricketing history, I here venture to report it.

When they first asked me to play I thought they were mad. Storwell-on-Sea is a village on the south coast—I beg pardon; I believe it is called by the inhabitants a town. It is a pretty place, and not unknown—in the locality. It has a season and all that kind of thing, and it was during the season I was there. And one day a deputation of the inhabitants called on me at my lodgings to ask if I would lead the local cricket club to, say, victory. As I have said, my first impression was that they were mad; either that, or else that they were "playing it off" on the unprotected stranger.

I hinted so much to the deputation. The deputation smiled. The chief spokesman was the local barber; his name was Sapsworth. He explained that Mr. Wingrave had sent them there. Wingrave was the vicar; we were "up" together, and he must have known quite well whereabouts my cricketing form came in. I decided to crush the deputation before the thing went farther.

"To show you the sort of man you propose should captain you, I need only mention that it is more than fifteen years since I had a bat in my hand."

But the admission did not crush them: quite the other way. It opened the floodgates of their eloquence.

"That's nothing," Mr. Sapsworth cried. "There's Hedges here; we've had to put him in; he don't even know the rules of the game, and he's just turned sixty-one."

I glanced at Mr. Hedges, thus frankly referred to. He was a smiling, red-faced, bald-headed old gentleman, who, if not considerable in height, was great in girth. He would certainly have turned the scale at sixteen stone. I felt that, to cricketers who intended to play Mr. Hedges, any objections which I might urge would appear quite trivial.

"When is the match to be?" I asked.

"To-morrow," was the startling reply.

I was speechless. That I, after fifteen years' total abstention, should be asked to captain a team the members of which were entire strangers to me, and of whose individual styles of play I had not the faintest notion, in a match against an unknown foe, at four-and-twenty hours' notice, was a little hard to credit. It was altogether too preposterous. I told them so. But they could not be brought to see it.

The end of it was that I agreed to play. No man knows to what a depth of folly he can sink until he tries.

CHAPTER II

MR. BENYON BOWLS

The match was to be played on Mr. Stubbs's field. Mr. Stubbs was a local butcher. Mr. Sapsworth had kindly promised to come and escort me to the scene of action. He arrived at half-past nine, just as I was opening my morning's letters. On the way he gave me a chart of the country. It appeared that in batting we were not strong, in fielding we were weak, and that our bowling was more than shaky.

"But we shall pull through," Mr. Sapsworth added; "especially now," and he glanced at me.

"I hope you are under no delusion as to my powers, Mr. Sapsworth. I never was a first-rate cricketer, and, as I have already told you, it is more than fifteen years since I handled a bat."

"If you'll excuse my saying so, sir, I've generally noticed that them who doesn't say much does a deal."

That was one way of looking at it, no doubt; but if I did a deal, I could only say that it would be a pleasant surprise to me.

"And our opponents—what sort of a team are they?"

Mr. Sapsworth turned up his nose—not metaphorically, but as a matter of fact.

"If we're bad," he said, "they're wuss. There's only one thing I've ever seen those Latchmere blokes much good at, and that is cheating. You'll have to keep a sharp eye on them, or they'll have all our chaps out when they ain't; and they won't go out themselves, not even when you've bowled their three stumps down all of a row."

"Surely," I suggested, "those sort of questions are for the umpires to decide."

"Umpires!" Up went Mr. Sapworth's nose again. "They bring their own umpire, and he's got his own ideas of umpiring, he has. But we've got our own umpire as well as them."

I said nothing; but Mr. Sapsworth's words conveyed to my mind pleasant impressions of the strict rigour of the game.

When we arrived there was a goodly gathering already assembled in Mr. Stubbs's field. A tent was erected; in and about it was a nondescript collection of men and boys; some forty or fifty others, availing themselves of the opportunity afforded them for a little practice, were actually disporting themselves on the pitch on which we were presently to play. I consoled myself with the reflection that the worse the ground was the more my bowling would tell.

Mr. Sapworth introduced me to the crowd en masse. Several persons touched their caps to me; others nodded their heads; some grinned.

"Good-morning, gentlemen. We're going to have a fine day for our match. Our team all here?"

Mr. Sapworth took upon himself to answer; he had been searching about him with his eyes.

"They're here all right. I suppose those Latchmere chaps ain't come yet?"

They had not come, and they did not come for an hour or more. I employed the interval in becoming acquainted with the individual members, arranging the order of going in, and their positions in the field; matters in appearance simple enough, but more difficult in practice. But at last the preliminaries were settled somehow, and the Latchmere men appeared upon the ground.

Their captain, coming up, was introduced to me. I was informed afterwards that he was a blacksmith. I thought he was by the way in which he grasped my hand. His opening speech was a little surprising.

"We ain't going to play you if you've got eleven men, you know."

I inquired into his meaning.

"We've only got ten," he said. "And one of them's Soft Sawney, and another's Sprouts."

I do not know if those were the correct names of the gentlemen referred to, or only fancy ones by which they were known to their friends; but he laid his hand on two of his followers and hauled them to the front. One was a long, weedy youth, who, one saw at a glance, was more than half an imbecile; and the other was a portly old gentleman of fifty-five or six, with a corporation like a barrel.

Mr. Sapsworth intervened.

"What's that?" he cried. "We've got Hedges!"

He brought Mr. Hedges forward. I could not but feel that, to say the least of it, Mr. Hedges balanced Mr. Sprouts. If Mr. Hedges could run more than a dozen yards without pausing to take breath, I was almost ready to express my willingness to eat my hat.

"But we've only got ten men," persisted Mr. Barker. "You'll only have to have ten. If you think we're going to play against your eleven we won't play you at all, so that's all about it."

There was a prospect of unpleasantness even before the match began. It seemed that one of us would have to retire, in satisfaction of Mr. Barker's rather unjustifiable demand. I was about to retire myself—for I instinctively felt that, as a captain, I was no match for Mr. Barker—when a rather curious incident occurred.

On a sudden a newcomer appeared upon the scene. I say on a sudden, for no one had noticed his approach, and yet, all at once, there he was, standing between the Latchmere captain and myself. To me at any rate his presence was so unexpected, and, indeed, so startling, that I stared. He seemed to have come out of space. He was a big, burly fellow, with smooth cheeks, round face, bullet-shaped head, and sleepy-looking black eyes.

"Let me play for you?" he said.

For a moment Mr. Barker stared at the stranger in surprise, in common with the rest of us. Then he jumped at the offer.

"Let you! rather!" He thrust out his hand and caught the stranger's palm in his. But no sooner had he got it firmly gripped than he dropped it with an exclamation: "Why, what's the matter with you? Ain't you well? Your hand's as cold as a frozen corpse."

I went a little aside with Mr. Sapsworth.

"Who is he?" I asked.

"I don't know, and yet I seem somehow to have seen his face before. But let them have him. He doesn't look as though he were up to much."

He did not. Anyone looking less like a cricketer I have seldom seen. His costume was ridiculous. He had on a pair of large check trousers—a check of the kind which the Oxford tailor explained to the undergraduate was a leetle too large to be seen to advantage on a single pair of understandings. He had on a huge top hat, of a size and shape which would have made the fortune of a "lion comique." A red woollen muffler was wound several times round his neck, and his capacious person was enveloped in an enormous overcoat, the like of which I had never seen before. The day promised to remind us of the torrid zone, yet Mr. Barker had cried out that the stranger's hand felt cold.

In the toss for innings victory fell to us. So we went in. I led the van. My associate was a youth named Fenning. He was a mere lad, and looked too much of a lout to be much of a cricketer. Mr. Barker led the bowling. I soon saw that if he had any strength it was not as a bowler. If I kept my head, I told myself, and he carried away my bails, it would be owing to the ground; for a rougher piece of turf, I suppose, few wickets have been pitched upon. But I was far too nervous to take liberties even with Mr. Barker. And, indeed, when the first over was finished, and I found myself still in, I drew a long breath of self-congratulation.

The other bowler was, in his own line, as meritorious a specimen as his captain. So, on the whole, things were going better than I had expected. I had scored eleven, six off Mr. Barker, and the rest off his friend. Even Fenning had hit up two—literally hit up. I was really beginning to think that I was getting set, which, in my palmiest days had only happened once—thrice happy day!—when something took place which showed me, not for the first time, the advisability of never counting your chickens till the eggs are hatched.

Mr. Barker was just about to commence an over. He actually had the ball in his hand, when the substitute—the stranger who had volunteered to fill the place of the eleventh man—came marching right across the field. Mr. Barker saw him coming, and called out to him to stay where he was. But, wholly unheeding, the substitute strode on. He reached Mr. Barker, and, without saying a word, so far as I could perceive, he coolly held out his hand for the ball. I fully expected that the Latchmere captain would remonstrate, and not only remonstrate, but remonstrate strongly; but, to my surprise, he instantly surrendered the ball, and slunk rather than walked to the place which the stranger had just quitted. So the substitute was left to bowl.

Without doubt he was an eccentric character. Up to that moment he had been fielding in his woollen muffler, his overcoat, and, last but not least, his wonderful top hat. These, however, he now doffed, and laid in a heap upon the ground. Their disappearance revealed the fact that he wore a tight-fitting jacket which was the same wonderful pattern in checks as his trousers. From the look of him, I certainly never supposed that he could bowl. My surprise was, therefore, all the greater when I discovered that he could. His action was peculiar. He went right up to the wicket, and stood quite still, delivering the ball with a curious flourish of the wrist. Its pace was amazing. It pitched a good two feet to the off, and broke right in—perhaps aided by the ground, though he certainly had found a spot. I was so astounded by the pace—which reminded me of the old stories told of Lillywhite; you could hear it "humming" in the air—that I never even moved my bat. It was that which saved me. As it was the bat was all but driven out of my hand. I told myself that on the arrival of a second edition I should have to go. Yet I did manage to stop the next four balls—how, I have not the faintest notion; but the sixth—for it seemed that, in those parts, they bowled six to the over—took my middle stump, breaking it clean off at the top.

As I entered the tent the scorer cried out—

"What name?"

"Tom Benyon," replied the bowler.

Mr. Hedges, who was seated at the scorer's side, brought down his fist upon the trestle-table with a bang.

"I knew it was! I knowed him all along!" Mr. Hedges was in a state of odd excitement. "That chap who bowled you ain't a man, sir—he's a ghost."

"He manages to put a good deal of pace on the ball for a ghost," I answered.

"And so he ought to. Did you hear what name he said? He said Tom Benyon! There wasn't a better cricketer in all these parts than Tom Benyon used to be. He played up in Lunnon more than once, I know, and got well paid for playing too. But he always was a queer sort, was Tom. I knew him well. I saw him buried. And if it is him, and not his ghost, he ain't grown a day older these twenty years, he ain't."

I laughed. I supposed the old gentleman was jesting. But not a bit of it. When our second man had gone to the wicket Mr. Sapsworth drew me aside.

"I don't like the look of this," he said.

"Nor I," I answered, supposing he referred to Mr. Benyon's bowling. "He'll bring down our stumps like ninepins."

"It isn't that. It—it's the man," he said.

"Do you mean the ghost?" I asked jokingly.

"It's easy to laugh. But—" Mr. Sapsworth paused. I could see he was ashamed of himself, yet had his suspicions none the less. "I thought I had seen him before, and I had. It is Tom Benyon."

"He says he is Tom Benyon, and I suppose he should know best."

"Yes." Mr. Sapsworth fidgeted. "But Tom Benyon's been dead these twenty years."

"Dead!" I cried, and laughed. "He showed himself too much alive for me, at any rate."

"When I was a youngster," continued Mr. Sapsworth, "Tom Benyon used to come into my father's shop to be shaved. He was always on the drink. One morning I was all alone, minding the shop for father, when he came in, mad drunk. I never shall forget that morning, never. He made me sit in the shaving-chair, and set about to shave me. He soaped me all over—face and hair and all. I was that there frightened I couldn't make a sound. I never shall forget how I sat and watched him, with the soap all in my eyes, as he put an edge upon the razor. Then he set about shaving off my hair. He had got off about half of it, and I was streaming with blood, when who should come in but my father. If he hadn't Tom Benyon would have made an end of me."

He paused. I perceived that the mere recollection of his little adventure affected him unpleasantly.

"There was something queer about his death. Some people said it was drink had done for him, some of 'em said he had done for himself. Anyhow, the whole country-side was at his funeral. I was there. I remember it as plainly as though it was yesterday."

While I was looking at Mr. Sapsworth, and pondering his words, there came the sound of laughter from the middle of the ground. It was not a loud laugh, but it was a distinctly disagreeable one. I looked round. Mr. Benyon was laughing at Mr. Fenning's discomfiture. He had served him as he had served me—he had taken his middle stump right out of the ground. I turned to Mr. Sapsworth.

"You follow."

"Me!" Mr. Sapsworth turned several shades whiter. "Me!" He looked about him with a frightened air. "Mr. Trentham, I—I can't," he said.

"Nonsense, Sapsworth! You don't mean to say that you are going to allow yourself to be frightened by any nonsense about a ghost, and in broad daylight too!"

The little man did not look by any means reassured by my tone of derision. He seemed more inclined to take to his heels than to take his place at the wickets. It is not impossible that he might have done so had he not been addressed from a different quarter.

"Bob Sapsworth!" It was Mr. Benyon calling to the little barber right across the field. "Come and be shaved!"

I own that I myself was startled. The words were apposite, to say the least of it. We had just been speaking of Mr. Sapsworth's experience of the shaver's art as practised by Mr. Benyon's hands, and here was Mr. Benyon's namesake inviting him, if not to be cut, at least to come again. On Mr. Sapsworth the effect of the invitation was surprising. He had on his pads, his bat was in his hand. Without a word he shuffled towards the stumps. If ever I saw a man go to the wickets in a state of "mortal funk," I saw him then.

I myself moved towards the scoring-tent. The state of things within it at once impressed me as peculiar. It had been filled, a little time ago, with jovial faces. Now, the owners of those faces might have been attendants at a funeral. And many a man has had a livelier following to the grave than I saw assembled then.

Fenning came shambling into the tent. I spoke to him.

"Mr. Benyon's bowling was too much for you, eh, Fenning?"

Unless I am mistaken, Mr. Fenning wiped a tear out of his eye. He certainly put up his hand and rubbed the optic with his knuckles.

"I never seed such bowling! 'Tain't fair!" he said.

"What is there unfair about it, Fenning?"

"It comes so sharp. I never seed the ball afore there was my wickets down."

I smiled. Not so the company. They regarded Mr. Fenning's words with different eyes. Mr. Hedges gave expression to the general opinion.

"You ain't never seen such bowling afore, and you won't never see such bowling again. 'Cause why? 'Cause it's a ghost that's bowling, not a man!"

Mr. Fenning looked about him with open eyes, and with open mouth as well. "A ghost!" he mumbled.

"A ghost!" said Mr. Hedges.

I expostulated.

"Come, Mr. Hedges, you frighten the lad. I am surprised, too, that a man of your age and experience and wisdom should talk nonsense about ghosts."

Mr. Hedges looked up at me a little sharply.

"If he ain't a ghost, what's become of the things that he's took off?"

I asked him what he meant. He pointed across the ground.

"He took off his hat and his coat and his scarf, and he laid 'em on the grass. He ain't touched 'em, and no one ain't took 'em, yet they're gone! We saw 'em go. If he ain't a ghost, what's become of the things that he's took off?"

Mr. Hedges grew a little excited. I looked in the direction in which the old gentleman was pointing. The garments he referred to had apparently vanished, but, of course, their disappearance was susceptible of a most natural explanation. I should have maintained this proposition with more confidence had it not been for something which immediately occurred.

Mr. Benyon was preparing to deliver his first ball to Mr. Sapsworth, and as I eyed him I noted the extremely unworkmanlike attitude in which Mr. Sapsworth awaited the delivery. Preparatory to delivering the ball Mr. Benyon divested himself of his remarkable coat, which matched his trousers, and in so doing disclosed a waistcoat which matched his coat. Neatly folding up the garment, he laid it beside him on the ground. No sooner did it touch the ground than it disappeared. I am unable to say how, but it did, and that before the eyes of all the lookers-on. This singular behaviour on the part of that curious garment took me by surprise.

After that I was prepared to excuse a certain amount of nervousness on the part of Mr. Sapsworth. To Mr. Benyon Mr. Sapsworth's nervousness seemed to afford positive pleasure. He cried, in a tone which was perhaps meant to be jovial:

"Now, Bob Sapsworth, prepare to be shaved!"

The ball went from his hand like lightning. Mr. Sapsworth yelled. Mr. Benyon sent down his second ball—whack! not against the bat, but, I should say, as nearly as possible against the same portion of Mr. Sapsworth's frame which it had struck before. Any cricketer might have been demoralised after receiving two such blows, but he would at least have tried to get out of the way of the ball instead of in it. Mr. Sapsworth placed his person exactly where the ball might be expected to come, and, for once in a way, expectation was realised—it did come. The third, fourth, and fifth balls found an exactly similar billet, and the sixth not only knocked his bat out of his trembling hands, but all three of his stumps clean out of the ground.

"I said I'd shave you, Bobby!" shouted Mr. Benyon, as the victim went limping from the place of execution.

"Next man in," I said.

"I ain't going in," courteously rejoined the player whose turn it was to follow. I was about to ask him why, when I was saved the trouble by Mr. Benyon.

"Jack Hawthorn!" Oddly enough, the man's name was Hawthorn, though how Mr. Benyon came to know that he was next man in is more than I can say. Mr. Hawthorn was a huge fellow quite six feet high; but at the sound of Mr. Benyon's voice he rose, docile as a child. "I'm waiting for you."

Without pads Mr. Hawthorn went striding across the turf, content to use the bat which Mr. Sapsworth had left lying on the ground. That hero came limping into the tent.

"It's a ghost," he said.

I could not but feel that the fellow was something of a cur. To this feeling I gave expression.

"Ghost or no ghost, rather than let him pound me all over the body with the ball, I would have made one try to hit at it. And you told me that you were an all-round player."

No doubt the man must have been suffering considerable pain, but I was too much annoyed at his cowardice to feel for him. Besides, the whole thing was so preposterous.

Undoubtedly, as a trundler Mr. Benyon was superb. I have no hesitation in saying that I do not remember to have seen finer bowling than his on any ground in England. He combined two things which, so far as I am aware, are not to be found together in any living player—pace and break. But it was not his bowling, fine as it was, which promised to work our ruin, so much as the absurd belief entertained by the members of the team that he—check trousers and all—was a ghost. An idea came into my head. I resolved that I would ask him, point-blank, in the face of all the people, if he was a ghost. If his answers did not satisfy the doubters nothing would.

The opportunity occurred just as he was about to begin his following over. Moving from the tent, I advanced towards the wickets.

"Excuse me, Mr. Benyon, but before you commence to bowl might I speak to you a word?"

He turned and looked at me. As he did so I was conscious that, in the most emphatic sense of the word, his appearance was peculiar. He looked as though he were a corpse, and an unhealthy corpse to boot—the sort of corpse that no man would spend a night with willingly. And this unpleasant appearance was accentuated by his ridiculous attire. Fancy a dead man, of a bloated habit of body, taking his walks abroad in a suit of checks—each check twelve inches square! I was so uncomfortably conscious that Mr. Benyon did not look a clubbable kind of man that I faltered in my speech.

"You will excuse me, Mr. Benyon, if the question I am about to put to you appears to you even worse than absurd, but the members of my team have some ridiculous notion in their heads that you are a certain Tom Benyon who died twenty years ago, and who now lies buried in the churchyard. I am sure, therefore, you will forgive my asking, are you a ghost?"

Mr. Benyon eyed me, and I eyed him—not willingly, but because, for some reason or other, I could not help it. At last he answered, speaking in a sort of shout,

"I am."

Of course such an answer was absurd—ridiculously absurd. As I sit here writing no man could be more conscious of its absurdity than I am. But then it was not that I was so conscious of as of a cold shiver going all down my back, and of a sort of feeling as though Providence had sent me out into the world knock-kneed. I struggled against a strong inclination to sit down upon the turf and stop there. But being at the same time dimly aware that I was making an unexampled fool of myself, I made a frantic effort to regain the use of my tongue.

"Oh, you—you are a ghost! I—I thought so. Tha—thanks."

How I got back to the tent I have not the faintest notion. But I do know that after that exhibition of the sort of stuff that I was made of, disaster followed hard upon disaster.

The first wicket—my own—had fallen for thirteen runs. The second, and the third, had seen the score unaltered. Hawthorn was the fourth man in. He was so fortunate as to appear upon the scene just as I put my fatal question—it was to give him a chance I put it. The answer settled him—that is, if there was anything left to settle. I am not able to state exactly what became of him, but I have a clear impression that he was out at the end of the over. Moreover, of this I am well assured, that nine wickets fell without an addition being made to the score. I suppose that is, in its way, a record.

Whether Mr. Benyon owed the inhabitants of his native place a grudge the evidence before me does not enable one to decide; but, if he did, he certainly paid it in full that day. Although he bowled at the wickets he hit the players first. Nor was this, so far as appearances went, in any way his fault; they seemed to have a singular knack of getting just in the way of the ball. The order of the innings was this:

the ball hit each man five times, and the wickets once. At the end of each of Mr. Benyon's overs a batsman returned to the tent a sadder and a lamer man.

One case in particular was hard. It was the case of Mr. Hedges. He was the last man in; when his turn came, with the score still at thirteen runs, he stuck to his seat like glue.

"Won't somebody go in for me?" he asked, as he saw his doom approaching. "I ain't no cricketer," he added, a little later on. "Now am I?" He asked the question of his friends, but his friends were still. He addressed himself to Mr. Sapsworth. "Bob Sapsworth, you asked me to play, now didn't you? You says to me, 'If you play, William Hedges,' you says, 'I shouldn't be surprised but what the gent as we're going to ask to captain us stands you a free lunch,' you says, 'not to speak of drinks,' you says." I pricked up my ears at this, but held my tongue. "But you says nothing about being bowled at by a ghost, now did you now; I ask you, Bob Sapsworth, did you now?"

Mr. Sapsworth was silent. The old gentleman went on:

"I shan't go in," he announced. That was when the ninth batsman had received Mr. Benyon's first ball— upon his person. "Nothing shan't make me go in to be bowled at by a ghost." This second announcement followed the delivery of the second ball upon the batsman's person. "I ain't no cricketer, and I don't know nothing about the rules of the game, and I ain't going to stand up to be chucked at by a ghost," and Mr. Hedges struck his fist upon the board. There came a yell from the wickets; Mr. Hedges gripped his seat tightly with his hands. "I won't go in!" he cried. Another ball, another yell. Mr. Hedges repeated his determination over and over again, as if in its reiteration he sought for strength to keep it. "I won't! I won't! I won't!"

The last ball of the over, and the ninth of our hopes had fallen. A pause ensued. The batsman came limping towards the tent. Mr. Hedges' time was come; he clutched at the seat with the frenzy of despair.

"Bill Hedges!" sang out Mr. Benyon; but Mr. Hedges gave no sign. "Bill Hedges!" Still no reply. "Bill Hedges, have I got to come and fetch you?"

At that awful threat the old gentleman did rise. His ample form went waddling across the ground.

"I—I'm a-coming, Tom. I—I ain't no cricketer, Tom. Do—don't you be too hard on me. If you must hit me, let it be behind."

"Where's your bat?"

The inquiry came from Mr. Benyon. Mr. Hedges had arrived at the wicket without that batsman's requisite. He scratched his head.

"My bat? I—I don't want no bat. I—I ain't no cricketer. You can hit me quite as well without it, Tom."

"Go and get your bat!"

Mr. Hedges went and got it. When he had it it was evident that he had but rudimentary notions of its uses. He held it gingerly, round side foremost, as though he were afraid that if he grasped it tightly it would burn him.

"Bill Hedges, do you remember those drinks you paid for me the Saturday week before I died?"

"No, Tom; I can't say rightly as how I do."

"You did. It was at the 'Crown and Anchor.' I had no money. I said if you'd stand Sam I'd pay you back again; but I never did. I'll pay you now."

Mr. Benyon paid him, five times over. The old gentleman bore it like a lamb. Whack—whack—whack—whack—whack! and the fall of his wicket at the end. As he returned towards the tent he wiped his wrinkled brow.

"I always said I wasn't no cricketer, and I ain't," he said.

CHAPTER III

AND BATS

Our innings was over—for thirteen runs. We sat there, moping in a crowd, I among the rest, when Mr. Benyon, bustling up, reminded me of my duties as a captain.

"Now then, turn out. Send your men into the field. We can't stop here all day. I'm first man in; soon I'll have to go, and I haven't had a smack at a cricket-ball these twenty years!"

We looked at each other. One part of his address gave us a certain gratification—that part in which he stated that he soon would have to go. We turned out. I suppose a more unpromising set of fieldsmen never yet took their places in the field. The Latchmere men went slouching towards the tent; some of them, I noticed, instead of going in stole towards the rear. These, I suspect, stole off the ground; I never set eyes on them again.

"Mr. Trentham, I—I can't bowl," whispered Mr. Sapsworth to me as we moved across the turf.

He and I had agreed that we should start the bowling. I confess that I felt no more inclined to act up to the letter of our agreement than he did. But Mr. Benyon intervened.

"Now, Bob Sapsworth, you take the bowling one end, and let your captain take the other. Captain, you take first over."

I obeyed without a murmur. It might have been quite a usual thing to see in a match a member of one team ordering about the captain of the other. I do not think that our field was arranged on scientific principles; I may certainly claim that I had nothing to do with its arrangement. There is a suspicion floating through my mind that at one or two points—two, or more—men were placed unusually close together. For instance, at deep mid-off—very deep mid-off—Mr. Hawthorn and Mr. Hedges were not only doing their best to trample on each other's toes, but each was seeking for a place of security behind the other's back.

Mr. Barker shared with Mr. Benyon the honour of being first man in. The Latchmere captain, as a captain, had become quite as much a figurehead as I had. His bearing was indicative of extreme depression. I think he had learned that to take, off-hand, the first substitute who offered, was, now and then, unwise.

To enable him to bat with more advantage, Mr. Benyon had removed his waistcoat, which matched his trousers and his coat. What he had done with it I cannot say; possibly it had vanished, with his other garments, into air. Now he had on a bright red flannel shirt—his tastes in costume seemed a trifle lurid—the sleeves of which were turned up above the elbows. His pose was almost as peculiar as his costume. He stood bolt upright, his legs together, his feet drawn heel to heel; not at all in the fashion of a modern cricketer, who seeks to guard his wickets with his legs. His bat he held straight down in front of him, the blade swinging gently in the air.

I am afraid I wasted more time in preparing to deliver my first ball than I need have done; but if Mr. Benyon had not had a smack with a bat for twenty years it was a good fifteen since I had bowled a ball. After such a lapse of time one requires to pull oneself together before exhibiting one's powers to a cricketer of Mr. Benyon's calibre. He, however, did not seem to recognise the necessity which I myself felt that I was under.

"Hurry up, sir! Don't I tell you that soon I'll have to go?"

I hurried up. I gave him an overhand full pitch which would have made a decent catch for point, if point had been close in, which he wasn't. However, in any case Mr. Benyon would have saved him the trouble. He hit the ball a crack the like of which I had never seen before. He drove it over the hedge, and over the trees, and up to the skies, and out of sight.

"I don't think that's a bad little smack to start with," he observed. "I like your kind of bowling, mister. I suppose that's a boundary." He called to the scorer—if there was one, which I doubt—"Put down Tom Benyon six!" He turned again to me. "It's no good wasting time looking for that ball. I've another in my pocket you can have."

He put his hand into his trousers' pocket. Those remarkable garments fitted him like eel-skins. I had certainly never supposed that he could by any possibility have such a thing as a cricket-ball in one of the pockets. But it appeared that he had. He drew one out and threw it up to me.

My second ball was a colourable imitation of my first, only this time it was wide to leg. To long-leg Mr. Benyon sent it flying.

"Put down Tom Benyon another six!" he cried. "I do like your bowling, mister. I've got another ball which you can have."

He produced a second ball from the same pocket from which the first had come. I could scarcely believe my eyes. But I was discovering, with Horatio, that there were more things in heaven and earth than had been contained in my philosophy. Since Mr. Benyon professed such affection for the style of bowling which I favoured, I sent him down another sample. This time it was fairly straight—by which I mean that it would not have pitched more than a yard from the wickets if Mr. Benyon had allowed it to pitch, which he didn't. He treated it as he had done the first—he drove it, with terrific force, right above my head.

"Never mind about the ball," he said. "I've got another in my pocket."

He had—the third. And in the same pocket from which the other two had come.

My fourth ball he treated to a swipe to square-leg. He seemed to have a partiality for swiping. Quite unnecessarily he allowed that this was so.

"I do like a ball which I can get a smack at," he remarked as he produced a fourth ball from the same pocket of his tightly-fitting trousers which had contained the other three. "A swipe does warm me so. Your kind of bowling, mister, 's just the thing."

It was kind of him to say so; though, to my thinking, his remark did not convey a compliment. When he sent my fifth ball out of sight I wished that his love for swiping had been less, or my bowling of another kind. The sixth, however, which he also produced from the same wondrous store contained in his breeches pocket, he contented himself with what he called "snicking."

"That's what I call a pretty snick," he said.

The "snick" in question was a tremendous drive to deep mid-off. It was stopped, quite involuntarily, by Mr. Hawthorn and Mr. Hedges. So far as I could see, it stunned the pair of them. Neither of them made the slightest attempt to return the ball.

"Run it out!" cried Mr. Benyon. He and Mr. Barker began to run. They ran four, and then they ran two more, and still the ball was not thrown in. Mr. Benyon urged the fielders on. "Hurry up, Bill Hedges!"

Mr. Hedges did not hurry up; he never could have hurried up, even if his manner of "fielding" the ball had not wholly deprived him of his wind. But the ball was at last thrown in—when the pair had run eleven. Forty-one runs off his first over was a result calculated to take the conceit out of the average bowler. And Mr. Benyon's last performance, his "snick," had placed him at the other wicket, prepared to receive Mr. Sapsworth's bowling—when it came.

"Now, Bob Sapsworth, I'll have a smack at you!" he said.

He had. I felt for Mr. Sapsworth. But since I had suffered it was only fair that he should suffer too. Crack—smack—whack went the balls out of sight in all directions. And for each ball that disappeared Mr. Benyon produced another from his breeches pocket. I felt that these things must be happening to me in a dream. I was rapidly approaching the condition in which Alice must have been in Wonderland— prepared for anything.

Time went on. Mr. Sapsworth and I bowled over after over. Mr. Benyon was making a record in tall scoring. No performance of "W. G.'s" ever came within many miles of it. And the balls he lost! And the balls which he produced! And the diabolical ingenuity with which he managed, at the close of every over, to change his end! If Mr. Barker did no hitting, he did some running. He never had a chance to make a stroke, but his partner took care to make him run an incredibly large odd number as a wind up to every over. Mr. Benyon did not seem to be distressed by the exertion in the least; Mr. Barker emphatically did.

Mr. Benyon had buoyed us up by his statement that he would soon have to go. His ideas of soon were different from ours. I suppose, at the outside, our innings had lasted half an hour. How long we bowled to Mr. Benyon is more than I can say. I know that I bowled until I felt that I should either have to stop or drop. By degrees one fact began to be impressed upon me. It was this—that the number of spectators was growing smaller by degrees and beautifully less. Originally there had been quite a crowd assembled. In course of time this had dwindled to half a dozen stragglers. A little later on even these had gone. And not only spectators but cricketers had disappeared. If my eyes did not deceive me, there was not a member of the Latchmere team left on the ground. They had had enough of Mr. Benyon—or his ghost.

What was more, some of our own team took courage, and leg-bail. I caught one of them—the lad Fenning—in the act of scrambling through the hedge. But I had not the heart to stop him. I only wished that I had been so fortunate as to have led the van.

The thing grew serious. So far as I could see, Mr. Hawthorn, Mr. Hedges, Mr. Sapsworth, and I were the only members of the Storwell team left on the ground. And the reflection involuntarily crossed my mind—what fools we were to stay! The amount of running about we had to do! And the way in which Mr. Benyon urged us on! The perspiration was running off from us in streams—I had never had such a "sweater" before!

"I do like your kind of bowling, mister," Mr. Benyon would constantly remark.

If I had had an equal admiration for his kind of batting we should have been quits, but I had not; at least not then.

A little later, looking round the field, I found that Mr. Hawthorn had disappeared, and that Mr. Hedges, stuck in a hedge, was struggling gallantly to reach safety on the other side. It was the last ball of Mr. Sapsworth's over. Mr. Benyon ran thirteen for a hit to leg. He made Mr. Barker run them too—it was the proverbial last straw. As Mr. Barker was running the thirteenth run, instead of going to his wicket he dropped his bat—the bat which he had never had a chance to utilise—and bolted off the field as though Satan was behind him. Mr. Benyon called out to him, but Mr. Barker neither stopped nor stayed. It seemed that the match was going to resolve itself into a game of single wicket.

To make things better, when I came up to bowl I perceived that Mr. Sapsworth's power of endurance had reached its tether. The position he had taken up in the field had not much promise of usefulness. He first stood close up to the hedge, then he stood in the middle of the hedge, then—I doubt if he stood upon the other side. But at least he had vanished from my ken. And I was left alone to bowl to Mr. Benyon. That over!

"I do like your kind of bowling, mister," he observed when, as usual, he sent my first ball out of sight. "Never mind about the ball. I've got one in my pocket you can have."

He had. He produced it—always from the same pocket. It was about the second thousand.

"It does warm me so to swipe." This he said when he had sent my second ball on a journey to find its brother. Then a ball or two later on, "I call that a tidy smack." The "smack" in question had driven the ball, for anything I know to the contrary, a distance of some five miles or so.

The next ball I fielded. It was the first piece of fielding I had done that day, and that was unintentional. It laid me on the ground. It was some moments before I recovered myself sufficiently to enable me to look round. When I did so no one was in sight. I was alone in the field. The opposite wicket was deserted. The bat lay on the ground. And Mr. Benyon had gone!

Richard Marsh – A Short Biography

Richard Bernard Heldmann was born on 12th October 1857, in St Johns Wood, North London, to parents Joseph Heldmann and Emma Marsh.

Shortly after his birth his father became ensnared in a bankruptcy proceedings which enforced the abandonment of a career as a merchant for that of a schoolmaster at a school in Hammersmith, West London.

By his early 20's the young Heldmann, showing a talent for writing, began publishing fiction. In 1880, he began to publish works of boys' school and adventure stories for the myriad magazine publications all eager for good well-written content. The most important of these was Union Jack, one of the better quality boys' weekly magazine associated with the popular authors G. A. Henty and W.H.G. Kingston.

Heldmann was promoted to co-editor in October 1882, but his association with the publication ended suddenly in June 1883. After this, Heldmann published no further fiction under that name.

The reason at the time was not immediately apparent but in April 1884 Heldmann was sentenced to 18 months of hard labour for issuing a series of cheques, all forged, in France and Britain the year before.

In order to be well away from the scandal and damage this had caused to his reputation Heldmann adopted a pseudonym on his release from jail. Shortly thereafter the name 'Richard Marsh' began to appear in the literary periodicals. The use of his mother's maiden name seems both a release from the criminal record now associated with his given name and a lifeline to a fresh beginning.

A stroke of very good fortune arrived when his novel The Beetle was published in 1897. There had been more than a few previous publications of his works but The Beetle would turn out to be his greatest commercial success and added some much-needed gravitas to his literary reputation. The story concerns a mysterious oriental person who follows a British politician to London, and then wreaks havoc with his powers of hypnosis and shape-shifting. The Beetle has some similar aspects to certain other novels of the period, including those such as Bram Stoker's Dracula, George du Maurier's Trilby, and Sax Rohmer's many Fu Manchu novels. Like Dracula, and also the sensation novels written by Wilkie Collins and others during the 1860s, The Beetle is narrated from the various viewpoints of multiple characters to create suspense. The novel is also layered with many themes and issues of the Victorian era including women's rights, unemployment, urban poverty, radical politics, homosexuality, science, and Britain's imperial adventures, particularly in regard to Egypt and the Sudan. The Beetle sold out upon its initial print run and thereafter sold well for the next several decades. After Marsh's early death the novel's story was made into a film and adapted for the London stage, both in the 1920's.

It should also be noted that in the year of its first publication it outsold Dracula, then also in its first year of publication. In hindsight a remarkable achievement.

Marsh was a prolific writer and wrote almost 80 volumes of fiction as well as many short stories, across several genres from horror and crime to romance and humour.

However, at horror he was particularly adept. Works such as The Goddess: A Demon (1900), in which an Indian sacrificial idol comes to life with murderous resolve, and The Joss: A Reversion (1901), whose central premise is that of an Englishman who transforms himself into a hideous oriental idol are prime examples.

An important element of many of Marsh's novels is the investigation of the mystery. Several of his novels are centered on the crime and its subsequent detection. In the novel Philip Bennion's Death (1897) a bachelor is discovered dead the day after discussing Thomas De Quincey's essay on murder as a fine art, and his neighbour and friend begin efforts to solve his death. In The Datchet Diamonds (1898) a young man who has lost a fortune on the stock market mistakenly swaps bags with a diamond thief, and then find himself pursued by both the thieves and police. In A Spoiler of Men (1905), Marsh puts together crime and science-fiction; the gentleman-criminal villain renders people slaves to his will by a chemical injection.

As with many authors success with popular fiction was never quite enough. He also wanted to be regarded as a serious author. His novel A Second Coming (1900) imagines Christ's return to an early-20th century London and is his most well-handled attempt in that pursuit.

His prolific output of short stories ensured his being published in a plethora of magazines including Household Words, Cornhill Magazine, The Strand Magazine, and Belgravia, as well as in a number of short story book collections. These collections; The Seen and the Unseen (1900), Marvels and Mysteries (1900), Both Sides of the Veil (1901) and Between the Dark and the Daylight (1902) all feature an eclectic mix of humour, crime, romance and the occult.

He also published several serial short stories. Here he was able to develop characters whose adventures could be related in discrete stories across numerous editions of a magazine. An example is Mr. Pugh and Mr. Tress of Curios (1898). They are rival collectors between whom pass a series of bizarre and disturbing objects—poisoned rings, pipes which seem to come to life, a phonograph record on which a murdered woman seems to speak from the dead, and the severed hand of a 13th-century aristocrat.

During his career he sometimes came up with characters or stories ahead of their time. His character Miss Judith Lee, a young teacher of deaf pupils whose lip-reading ability involves her with mysteries that she solves by acting as a detective was very pro-active in this regard.

Richard Marsh died from heart disease in Haywards Heath in Sussex on 9th August 1915.

Several of his novels were published posthumously.

Richard Marsh – A Concise Bibliography

As Bernard Heldmann
Boxall School: A Tale of Schoolboy Life (1881)

Dorrincourt [Union Jack, April-September 1881]
Expelled: Being the Story of a Young Gentleman (1882)
Daintree (1883)

As Richard Marsh
Capturing a Convict (Strand Magazine 1893)
The Devil's Diamond (1893)
The Mahatma's Pupil (1893)
The Strange Wooing of Mary Bowler (1895)
Mrs Musgrave—and her Husband (1895)
The Mystery of Philip Bennion's Death (1897)
The Crime and the Criminal (1897)
The Duke and the Damsel (1897)
The Beetle: A Mystery (1897)
The House of Mystery (1898)
Under One Cover: Eleven Stories by S. Baring-Gould, Richard Marsh, Ernest G. Henham, Fergus Hume,
Andrew Merry and A. St John Adcock (1898)
Curios: Some Strange Adventures of Two Bachelors (1898)
Tom Ossington's Ghost (1898)
The Datchet Diamonds (1898)
The Woman with One Hand and Mr Ely's Engagement (1899)
In Full Cry (1899)
Frivolities: Especially Addressed to Those Who Are Tired of Being Serious (1899)
The Purse Which Was Found
For One Night Only
Returning a Verdict
The Chancellor's Ward
A Honeymoon Trip
The Burglar's Blunder
Ninepence
A Battlefield Up-to-date
Mr. Harland's Pupils
A Burglar Alarm
A Lesson in Sculling
Outside
The Chase of the Ruby (1900)
An Aristocratic Detective (1900)
A Hero of Romance (1900)
The Seen and the Unseen (1900)
The Goddess: A Demon (1900)
Ada Vernham, Actress (1900)
A Second Coming (1900)
Marvels and Mysteries (1900)
The Long Arm of Coincidence
The Mask
An Experience
Pourquoipas
By Suggestion

Violet Forster's Lover (1916)
The Adventures of Judith Lee (1916)
Sam Briggs, V.C. (1916)
Coming of Age (1916)
The Great Temptation (1916)
The Deacon's Daughter (1917)
On the Jury (1918)
Orders to Marry ([1918)
Outwitted (1919)
Apron-Strings (1920)

Periodicals

For Debt, Windsor Magazine (January 1902)
Returning a Verdict, Cornhill Magazine (January 1896)
The Lost Duchess, Cornhill Magazine (January 1895)
Mrs Riddles Daughter, All the Year Round (17 March 1894)
An Episcopal Scandal, Cornhill Magazine (February 1894)
A Rubber or Two, All the Year Round (16 September 1893)
A First Night, Cornhill Magazine (April 1893)
The Mystery of Philip Bennion's Death, Household Words (3/10/17/24/31 December 1892)
The Princess Margaretta, Household Words (3 December 1892)
The Puzzle, Cornhill Magazine (November 1892)
A Victim to Art, All the Year Round (2 July 1892)
The Burglar's Blunder, Derby Mercury (24 June 1891)
Pourquoipas, All the Year Round (9/16 May 1891)
The Pipe, Cornhill Magazine (March 1891)
When Greek Joined Greek, Household Words (6 September 1890)
His First Experiment, Cornhill Magazine (September 1890)
"Mignonette", All the Year Round (9 August 1890)
The Long Arm of Coincidence, Household Words (24 May 1890)
The Match of the Season, Cornhill Magazine (May 1890)
A Set of Chessmen, Cornhill Magazine (April 1890)
A Dream of Diamonds, Household Words (7 December 1889)
My Uncle's Flirtation, Household Words (16 November 1889)
"Em", Household Words (2 November 1889)
The Barnes Mystery: An Adventure of Judith Lee, Strand Magazine (October 1916)
"Scandalous!", Strand Magazine (August 1916)
What Fell on her Hat, Strand Magazine (April 1916)
The Adventures of Sam Briggs: On the Film, Strand Magazine (March 1916)
A Set of Chessmen, Cassell's Magazine of Fiction and Popular Literature (Dec 1915)
Sam Briggs Becomes a Soldier: A Fighting Man, Strand Magazine (December 1915)
Sam Briggs Becomes a Soldier: On the Way Home, Strand Magazine (November 1915)
Sam Briggs Becomes a Soldier: An Official Mistake, Strand Magazine (October 1915)
Sam Briggs Becomes a Soldier: In their Own Gas, Strand Magazine (September 1915)
Sam Briggs Becomes a Soldier: Sanctuary, Strand Magazine (August 1915)

Sam Briggs Becomes a Soldier: In the Nick of Time, Strand Magazine (July 1915)

Sam Briggs Becomes a Soldier: A Night Surprise for the Germans, Strand Magazine (June 1915)

Sam Briggs Becomes a Soldier: In the Trenches, Strand Magazine (May 1915)

Sam Briggs Becomes a Soldier: Baptism of Fire, Strand Magazine (April 1915)

Sam Briggs Becomes a Soldier: Two Stripes, Strand Magazine (March 1915)

Life in the King's New Army: Jack Carpenter's True Story, VI: Career for our Boys, Daily Mail (27 February 1915)

Life in the King's New Army: Jack Carpenter's True Story, V: The Tailor and the Man, Daily Mail (26 February 1915)

Life in the King's New Army: Jack Carpenter's True Story, IV: Hutments', Daily Mail (25 February 1915)

Life in the King's New Army: Jack Carpenter's True Story, III: First-Rate Fighting Men', Daily Mail (24 February 1915)

Life in the King's New Army: Jack Carpenter's True Story, II: The Berwick Borderers, Daily Mail (23 February 1915)

Life in the King's New Army: Jack Carpenter's True Story, I: Crossed Swords, Daily Mail (22 February 1915)

Sam Briggs Becomes a Soldier: A Man in the Making, Strand Magazine (February 1915)

Sam Briggs Becomes a Soldier: Sam Briggs Becomes a Soldier, Strand Magazine (January 1915)

The Amazing Visitor, Strand Magazine (December 1914)

Looping the Loop: An Adventure of Sam Briggs, Strand Magazine (August 1914)

The Torch, Strand Magazine (October 1913)

"Gaiety" Abroad, Strand Magazine (September 1913), 274-82

A Self-Appointed Guardian, English Illustrated Magazine (August 1913)

For the Cause, Strand Magazine (April 1913)

The Adventures of Judith Lee: The Affair of the Montagu Diamonds, Strand Magazine (February 1913)

The Adventures of Judith Lee: Mandragora, Strand Magazine (August 1912)

The Adventures of Judith Lee: "8 Elm Grove—Back Entrance", Strand Magazine (July 1912)

The Adventures of Judith Lee: The Restaurant Napolitain, Strand Magazine (June 1912)

The Adventures of Judith Lee: Uncle Jack, Strand Magazine (May 1912)

The Adventures of Judith Lee: Was It by Chance Only? Strand Magazine (April 1912)

The Adventures of Judith Lee: Isolda, Strand Magazine (March 1912)

The Adventures of Judith Lee: "Auld Lang Syne", Strand Magazine (January 1912)

The Adventures of Judith Lee: The Miracle, Strand Magazine (December 1911)

The Adventures of Judith Lee: Matched

The Burglary in Berkeley Square, Pearson's Magazine (December 1908)

The River of Light, Strand Magazine (December 1908)

The Girl in the Light Blue Dress, Strand Magazine (October 1908)

O'Rourke of the Saucy Sixth, Grand Magazine (June 1908)

The Adventures of Sam Briggs: The Limerick, Strand Magazine (February 1908)

The Adventures of Sam Briggs: The Star of Romance, Strand Magazine (July 1907)

The Adventures of Sam Briggs: A Social Evening, Strand Magazine (April 1907)

My Best Story and Why I Think So No. 21: The Strange Occurrences in Canterstone Gaol, Grand Magazine (October 1906)

The Adventures of Sam Briggs: That Hansom, Strand Magazine (May 1906)

The Adventures of Sam Briggs: Her Fourth, Strand Magazine (December 1905)

The Adventures of Sam Briggs: A Modest Half-Crown, Strand Magazine (November 1905)

The Adventures of Sam Briggs: The Gift Horse, Strand Magazine (March 1905)

My Wedding Day, Strand Magazine (January 1905)

The Adventures of Sam Briggs: The Girl on the Sands, Strand Magazine (October 1904)

The Parson, the Soldier, and the Child, London Magazine (November 1903)

The Girl and the Boy, London Magazine (October 1903)

By Whose Hand? New Short Novel by Richard Marsh, Answers (1 August – 31 October 1903)

A Girl Who Couldn't, Strand Magazine (January 1903)

The Kit-Bag, Windsor Magazine, 17 (January 1903), 298-309

Their Reasons: Two Hitherto Unreported Conversations, House Annual (1902)

At Large: Being the Strange Perils and Experiences of George Otway, Suspect, Answers (12 July - 27 December 1902)

The Handwriting, Strand Magazine (June 1902)

La Haute Finance, Windsor Magazine (March 1902)

A Wonderful Girl, Strand Magazine (March 1902)

Skittles, English Illustrated Magazine, (February/March 1902)

Breaking the Ice, Strand Magazine (February 1902)

My Aunt's Excursion, Windsor Magazine (January 1902)

The Haunted Chair: The Story of a Strange Mystery, Harmsworth London Magazine (January 1902)

Miss Donne's Great Gamble, Strand Magazine (November 1901)

The Man in the Glass Cage; or The Strange Story of the Twickenham Peerage, Manchester Times, (6 September – 27 December 1901

The Adventures of Augustus Short: Things Which I Have Done for Others, and Wish I Hadn't: The Address Which I Gave for Rudman, Cassell's Magazine (November 1901)

The Adventures of Augustus Short: Things Which I Have Done for Others, and Wish I Hadn't: Jones's Love Affair, Cassell's Magazine (October 1901)

The Adventures of Augustus Short: Things Which I Have Done for Others, and Wish I Hadn't: The Duel I Fought of Jarvis, Cassell's Magazine (September 1901)

The Adventures of Augustus Short: Things Which I Have Done for Others, and Wish I Hadn't: Griffin's Offspring, Cassell's Magazine (August 1901)

The Adventures of Augustus Short: Things Which I Have Done for Others, and Wish I Hadn't: McCulloch's Shoes, Cassell's Magazine (July 1901)

The Adventures of Augustus Short: Things Which I Have Done for Others, and Wish I Hadn't: The Fitzroy-Jenkinsons' Rooms, Cassell's Magazine (June 1901)

Staggers, Windsor Magazine (April 1901)

How I Drove a Motor Car for Randal, Strand Magazine (April 1901)

The Disappearance of Mrs Macrecham: The Amazing Story of a Strange Cat, Harmsworth Monthly Pictorial Magazine (March 1901)

The Irregularity of the Juryman, Strand Magazine (December 1900)

The Strange Fortune of Pollie Blythe: The Story of a Chinese "God", Manchester Times (12 October 1900 – 8 February 1901)

Pugh's Poisoned Ring, Harmsworth Monthly Pictorial Magazine (October 1900)

Willyum, Penny Illustrated Paper and Illustrated Times, (26 May 1900)

Willyum, Hampshire Telegraph and Naval Chronicle (26 May 1900)

The Goddess: A Demon, Manchester Times (12 January – 30 March 1900)

The Stolen Treaty, Manchester Times (27 October 1899)

For One Night Only, Answers (8 April 1899)

In Full Cry, Manchester Times (3 March – 9 June 1899)

The Colonel's Cane, Cassell's Magazine (February 1899)

The Burglary at Azalea Villa, Manchester Times, (13 January 1899)

The Burglary at Azalea Villa, Newcastle Weekly Courant (14 January 1899)

Our Christmas Burglar, Answers (17 December 1898)

Something to his Advantage, Manchester Times (7 October – 4 November 1898)

A Lesson in Sculling, Newcastle Weekly Courant (October 1898)

That Five Hundred Pound Price, Harmsworth Monthly Pictorial Magazine (September 1898)

The Chancellor's Ward, Harmsworth Monthly Pictorial Magazine (August 1898)

The Ossington Mystery, Ipswich Journal (1 April – 17 June 1898)

The Duchess of Datchet's Diamonds, New Zealand Graphic and Ladies' Journal (New Zealand) (7 May – 25 June 1898)

The Peril of Paul Lessingham: The Story of a Haunted Man, Answers (13 March – 19 June 1897)

The Purse Which Was Found, Answers (17 April 1897)

The Rector and the Curate, Answers (19 December 1896)

An Illustration of Modern Science, Pall Mall Magazine (November 1896)

A Battlefield Up-to-Date, Idler Magazine (August 1896)

Twins, Idler Magazine (January 1896)

Lady Wishaw's Hand, Leeds Mercury (January 1895)

Young George, St Nicholas (March 1894)

Exchange Is Robbery, Idler Magazine (December 1893 - January 1894)

The Tipster: An Impossible Story, Home Chimes (December 1893)

The Influence of Women, Home Chimes (November 1893)

By Deputy: A Reminiscence of Travel, Home Chimes (October 1893)

Rivals, Home Chimes (September 1893)

Capturing a Convict, Strand Magazine (August 1893)

A Burglar Alarm, Home Chimes (June 1893)

Music Halls and Theatres, Home Chimes (March 1893)

A Strange Bride, Manchester Times (6/13 January 1893)

The Mask, Gentleman's Magazine (December 1892)

A Vision of the Night, Strand Magazine (December 1892)

Nelly, Home Chimes (November 1892)

A Prophet: A Story, New England Magazine (October - November 1892)

Mr Harland's Pupils, Home Chimes (August 1892)

The Brothers in Grey, Home Chimes (April 1892)

The Half-Back, Derby Mercury (March 1892)

The Half-Back, Home Chimes (February 1892)

The Violin, Home Chimes (December 1891)

The Short Story, Home Chimes (August 1891)

Magical Music, Gentleman's Magazine (May 1891)

A Honeymoon Trip, Home Chimes (April 1891)

Mitwaterstraand, Time (September 1890)

A Pack of Cards, Longman's Magazine (August 1890)

The Burglar's Blunder, Ladies' Journal (Canada) (1 July 1890)

The Strange Occurrences in Canterstone Jail, Blackwood's Edinburgh Magazine (June 1890)

A Substitute: The Story of My Last Cricket-Match, Longman's Magazine (June 1890)

The Burglar's Blunder, Gentleman's Magazine (May 1890)

A Silent Witness, Belgravia (October 1889)

A Bed for the Night, Belgravia (Summer 1889)

Payment for a Life, Belgravia (Summer 1888)

www.ingramcontent.com/pod-product-compliance
Lightning Source LLC
Chambersburg PA
CBHW072123170626
46813CB00004B/1676